The House by the Side of the Road

CHRIS COWGILL

Tregenna Press
Riverside, California USA

Published in the United States by Tregenna Press
Riverside, California.

Library of Congress Cataloging-in-Publication Data
Cowgill, Chris [2022]
The House By The Side Of The Road
Chris Cowgill.
ISBN: 978-1-7923-8553-7

www.chriscowgill.com

Cover Design by Tim Green
Edited by Kyle Cowgill
Edited by Karen Pierpoint
Winn Barn In Snow photograph Copyright © [2009] [Gary Hamburgh]
Author photograph copyright © [2019] [Emilie Hendryx]
All Scripture quotations, unless otherwise indicated, are taken from the King James Version of the Holy Bible
Excerpts from "The House By The Side Of The Road", poem, Copyright © [1898] [Sam Walter Foss] Public Domain
Excerpts from "Come Thou Fount", hymn, written [1758] [Robert Robinson] Public Domain
Waltzing Matilda by Marie Cowan and AB Paterson, Courtesy of Carl Fischer, LLC, All rights reserved. Used with permission.
"The Family Psalm", poem, Copyright © [1985] [Karen Pierpoint] Used by permission
Image of Kenoyer barn, Albion, WA: drawn by F. Rebecca Skeever

Printed in the United States of America
First United States edition

For Mother,

whose prayers have surrounded us

from the beginning.

CONTENTS

THE CONFESSION

Disneyland may be called the "Happiest Place On Earth", but one day in 1993 the promise did not deliver.

I spent that day standing in long lines with my father, as he poured out to me the events you are about to read. It was strange, inching along with him that day as he confessed to things I did not wish to know, or want to hear. My sister noticed what was happening, and began to tag-team with me. Thus, we shared the burden.

My father had not meant that day to provide details for a book, and I had not known I would write one. He later told me to share the story if I thought it might stand as a warning, and a promise, that the Grace of God will heal any who ask it of Him.

This is that story. I have changed some names to protect individuals' privacy. These are my memories, from my perspective, and I have tried to represent events as faithfully as possible.

Chris Cowgill

PENNIE AND LANDON WEST

"I am certain that the step we took is one we shall never regret, and I think I speak for the both of us when I say we will be gloriously happy for the rest of our lives."

LANDON WEST

July 10, 1943

PROLOGUE: WHAT HAPPENED INSIDE

1958

THE SMALL BLOND GIRL HESITATED, casting her eye on the house across the street. It was not a busy street, but she would cross it only after looking both ways twice. Jenny was eight years old and should enjoy a long life (Mother had said) if she followed this one simple rule. If she didn't, well then, dreadful things might happen.

As if to prove this point, a little gray car came drifting over the hill in her direction. She drew back but did not worry, for the driver, hands clutching an oversized steering wheel, was Ralph Tucker. He was as tame as an elderly tortoise, never known to gather momentum. Jenny knew she could dart across the street in plenty of time, but such a dart might frighten Mr Tucker. So she waited.

Everyone liked the kind and generous Mr Tucker, whose relatives populated the town and strengthened its good reputation. Jenny and her sister were sometimes invited to his house for milkshakes, seated upon silver stools at his silvery kitchen counter. Mr. Tucker possessed an authentic ice cream mixer, the kind you would find in a cafe downtown. The girls watched, enchanted, as he scooped in the vanilla ice cream, the chocolate sauce, and the milk. Then at the push of a button, there it was - magic on a hot summer's day.

Jenny waved him past and crossed the road, skipping up the steps to Emily's door. She knocked, and waited.

Emily might be at home - Jenny hoped so - but she also might not be, on account of being a small, busy dancer. She and their friend Kim could tap, do ballet, and use "toe shoes", all while wearing the most delicate and flowing costumes. Jenny thought they made Emily look exactly like a tiny, exquisite green fairy.

As small girls, Emily and Kim had been 'discovered' by an agent who put them on television. It was the strangest thing to see the normal

Emily at her house one minute, and then to go home and see her on TV the next, wearing stark layers of makeup. Miss Shirley from up the lane disapproved of little girls wearing makeup on TV, and said it made them look "loose". Jenny didn't know of anything that looked "loose" on Emily, and thought it was enchanting to have two such famous friends. She felt lucky, and not at all jealous.

Emily and Kim's mothers, Marion and Margaret, were kept busy driving their remarkable daughters around. Marion and Margaret were interesting people who said interesting, gossipy things when they thought no one was listening. Jenny really never knew what topic one of them might broach, so she stayed alert just in case.

When she had just about given up waiting, the door finally opened and there stood, not Emily or her mother, but Margaret, waiting for them to come home. No one's house was ever locked in Weston.

"Hello," said Margaret. "They're in Pendleton, but should be back soon. Do you want to come in and wait?"

She said she would, thank you, and came in to sit on the living room sofa.

"Would you like a glass of water?" the woman asked. But Jenny politely declined, and Margaret didn't say anything for a while. Instead, she walked nervously around the room, taking in deep breaths and making Jenny feel equally nervous.

Then the woman sighed as if having come to a difficult decision. She stared at the girl for a moment, then said, "There is something I think you ought to know." Jenny looked up.

"Know?" she asked.

"Yes. I think you should know about your father."

Jenny knew about her father. At least, she knew everything about him that someone like Margaret would know. His name was Landon, and he sang beautifully. He worked hard at the Crop Insurance, where he stayed all week until he came back home each Friday.

"I know about my father," she said. "He works at..."

"Yes, I know you know that," interrupted Margaret. "I meant, there are - other things you should know about your father."

At that moment they heard Marion's car turning into the driveway, and Jenny jumped up to leave.

"He goes with other women," said Margaret, in a sudden rush of words.

The girl stopped.

"Where?" she asked, eyes wide. "Where does he go with them?"

"Well, I mean he – goes to other places and stays with them. He stays all night with them," she finished, and sat down with an air of accomplishment, as if having done her duty. Jenny noticed that Margaret's face had become red.

But the woman's words mystified her. Why would anyone's father stay all night with somebody? Jenny sometimes stayed all night with a friend, for instance Emily, and had dinner with her parents, then woke up the next morning to go back home. She didn't know grownups stayed overnight too.

"I just thought you should know..." the woman mumbled.

Jenny started toward the door and said, "I have to go now,"

"But Emily is back," said Margaret.

"I said, I have to GO!!!" Jenny shouted that last word in the direction of Margaret's red face, and all at once broke for the door. She flew out of it and down the steps, a suffocating feeling creeping over her about the thing she had heard; about people staying overnight with other people; about her father. Jenny thought about her parent's bedroom, and knew her mother slept in it at the same time her father slept. A sudden and terrible vision came to her of some strange woman in that room instead of Mother. This thought made her dizzy.

Having gotten out of the car, Emily saw her running and called out, "Hello! But where are you going?"

Jenny became distracted by these things and nearly forgot to look both ways twice. As she did, and as she crossed the simple small town street, she pushed Margaret's words out and away. She would forget them, escape from them. She had reached the safety of her own front yard when she heard Margaret's voice calling out after her. But Jenny ran on, up the steps and onto her porch. The door opened, and there stood her beautiful mother in the hallway, looking concerned.

"What is it?" Pennie asked, studying her daughter's white face.

In that moment, the moment when her mother let her into the house and asked, "What is it?" Jenny did not know. Her mind became suddenly blank. The appalling words, the burden they offered, and the woman who had taken it upon herself to lay that burden, had all swiftly, and mercifully, disappeared.

PART ONE

THE KENOYER WAY

CHAPTER ONE

Like The Wind Through The Trees

1924

It was a simple prayer, dear to him now and as natural as breathing. For twenty agonizing hours Ike Kenoyer had breathed it, pacing outside her door. He could hear unfamiliar, disquieting things, and wanted very much to go in. But fathers were forbidden, and although Ike was a big man and could have forced his way, that would upset Ida. Ida stood at a precipice that might take her and the child beyond his reach, and this he could not bear; so he prayed on as the twenty hours stretched to twenty-one, then twenty-two and twenty-three...

"...let them live."

* * *

The pealing of a telephone broke the silence at midnight, rousing the Torgersons. Theirs was a peaceful household in which telephones seldom, if ever, rang at night.

In a moment there came a shout: "Ida's had a girl!" whereupon two pairs of strong, young feet pounded noisily along the corridor, down the stairs, and into the still-warm kitchen.

"A girl-baby!" they shouted, grasping hands and twirling around in front of the wood stove. The reality of being aunties lit their eyes like fire-crackers on the fourth of July. They had longed for a girl to cuddle and pet, and to dress in all the pretty clothes they could possibly make for her. There were already a number of things waiting to be worn, delicate tiny things which they, Stella and Louise, had labored endlessly over.

At seventeen, Stella had become the slender and delicate beauty - blond, as blue-eyed as any Norwegian daughter, and filled with all that is sweetness and light. People were drawn irresistibly to Stella, for to see her was to laugh. Her sunny and often mischievous smile never left her face, and pleasantly infected the faces of everyone around her.

Eleven-year-old Louise, also blond and blue, spun around her older sister like a young puppy, with the firm conviction that anything Stella ever said or did - even to almost burning the house down - was unimpeachable.

"Clarence, come down here!" Stella shouted up the staircase. "It's a girl, don't you know?"

Their brother moaned at them from the comfort of his bed, but declined to stir.

"Oh, Clarence, how can you be so ho-hum?" she cried. But Clarence, in true Clarence fashion, had already pulled the pillow up over his head and gone back to sleep. Babies could wait.

Stella herself waited until almost daylight, then rode like the wind through the trees. Her bicycle swiftly ate up the eleven miles to the little house where slept her sister's darling baby. Leaving the bike in the yard, she crept quietly up the stairs to the bedroom where Ida lay, exhausted from her twenty-four hour ordeal. Ike sat nearby, his eyes upon the small peaceful bundle that was his daughter. He looked up as Stella entered.

"How are they, Ike?" she whispered. "Was it alright?"

He yawned and shook his head. "It was hard on her. It took too long. But they're both well enough now." He didn't like to think of the frightening labor or the struggling doctor, and how it took the arrival of a midwife to save both mother and child.

"What are you going to call her?" Stella asked.

"Her name is Pennie," said Ike. "Pennie Mae."

"Pennie Mae Kenoyer," Stella whispered, gazing down at the wisps of dark hair visible above the blanket. "A perfect angel." She stooped to gently pick up the child.

"Well hello, my small darling," she said. "I am your Aunt Stella, and you and I are going to be terrific friends. Your mother is my best friend, and I shall expect you to carry on the tradition."

The baby opened her eyes and looked, with the stunning precision of all newborns, straight into Stella's. The eyes were a startling blue, almost azure, and regarded her aunt solemnly. Ike stepped out to his chores as aunt and niece sat in a companionable silence. Stella looked over at her sleeping sister, suddenly filled with a grateful love. Ida had made it through, bringing with her this tiny, adorable treasure. But it had taken twenty-four hours! Stella shuddered at the thought.

Placing Pennie back into her crib, Stella patted the little head and murmured a quiet prayer over her. "Goodbye, my darling," she whispered, leaving the silent house and racing toward home and the waiting Louise. There was only one bicycle, and it wasn't built for two.

Ike and Ida approved of their small, blue-eyed daughter. From the beginning he held her on his knee, telling her the stories he had learned as a child. No one could chronicle the past the way her father did. In his big voice, he could make the stories funny, or lively, or (if Ida wasn't around) deliciously scary. She especially shivered when he told his old Indian stories, which included elements such as hatchets, or arrows, or scalps.

Ida, for her part, loved making Pennie little white dresses and tying pretty bows in her soft brown hair. Each night Ida tucked her in and kissed the silky little head, saying, "Good night, sleep tight! Sweet dreams." Pennie memorized these words, and grew to love the voice that uttered them. Never was there a sound so soft and kind, with a surprising touch of humor when she needed it. Pennie felt that sleep, for her, might never truly arrive without it.

CHAPTER TWO

So Long As Her Father Was Near

1926

Pennie stood at the very edge of her small porch, and felt hungry. Dawn lightly brushed the horizon with that rare gold you only see in a forest, and she still wore her little white nightcap and gown. Anyone passing might think she was about to step off. But she wasn't. She wouldn't. Mother had said never to leave the porch, and at age two, Pennie already thought in terms of boundaries.

But something else kept her safely on that porch. A few feet from the little girl's tiny self stood a cow, solemnly chewing her cud. Pennie regarded the creature with suspicion because of its enormity, and sometimes dreamed it would come to "get" her. They called the cow Daisy.

The summer had been hot in the valley below, but she and her father and mother had come up to work in these logging mountains where it felt lovely and cool. They had ridden together in a pony cart, and Mother had brought her pans and her plates. These pretty things were set up in the cabin, and Pennie liked watching her mother using them. When she did, it usually meant something nice to eat.

This notion of eating reminded her again of her tummy, so she walked over to the top step where her father sat, sharpening his axe.

"You are up early today, Penn," he said. She liked that name, "Penn", because no one but her father ever used it.

"I'm hungwy," she piped.

Out of habit she glanced around for the cow, and saw it standing in the cool shade of the trees. Pennie did not fear it so long as her father was near, so she forgot about Daisy and climbed up into his lap.

For a man of his stature, Ike was remarkably gentle. His hair shone blacker-than-black, and his similarly dark eyes twinkled kindly whenever he looked at her. His words were few, but his voice sounded big. Pennie liked its bigness because she could always determine his whereabouts. Her father made her feel safe in that far away cabin, miles from any other little girls or houses. His big voice often made Mother laugh. Pennie liked it when her mother laughed, for it sounded exactly like a soft and shimmering bell.

"You're hungry, eh?" said Ike.

Pennie nodded.

As she watched with interest, he began fiddling with something in his pocket, finally bringing the something out of its folds. "Here you are, Penn," he said, and handed her an apple. The big, shiny red apple made Pennie take in her breath. She had rarely seen such an apple as this, so bright and so big.

"Take it on into the house, I'm going to chop up this wood before your mother gets back."

"Where is she?" Pennie asked, chewing her first bite.

"She is helping Edna," he said vaguely. Edna, wife of another logger, would have a baby that day. But about this Ike said nothing.

Pennie watched as her father went behind the house. Presently she heard him chopping, and knew he wouldn't stop until he had enough for Ida to do her baking.

The apple was big for so small a girl, so she grasped it with both hands and took another satisfying bite. Chewing it, she felt a change. Daisy had moved. Pennie looked cautiously around, and saw the cow making its way toward the porch, both huge eyes on the apple in her hands. Daisy preferred apples, and looked as if she meant to have this one. Pennie backed slowly toward the door, then held her ground. The cow was chewing. She was chewing.

Daisy paused at the bottom of the steps, and to Pennie's horror, she lifted a hoof. Thump. Then the next hoof rose unsteadily to the next step, and the next. A cow in the distance is almost bearable, but a cow up close could not be tolerated. Pennie ran inside and climbed up onto the big bed. She saw the space between the bed and the wall, and to this sanctuary she scrambled, all the while holding tightly to her beloved apple. She watched the door from her hiding place, and listened. Nothing happened for a while, until she heard the solid sound of hooves upon the wooden boards of the porch. Then the unthinkable happened: first its nose, then its eyes and head came through the door. Pennie's worst nightmare had come true. The cow was coming to get her!

She thought suddenly of her father, and his wood pile, and his axe.

"DADDY!!!" she screamed. But the cow stepped slowly on until both head and shoulders were inside the cabin. Surely it could not get to her, safely between the big bed and the wall...

But Pennie did not need to find out, for suddenly her father appeared, placing strong hands on the neck of the baffled cow.

"Sooo, Boss," he gently murmured. "So, Bossy Bossy." Pennie had never heard his voice so gentle or so firm. Through some miracle of will and words, Ike turned and eased the gigantic bovine out through the door. But there she stopped. Up the steps had been one thing. Down again would be, for Daisy, out of the question. But Ike had another apple, and eventually lured her safely down onto the dirt below.

"Ike, what on earth?" came Ida's voice through the trees. She sounded tired, and had felt thankful to be home again - until she saw the huge form of Daisy lumbering down the porch steps, led by Ike. She ran to where he stood, his hand on the neck of the hapless creature. "Whatever was she doing up there?"

"Well, Penn had an apple, and..."

"Oh, the poor thing," she said, starting quickly toward the steps. "And I don't mean Daisy!" Pennie still stood wedged between the bed and the wall, apple in hand, chewing. Ida could see the movement of her little night cap above the bed spread.

"Well, Pennie, did you meet up with that old cow today?" asked her mother, chuckling.

Pennie swallowed and nodded. "I was hungwy," she replied, and took another bite.

That summer Ike chopped and stacked logs with the other men all day long, until the sun went down and he could go home to his girls. Girls seemed to surround him, especially since the birth of baby Dorothy in mid-summer; but Ike didn't appear to mind it.

Evenings were her favorite time of day, when Dorothy had been put to bed and Ike held Pennie on his knee to tell her stories. This goodness happened every day, day after day, until she thought it might go on happening forever.

But one morning in late summer, Pennie saw her mother tucking her pretty dishes back into their box. Ida stood at the table, wrapping each piece in a cloth so none of them might break. The cabin looked strange and empty without them. When the box became full, her father carried it out to the pony cart. Pennie did not know it, but he had finished logging these woods, and they would now be going home. When she heard this, she did not want to go to a home she no longer remembered. This was the home she remembered, and the tears began to fall.

Ida held her and gently kissed the top of her silky head as they drove away. The cabin grew smaller with each step of the pony, until nothing stood behind them but the trees. They were pretty trees and Pennie liked to ride in them; but they had swallowed up her cabin.

Little did she know there was something better out ahead, waiting for her and for little Dorothy. Ida knew it and Ike knew it, and did not weep as Pennie wept. They knew the "something better" and were looking forward, not back.

"It's that way with Heaven too, Penn," said her father. "This old earth gets to feeling mighty comfortable, and we don't like to leave it. But out ahead? That'll be Heaven. That'll be Home. Just you wait."

CHAPTER THREE

Something Better Out Ahead

1929

The town of Albion, Washington housed 241 people that year, including a great quantity of Kenoyers. Ike's mother, famous for her farmland and her wealth, lived there. Her real name was Eva May, but nearly everyone called her Big Grandma. Pennie knew about Big Grandma, but could not exactly remember her. She thought of a woman standing in a wheat field, with her house behind her. The woman's hands were resting on her hips, and she was, in fact, Big.

Big Grandma was the boss of her house, Ida told Pennie, except for once a year. The once a year happened when Little Grandma came to visit.

"Why can't she be the boss of her house when Little Grandma visits?" asked Pennie.

"It is because Little Grandma is Big Grandma's mother," Ida said, smiling, "and Big Grandma must follow her rules whenever she is there. Little Grandma's rules come with her wherever she goes. It is their way."

Big Grandma had been left a prosperous farm widow when her husband, James, had died. She had been left even more prosperous when her second husband, William (also a farmer), had died. These two deaths had been very sad affairs, and Big Grandma had been very sad both times. But she set about making her farms even more prosperous than they had been with the expertise of two husbands. This made some of the lonely farmers in the area sit up and take notice, but Big Grandma vowed that three husbands in one lifetime would be one husband too many.

It was because of Big Grandma, who had given birth eight times, that Albion held so many Kenoyers. Pennie loved her aunts and uncles.

The uncles were all big, burly men who liked to toss her high into the air, and catch her when she came back down again. She screamed high-pitched whenever they did this, until her mother reminded her that "a lady must be decorous". But it is hard being decorous when someone is tossing you into the air.

The aunties were cheerful, busy ladies with busy kitchens, each one producing three massive meals every day, delicious and plentiful. After church on Sundays, they ate the delicious and plentiful together, and because of this, Sundays were extra jolly.

Pennie's aunts and uncles never seemed to be cross. Whenever she entered a room where they were sitting, they all noticed her and issued a booming "Hello!" and then laughed. They always laughed. Their Kenoyer voices were big like her father's, which meant that any room with them inside it became a loud room.

But her father was the biggest and loudest of all.

Ike loved and respected his mother's farm, with its vast acreage resplendent and impressive, greener than any emerald. Farming this land would be his future, and he worked it tirelessly. Whatever he might be doing with the wheat, or the cows, or the barn, his name would ring out across the fields: "Ike! You're needed." And Ike would always come.

Pennie never felt bored, and Big Grandma's barn was one of the many reasons why. How could anyone be bored when surrounded by such a barn? She crept about, high and low in search of the unknown.

One morning, she came upon a litter of kittens secreted away in the upper corner hay loft. Ecstatic, she ran down to the kitchen to share this good news. To her surprise, Big Grandma said she could have her pick of the litter.

"I've been waiting for you to find them," her Grandmother said, with a smile. "They are old enough to leave their mama, now."

Pennie carried the sweet thing home, ecstatic.

"Big Grandma gave me this kitten today, Mother," she said.

"That is a sign of Big Grandma's fine generosity," said Ida kindly.

"She should be a mite less generous, in my opinion," said Ike's voice from behind his newspaper, low and a little bit growly.

"Why is that, Daddy?" asked Pennie, suddenly afraid Tipsy might be sent back. She loved him already, with his black, smooth fur, and his white-tipped tail. "Isn't it alright that I have him?"

But the subject became mysteriously changed, and Pennie was left to wonder at her father's growl. She did not know that he was worried, and that his worried look was already spreading to others, as if storms were coming their way and no one knew when they would arrive.

And yet these grownup concerns did not touch Pennie or her cousins. For them, Albion simply offered home and family, and lots of houses to go and visit. Pennie liked all of the houses, but Uncle James's was her dearest favorite because it contained a library. She loved books, and tried to visit it at least once each week.

Her uncle kept his front door unlocked, as all doors always were in Albion. But Pennie knocked politely, and her aunt opened the door with a broad smile.

"Well, Pennie!" she smiled, one bright afternoon. "The library? Of course, go ahead on up.."

Cheerful voices drifted out from the kitchen where her cousins lounged, laughing and eating cake. Aunt Betty's cakes were famous, especially popular on baking day. But Pennie turned toward the front stairs and climbed them, counting as she went. The fifteenth step led to a long hallway, at the end of which stood a heavy wooden door, slightly ajar. Pushing it open, she stepped inside and caught her breath: there they were, row upon row of books covering every wall and every shelf, giving off the most gratifying, bookish aroma. Pennie loved every inch of this room, and would forever think of these, and of all books, as friends.

But the library held something even more breathtaking than the books. All along its upper shelves stood animals, real animals that appeared to be alive. Encased in glass, Pennie could see them as they had once been in the wilderness. She gazed from one gleaming case to the next, the little fox sitting with its tail so broad and held so beautifully high; the variety of birds, large and small, peering out at Pennie as if they could see her. She particularly liked the badger.

How thankful her cousins should be to have such a room in such a house! But they seemed to have grown accustomed to it, and rarely went in. Her interest in it puzzled them, but they didn't mind. It was Pennie's way.

She soon found the stack of Uncle James' newest books, and lifted the top one. Age five, Pennie could not yet read so she perused the cover for a whisper of what might be found inside. To her surprise, this particular book cover frightened her. Devilish creatures, colored a fiery red with strange, snaky arms, were reaching out to catch someone. She put the book down, thinking and wondering. Then her curiosity got the better of her and she picked it up again.

She did not know it, but the book in Pennie's hands was Dante Alighieri's Inferno. Her uncle had no earthly idea she would come upon it, for it was not a book intended for children. But leafing through the images inside, she thought the message might have something to do with what the preacher called Sin. Pennie had been brought up going to church and held a loose understanding that Sin was "doing something bad". She knew she had sinned, because the Bible said she had. Everybody had. Pennie could not quite name these sins of hers but she sensed them, and sincerely hoped she had been forgiven them. If so, the Bible said she would go to Heaven when she died.

But what if she sinned, and then immediately afterward (as sometimes children did), she died? Mightn't that make her go to the other place? She and her cousin Irma had discussed this, and it frightened her. The preacher told them the other place was called "Hell", and that it was very dangerous. Dante's pictures hinted what Hell might look like, and the pain its occupants might experience. One sufferer (Pennie learned later that it was the Pope) had been buried upside down in sand, an evil creature smacking his exposed feet with a horned stick. This image gave her such a fright that she shut the book with a snap, and tip-toed out of the room.

"Oh, there you are!" said her Aunt as Pennie came down the stairs. "There's still cake on the table. Chocolate..."

Pennie had never declined a slice of her aunt's deliciously moist, buttery chocolate cake. But she did not want cake, now. She wanted Mother.

CHAPTER FOUR

Like Water On A Hot Summer's Day

The stock market crashed one late October morning in 1929. Pennie had scarcely known fear before that day, but now everything changed, as if hostile clouds had drifted over the town and blocked out all the fun and all the laughter.

Ike and Ida had something to be worried about because over time, Big Grandma had loaned a great deal of her money to other farmers. This generosity had troubled Ike, for the wheat, barley and peas were not producing the income they once had, and farmers were feeling the pinch. One by one they came to Big Grandma, who did not feel it, asking her for loans which she generally gave. The farmers did not go to the banks for these loans, which made Ike uneasy. But his mother did not appreciate his advice.

"They'll pay me back when things improve," she assured him. But when things did not improve, the farmers could not pay her back. They wanted to very much and were very sorry about it. But their money had gone, and soon, so had hers - evaporated like water on a hot summer's day.

Albion became a changed town. Goodbyes rang out as families left to find work elsewhere, and fathers had to leave their families behind. Even Ike and Ida, who finally found logging work in Idaho, had to go.

"I'm sorry you must," Big Grandma said when Ike stopped by for a box of supplies. "I hate to think of Pennie having to leave Albion. The girl sets such store by it."

"She is resolved to make the most of this, Mother, same as you."

As he drove away, Big Grandma looked out at the land which had all once been hers. Bit by bit her land, including farmland in Idaho, went under auction, and for the first time she found herself with debts to pay.

At last she saw what Ike had seen, and knew what he had known. If only she had listened.

Dorothy, not yet four and unaware of the change ahead, was to stay in Albion with Big Grandma. As Ike, Ida, Pennie and baby Barbara drove away, Pennie leaned out the car window to wave at the little girl and saw her, through the cloud of dust, break away in an attempt to follow.

"Mama!" she cried, but Big Grandma caught her gently up, turned around, and carried her into the house.

A few hours later, Pennie stood on a porch in Milton to watch, with Grandma Torgerson, as Ike's car disappeared in another cloud of dust. She could see both her parents and small Barbara standing behind them in the back seat. But this time there were no tears and no running, for Pennie was a big girl of six. There were tears inside her, but she must cry them later.

Dorothy and Pennie did not see their parents again for a year.

That first evening, Pennie crept up to the spare room and lay in the dark silence, picturing her mother in the mountains, putting Barbara to bed in a tent. It probably wasn't very easy, and Barbara probably wasn't very happy. But at least she got to be with Mother. Surely any hardship could be faced if you were with Mother.

The spare room door opened, and Pennie saw her Grandmother's silhouette outlined by the hallway light. Grandmother's face always smiled naturally, and Pennie could sense it smiling over at her now.

"Hello my dear," said Grandmother in her Norwegian accent. "Are you settling in?" She came to sit on Pennie's bed, and took up the little hand.

Pennie sat up. "I am fine, Grandmother."

"Well, that is as it should be. You are a great brave girl to come all this way and stay here with us. We feel you are God's gift to us this year."

Pennie nodded. Grandmother hugged her, prayed with her, and tucked her in all nice and snug. "Good night, sleep tight! Sweet dreams…" Grandmother said.

Pennie's eyes opened wide. Grandmother knew the nice words Mother used at bedtime! She squeezed the care-worn hand again, and smiled. Grandmother winked. "I am her mother, after all..."

When she was alone, Pennie remembered something that lay deep inside the box of belongings her father had carried for her up the stairs. She climbed out of bed, made her way to the box, and reached deep inside. There it sat, at the bottom - a new Bible, the one her father had given her on her birthday. Pennie could not yet read it, but she carried it back to the bed, climbed up, and fell asleep with its comfort and words clasped to her heart.

On Christmas morning, Pennie woke early and found her grandfather already downstairs, waiting in his chair by the fire. The scene below her looked enchanting, ivy and holly placed gracefully around the room, the tree decorated and simple gifts scattered beneath it. Pennie's eyes shone.

"Well, Merry Christmas!" Grandfather exclaimed as she came down the stairs. Pennie climbed onto his knee and replied, "Merry Christmas, Grandfather." Gazing at the magnificent tree, she thought of something.

"Is this where the Christmas tree stood the night Mother and Aunt Stella lit the candles?" She looked up at him and saw that his eyes had begun to twinkle, as they did whenever he found something twinkle-worthy.

"Well," he said, "yes. This is precisely the place. The tree was a particularly tall one that year, and it took a deal of work to place all those candles." He sat in silence, remembering.

Presently, Pennie said, "May you tell me the story, Grandfather? My mother is not eager to tell it." He smiled, and told Pennie of the night Ida and Stella very nearly burnt themselves and this lovely house to a crisp, secretly lighting the candles on the tree.

"Your grandmother and I were at a church meeting, and the girls took it into their heads to light the candles after I warned against any such notion. We could see the little fires through the window as we walked home. And then, we ran." They sat companionably, thinking of Grandfather running home in the snowy darkness.

"It goes to show that no matter how sensible you think people are, they can still surprise you."

"Grandma said that Providence brought you home."

"He did indeed, my dear," he said, patting the top of Pennie's head for her splendid wisdom.

"I can read now, Grandfather," she said, seeing as how she had his full and rapt attention.

"You don't say!" he cried. "Please do read something to me, for I am eager to hear it. Do you have a book?"

"Oh yes!" she said, and disappeared up the stairs.

He expected her to bring him a school primer with word lists all down the page. So when Pennie came back with her Bible, his face lit up.

"The Bible, eh?" he exclaimed. "My favorite! Let us commence."

She didn't know if she could do it, for the Bible is large and heavy, filled with large and heavy words. But she would try.

Pennie opened the Bible to Genesis chapter one, hoping it would be alright; hoping not to make a mistake and disappoint Grandfather. She looked down at the page, cleared her throat, and from her mouth came the four most honorable, most important words in this wide, wide world.

"In the beginning, God..."

Grandfather listened, and heard the creation passages as he had never heard them before, ringing more clearly than ever they had rung. Thankfully, he wasn't required to speak just then, for he wouldn't have been able to. There seemed to be a lump in his throat.

On the day of her parents' return in the spring, Pennie had no earthly idea they were coming. People did not notify one another of their comings and goings in those days. They just came, and they went.

As Pennie stood on a ladder in the apple orchard, a familiar looking Buick turned down the lane. The driver wore a soft brown hat, and a blond lady beside him held a sort of bundle. And didn't the curly-headed little girl standing on the seat look sort of Kenoyer-like? Pennie shouted something incoherent, jumped off the ladder, and ran. All of her bravery and loneliness throughout the year-long separation fell away as she sprinted into the strong arms of her father.

"I almost didn't recognize you, Penn!" he said, picking her up. "You must've grown a foot." The Torgersons heard the loud voice and came out to join in the excitement.

Pennie went to hug her mother, but something made her hesitate. There was a change in Ida, a subtle difference in shape.

"We have a surprise for you, Pennie," said Ida, answering the unspoken question.

Pennie glanced around, wiping her tears. "A surprise? Where?"

Ida gently opened her bundle, and out popped a tiny, impish face that looked like a carbon copy of Ike's.

"This is baby Alan," said her mother. "And he is your birthday present, being born so close to March 19!" The little face suddenly wrinkled itself up, and uttered something very like a "Quack", making them all laugh.

Before long, Ike carried Pennie's box back down to the car as her grandmother, grandfather, Stella, Louise, and Clarence all gathered on the porch. It was strange to see those five loving faces looking so beautiful and so sad. They each hugged her, saying their goodbyes.

"Don't grow up too quick, now," said Clarence, looking wistfully down at her.

Unable to speak, Pennie climbed into the back seat with little Barbara, who no longer knew her and made as if to clamber into the front.

"No, Barbara." said Ike, inflexibly. "Back seat."

The little girl burst into tears and looked daggers at Pennie. But she did what her father said.

Pennie leaned out of the window and watched the little group on the porch for as long as she could see them. The three women waved white handkerchiefs as Grandfather and Clarence stood, hands in pockets, stock still. When the car rounded the corner, Pennie quietly turned and reached forward to touch her mother's shoulder. Ida grasped her hand.

Neither of them spoke, but each knew what the other was thinking.

CHAPTER FIVE

An Orange Of My Very Own

1934

The Great Depression settled in hard, making itself felt around the world. Pennie was only five when it began, and now she couldn't remember any time before it. The children of the town knew the poem that would follow them all for a very long time:

Use it up,
Wear it out,
Make it do,
Do without.

Around Ike and Ida's table, the conversation now almost always turned to politics, for a Presidential election was looming.

"It isn't looking good for Hoover," said Ike, as the day drew near. A Republican, Herbert Hoover was of the mind that people did not need big government to solve their problems for them. He called this philosophy "Rugged Individualism" and believed in lower taxes.

Democrat Franklin Roosevelt, however, believed the government could pour money into a suffering economy, and bring it back to prosperity. He called this "The New Deal", which would mean a rise in taxes. The Kenoyers did not see eye to eye with Roosevelt.

"I wish I could vote," said Pennie. "The President needs all the help he can get." She would not reach voting age until the mid 1940's, but felt as if she knew enough now to make a wise choice.

But the ballots were finally cast without her. Herbert Hoover was Out, and Franklin Roosevelt was In. The newspapers hailed it as a landslide.

Opinions about this new President seemed endless. Roosevelt began generating lots of ideas for Programs to help the poor which caused something of a stir. Pennie wanted to know what a "Program" was and how it would help the poor. But the answer to this seemed vague and no one could explain it exactly.

Finally Ike said, "Well, Penn, I suppose a Program is something you put money into that never gives the money back." Pennie said it didn't sound very smart, and Ike said that is because you are a Republican. And then for the first time in weeks, he laughed.

One government program gave food to people who could not afford to buy it. They called this being "on relief", and a lot of people believed in it (the former President hadn't, and now he was Out). Ike and Ida did not hold with being on relief, as tempting as it might sound, or to take things like oranges and peanut butter from the government without paying for them. Although they hadn't tasted oranges or peanut butter in years, Ike said he would work for whatever food his family needed. That was the Kenoyer Way.

"We're not starving yet, girls, and we don't take hand-outs," their mother gently replied when the girls came home discussing the government oranges.

"But Mother," said Barbara, threatening tears, "Emily ran past me today carrying the most delicious looking orange! She said the government gave it to her, and that I could go and get an orange of my very own!"

But Ida said, "Others might take them, but we will not. I do not say others must not, because it is their own decision to do so. Go into the house now, dear, and cut yourself some bread."

"But why would I want boring old bread when I could have an orange of my VERY OWN…?!" wailed Barbara, running inside. The door slammed.

Her mother sighed, but their standards were firm. There would be no changing the Kenoyer Way.

"Do you know what I think, Pennie?" said her cousin Evelyn, the next day. Evelyn was like a loyal friend who just happened to be related.

The girls were sitting, as they often did, at the top of the railroad bridge to watch the trains going by below.

"What? What do you think, Evelyn?" replied Pennie, fondly.

"I think the Depression is going to go on and on, and never stop, and we are all going to get old, and sick, and die. We aren't going to have sugar, or butter, or go to the movies every day, ever again. That is what I think is going to happen."

"Surely not," Pennie protested. "Surely it will end. Maybe a war will end it, as my father sometimes says."

"He does? Because of Hitler? My father says that man is crazy, and doesn't see how he can make the Depression, or anything else bad, ever end, because he is bad himself."

Eventually the girls ran out of their fathers' opinions, and the conversation drifted elsewhere.

The next day, Pennie heard the rumble of an old truck pulling up the lane toward the house.

"Is that anyone you know, Ike?" said Ida, standing at the window. Several children sat in the bed of the truck, and a few adults were wedged into the front. The license plate on the truck said Oklahoma.

"No," said Ike. "Never seen them."

The Kenoyers had heard about Oklahoma's drought, which was often called "The Dust Bowl". Many people had tried to escape it, but this "bowl" seemed to have high sides and hardly anyone ever did.

"Howdy, folks," said the driver, as Ike and Ida came out to greet them. "We just come from Oklahoma City, and all's we need is a meal, if you've any to spare, that is, ma'am."

"Of course," said Ida, and went inside to get it ready. She always had something to spare, knowing there would be travelers, hungry children, people with no home. The children in the back of the truck sat looking at Pennie. They were thin, and she knew they must be thirsty because the dust seemed to have followed them all the way to Washington. She fetched a canteen and filled it with well water as the children watched with interest.

"Here is a drink for you," she said handing it to the eldest child, a boy.

The boy hesitated, and looked a question at his Pa. Pa nodded and the boy took the canteen, handing it around it to the younger children first. Only then did he take a drink himself. Pennie thought he looked like a man. A little man, but a man all the same; someone who'd had to grow up quickly and take responsibility for the younger ones.

When Ida came outside with the food, the family couldn't hide their eagerness. The children especially ate swiftly, their mother quietly watchful as she ate with a slow grace. Ida could see the woman had once been pretty, before the world changed. She said nothing, but her husband showed an interest in the surrounding land.

"Out in Oklahoma, everything's as flat as a table. No ridges. No cliffs. We can't believe these rolling hills." Then he gestured across the wide lawn toward a mountain range covered in snow. "And that mountain. It's a lucky man you are, sir, lookin' every day at that. This place is like another planet."

When they had finished eating, the boy gathered the utensils and placed them neatly on the porch. To Ida he politely nodded and said, "Thank you, Ma'am," and went back to the truck. Ida walked around to the passenger side. "There is an outhouse around the back," she said quietly to the mother, "and water, if you would like to freshen up."

But the woman shook her head, and Ida drew back, not wanting to insist. The truck started up, pulling slowly back down the dusty lane. The boy waved his hand toward Pennie as they rounded the bend, out of sight.

"Maybe they will find something better out ahead," said Pennie, hopefully. But her father wondered out loud if driving two thousand miles would make even a scrap of difference.

That evening as she sat on the porch with her father, Pennie said, "Evelyn thinks the Depression will never end. She said it will go on and on until everybody gets old, and sick, and dies."

Her father grunted. "Evelyn talks nonsense, or hadn't you noticed that yet?"

Pennie had, but didn't say so.

"She also thinks we'll never have sugar, or butter, or go to the movies every day ever again," she continued, deciding to make a clean breast of it.

"Did you ever go to the movies every day?" asked Ike.

"Well...no," Pennie admitted. "Not every day."

"Every week, then?" he persisted.

"No, not even every week."

"Well then, Penn, maybe there isn't all that much to worry about."

PART TWO

ANNA AND THE FARMER

CHAPTER SIX

He Just Didn't See Them

1920

In 1918 the Great War had ended, and the men came marching home. Some were whole and some torn, but they were all ready to start again.

"There will never be another war like the Great War," people said, and almost everyone believed them.

George West, at forty-one years of age, had looks, land, and eligibility. These qualities caused the young ladies of the town of Milton to sit up and take notice, but they made no headway.

His already worried mother worried over this, and said things like, "Now George, that Margaret Baker is awfully nice. Why don't I have her over next week for dinner?" But George hardly heard her. It wasn't that he disliked Margaret Baker and the other girls his mother recommended. He just didn't see them, even if they were in the same room. They were never the girl. For George West, although he hid this fact from everyone around him, had already fallen head-for-heels in love with a girl named Anna.

He had begun to notice her five years before, the spectacular contralto Anna Landon Compton, whom crowds of people traveled distances to hear. George could hardly believe such a celebrity lived in Milton, but even celebrities must live somewhere. Audiences sat mesmerized as she sang her way through any number of arias, all without so much as a note of music in front of her. George sat among the mesmerized, but thought her unattainable - as remote from him as a star in the heavens.

"George."

"Yes, Mother?" he said, absently. He had come upon a particularly interesting article on aerial crop dusting. New and innovative, many young farmers were keen. If only it could be affordable. Maybe…

"George. Anna Compton is an awfully nice girl, and her father's a doctor. We should…" She stopped, noticing the look on his face.

"You're not actually going to suggest she come over here for dinner, Mother."

"And why not? The girl is so accomplished, she would make the perfect wife for you. Why, everyone knows about her."

"Anna Compton could hardly be referred to as a girl, Mother. She's almost thirty."

"Yes, and it's high time she got herself married, too, you both do beat all…"

"Miss Compton is not interested in the likes of me and doesn't know I exist. So do stop talking about it. I want to read."

She looked hurt.

"Now that right there isn't true, George," she went on. "This is a small town, everybody knows you." George remained silent. "And if you don't do something about it, that g—, that woman is going to be scooped up by somebody else, and then it will be TOO UTTERLY LATE."

She finished with a sigh. And then George sighed. It was probably true, and he would probably regret it, but he didn't see what on earth he was going to be able to do about it.

But as the weeks became months, Anna stayed strangely single. This baffled George, who had started driving past her house hoping to accidentally see her. What he saw was a succession of suitors sitting, one at a time, on her porch swing. This irked him, because most of these suitors were younger men than he.

One evening while splitting wood, George's thoughts came to a head. The waiting and the wishing had gone on for over five years, and what if it was too late, as his mother suggested? George thought of his fleeting youth, and came to a sudden decision: *If I split this next piece of wood in one stroke, I'll go see Anna tomorrow. If not, I'll give her up once and for all.*

Imagining one of her young and grinning suitors, George took up his axe and swung with renewed purpose: up, around, and down it came, slicing the wood in a single precision cut. He smiled.

Tomorrow.

"I'm forty-one," he thought the next evening as he walked up her steps in his second-best suit. "She'll probably laugh me right off the porch."

George knocked nervously and waited. Nothing happened, so he knocked louder and waited again. As he turned and headed toward the steps, the door opened. He saw, not Anna, but her younger sister Sue, peering up at him.

"Oh hello, George. Here for a visit?" she asked, noticing the suit. "You're looking mighty dapper."

"Ah, yes Ma'am, ah, here to see Miss Compton." Sue stood quietly in the doorway, saying nothing at first. Then she appeared to make a decision.

"Well George, Anna isn't actually up to seeing anyone …"

George looked surprised. "Oh - well, I'll be on my way then," he said, beginning to move. But Sue reached for his arm. "Now just a minute, George, I'm not finished. Anna isn't supposed to see anyone, that is true enough, but I'm thinking she might just see you." She looked at him kindly. "Yes, I think you might fare rather better than anyone else right now."

She led the baffled George inside, and left him there. All around were the clear signs of a successful physician, understated but gleaming walnut furniture surrounding the blazing fireplace. To his right stood a neatly organized kitchen which looked as if a maid might have come and gone. He could see the unmistakable touches his daughters had maintained after their mother died. All this seemed a far cry from his little one room farmhouse.

Presently, a soft movement drew his attention to a door near the upper stairway. Anna stood with the support of her sister, looking at George as quietly composed as if she were on a stage. Her brown hair was somewhat mussed this evening, and her face had grown thinner.

But to George, she was the most fetching thing he'd ever seen.

"Hello, George," she said.

Words suddenly abandoned him, and George surprised himself by speaking the most ridiculous gibberish.

"Ah, yes...shall I, ah...Anna," he finished lamely.

His discomfiture did not seem to bother her, and in fact she appeared amused by it.

"I mean, hello," he finally said. "Are you alright?"

"Well, that's for the good doctor to say, George. I don't actually know."

She led him out to the porch swing, where they sat gazing out onto the street below. The now forgotten Sue cleared her throat and said, "I'll be in the living room if you need anything..."

George and Anna sat quietly side by side, rocking the swing and saying little as they watched the townspeople going past.

"I'm sorry you've been ill," he ventured.

"I'm not actually ill, George, but my legs are such a trouble that sometimes I don't know what I will do. The pain has been grueling."

George asked, "Is it rheumatism? My aunt had rheumatism. But she was old, and I hardly think you could both have the same affliction."

"It is, though, George. Even younger people can get it. There isn't much anyone can do, though, and none of the pills they give me are helpful. I hope you will pray for me..." She looked so sweetly up at him that George's heart gave a sudden lurch. His heart had never lurched before, and he liked the feeling.

"Take my mind away from it, will you George?" she asked him. "Tell me about your farm. Please."

In her own way, Anna eased this shy-by-nature man into conversation by touching on the one subject he liked the most, and knew the best. He told her all about it, and how long he had worked to pay each of his siblings in order to become the sole owner. "I've only got a few more payments to make," he said. "And when that happens, it'll be a Red Letter day."

Just then, a vision presented itself to George's mind - Anna Compton herself, standing with him on the porch of his tiny farm house. He suddenly knew she belonged there.

"Anna," he murmured.

"Yes, George?"

"May I - when you are better, of course - may I come and see you again?" She saw his red face, and smiled.

"Yes, of course you may come. I've been hoping you would for some time." George took her hand, and his heart gave another lurch as they sat together there. He suddenly realized that hand-holding had been vastly underrated.

"George," Anna said. "There is something I suppose I had better tell you."

He looked at her, and waited.

"I have only today taken a decision. I have decided not to go to the mission field."

George stared. "The mission field? I didn't know you were going to the mission field."

"Yes, I had planned to go. But now I am not. Not anymore. Dr. Calhoun is unable to give me clearance, George, because my condition prohibits it."

George suddenly said, "Why, that's wonderful!" and stopped. "Oh, I'm sorry. But the thought of you traveling and living so far from here would be...untenable." He squeezed her hand ever so slightly.

"Untenable?" she asked, squeezing his ever so slightly back.

George turned to look her square in the face. "Yes. It would be untenable, Anna, because if you were to be thousands of miles away in some African village, you wouldn't be, well, here." He swallowed. "With me..."

"But I am going to be here, aren't I, George? I'm not going away to any African village and because of that, you might as well come to dinner on Saturday, with Father and Sue and me." She smiled. "How would you like that?"

With a fleeting thought of his long-suffering mother, George said, "I suppose it would be... tenable." They both laughed.

They were still holding hands when Sue came out to the porch. "Anna?" she said. "I'm going out for a while now. Are you feeling well enough?"

Anna glanced at George and said, "Yes, thank you Sue, I am feeling well now. Wonderfully well…"

With a little smile, her sister stepped from the porch and strolled on down the street. They watched her go.

A first kiss is a blessed event, especially for two people who had long despaired of ever experiencing one. As this event took place, a passerby saw it, and soon the town grapevine became activated: "George West is paying court to Anna!" From house to house, the news spread quick as a spark on dry tinder. Even his mother heard, and abandoned her rolling pin, raising floury hands to the Heavens, and shouting, "Hallelujah! I knew I was right!"

George and Anna were soon engaged, disappointing the hopefuls on both sides.

"George, you are the hero of my family now," she said. "They are so relieved I'm not going to be an Old Maid, they can scarcely sit still. It's George West this, and George West that. I'm almost jealous."

When it became clear that she felt well enough, George drove Anna out to look over his acreage and see the West barn. Built in 1916 by his own two hands and the good help of others, the barn had become a sensation in the county. "It'll be a Century barn, you mark my words," he said. As they came around the bend, she saw it with new eyes.

"Here it is," he said with not a little pride.

"Oh my…" Anna said as they pulled up and parked directly facing it. She'd driven past, but had never been this close.

"What a marvelous barn. And you built it yourself. George, you are a singular man." It was magnificent, painted the bright red of most barns of the day, with crisp white trim, and surrounded by neat horse corrals. The two of them sat and stared at it.

"Now all we need is a house," Anna said sweetly.

"A house?" replied George in some confusion. His own little one-room house stood not far from the barn, ready for her to move into after the wedding.

"Yes, a house. That one is small, George, and our family, I am certain, is going to grow. Better to build it now, rather than later. Or never, of course. There is always never." George looked at his diminutive house, and then at Anna. He studied the profile of her face, self assured and rather determined. George did not wish to disturb those waters.

"Right, Anna," he said. "We'll build now."

"What a fine idea," she replied, with a nod and a smile.

They had long talks about the possibilities, deciding upon a "kit" home from the Montgomery Ward catalogue. Once the materials arrived, George built their house as painstakingly as he had the barn. He gave over a good deal of that spring to this endeavor, and to Anna's delight, the outcome was perfect.

It had their bedroom, the kitchen, a living room and something he called a den. They had a bathroom, but because of his deep-seated abhorrence of germs, it contained no toilet. Strangely, Anna went along with this quirk and declared an outhouse to be good enough for her

(George might be right about those germs). He created plenty of space for the house garden, which lay just outside their kitchen window. Anna could work there with a marvelous view of both garden and barn.

By the middle of June, the house was completed and they could be married. Anna beamed. You had to hand it to that George West. No man could match him for hard work, and once he put his mind to a thing, that thing would be accomplished.

And so, after the wedding on June 15, 1921, Anna moved her things into their new and adorable white house. The two of them stood on the little porch and surveyed their domain, hand in hand.

"Good morning, Mrs. West," said George, turning.

"Good morning, husband," said she. Then to her surprise and considerable chagrin (for she was not a small woman), George suddenly lifted her up and carried her in, across the threshold.

"George!" she exclaimed.

"Welcome home," he murmured.

CHAPTER SEVEN

It's Still A Honeymoon

1921

They took a month's honeymoon, heading south across the lush green fields of Umatilla County. Anna loved Oregon in the month of June, but had been so busy with teaching and performing that she rarely had time to get out and enjoy it. Well, now she would.

With an upcoming crop sale in July, George would have preferred a shorter trek. But Anna was keen to spend their first month free of farm concerns, so George had left it all in the capable hands of his farm manager. Mac Tompkins had the reputation of an astute administrator, and George harbored no fears.

"We'll be back before the sale, Mac," he said. "But my stipulated price and all the details are in the ledger if you need them."

"Yes, sir," said Mac, and George worried no more. That money would take him and Anna comfortably through the coming year, a good solid beginning.

Anna's hand rested lightly upon his as they drove, and both were smiling.

"What's that, George?" she said.

"Oh, just thinking out loud, I guess. About the crop. And, Anna - about something else I haven't told you."

"Oh?" she asked, with interest.

"I've finally paid off the farm. It's ours."

Anna grasped his hand, and squeezed. "How wonderful for you! I thought you might have, the way you've been smiling so."

"Well, there's been a lot to smile about," he chuckled, "and not just the farm."

She gazed out at the passing landscape, concluding once again that she had landed on her feet in marrying George. He was surprisingly sweet, for a farmer. And what other man of forty-two had full ownership of a prosperous farm with 475 acres? She smiled again and murmured, "Thanks be to God."

On the last full day of the honeymoon, their car broke down as they rolled into the town of Shaniko. George frowned and pressed the starter, but apart from a clicking noise from beneath the hood, nothing happened.

"Confounded car," he muttered in a tone Anna had never yet heard.

"Hmm," she replied.

At the service station, they were told the carburetor could be repaired, but they would have to wait two days for the parts.

"Two days!" cried George, in alarm.

"The Shaniko Inn is across the way, sir," said the mechanic, helpfully. "Plenty of rooms..." But he faltered when he saw the red face of his customer.

"Confounded car!" George repeated as they crossed to the hotel. The agitation over his crop back home had given him a headache. The sale would happen without him now, and he would simply have to wait.

"It's still a honeymoon," said Anna, who rather liked the looks of the hotel and did not mind the delay. But George fumed, and the moment they reached home two days later, he leapt from the car and dashed off in search of his manager. Anna went into her new kitchen, cheerfully oblivious to the drama taking place in yonder barn.

The news from Mac could not have been worse: he'd botched the deal by waiting too long, finally and desperately selling the crop at rock bottom.

"I'm sorry, George," he said, handing over the tell-tale ledger.

"Sorry?" said George, with a hard look. Seeing the figures, he let out

a great roar of "Thunderation!", as bad a curse word as George would use. This prompted some stiff language from the manager, defending his actions and accusing George of staying away too long.

"I was waiting for you!" he cried.

But shouting and cursing could not alter the fact that somewhere between Shaniko and Milton, their first year's income had disappeared. George thought what a complete simpleton he had been, traipsing off on a wedding trip when he had a crop to sell. He saw this as Anna's fault, for she had (unreasonably, he now felt) wanted the honeymoon.

She felt sorry, now, and said so. But of course being sorry would do nothing to recover their first year's income.

George sank wearily down on the bed in a stony silence.

At least I've paid off the place, he thought. No one can take that from me. He'd need to get those deeds filed with the county, though, and soon. He had meant to file them before the wedding, but time had gotten the better of him.

Reaching beneath the bed where he kept his strongbox, George stiffened. The strongbox wasn't there. He knelt to the floor to have a closer look but again, he found nothing. Had he put it somewhere else?

Had Anna? Surely not, for she didn't know about the strongbox. In a growing panic he searched every inch of the house, the bunkhouse, even the empty little house he had once occupied. With nowhere else to look, George had to face the truth that his strong box, and the ownership deeds it had contained, were gone.

The loss of their crop had been bad, but could not compare with the loss of those deeds. Just two days ago, he had been on top of the world; now, he may as well be a pauper. Anna once again came to his mind in an unreasonable rage. He lifted his heavy travel case and hurled it at full strength across the bedroom.

The resultant crash brought his wife running in from the kitchen. "What on earth, George?" she cried, concern lining her face. He looked slowly over at her, stern and formidable. She almost didn't recognize him.

"The farm deeds are gone," he said. It sounded like an accusation.

She stared at him. "Gone? But where?"

"How should I know? The strongbox is missing."

"But George - I thought you had already filed those deeds." She looked frightened. "Hadn't you…?"

She realized then that he hadn't, that they would presumably have to begin paying for the farm all over again. It came as a terrible shock, but she could think of nothing more to say than the "Oh dear.." that escaped her lips. She tried to approach him, to comfort him; but one defiant shake of his head discouraged the warm access she had enjoyed with him until now. Anna backed away toward the sanctuary of her kitchen, for this, at least, made sense to her. They had to eat, after all.

In the following weeks George refused to discuss the missing deeds, but quietly followed up on his own theories surrounding their removal. The answer had to lay somewhere in the family, so he went to his siblings one by one and asked them straight out. His sisters were surprised to hear of the disappearance, and would take not another penny from him. Their brothers, however, saw it differently, claiming George had "lost" the deeds and would simply have to pay the price.

He would never darken their doors again.

Another blow came from his own mother, who refused to testify in court on his behalf even though she knew the truth. The discussion became heated.

"No, George."

"What do you mean, 'No'?"

"I mean no, I won't go into that old court, not for nothin'."

"But I need your help, Mother, you must see that. My brothers came into my house boldly and took those deeds after I'd paid for them!"

"Do you think I would stand up in a courtroom and tell family secrets like that? You leave me out of this, George." And so, he had.

In this way, a chasm developed within the family that would never be fully healed - not in their lifetimes, at least. To their descendants, the lingering rift became a mystery, discussed and debated until the last sibling had finally died, and the questions had all lost their edge.

But time is a healer, if not of all wounds, then at least of some. Prosperous years did come, but George, from the year of the wedding, was a changed man. Whether by age or disappointment, he became harder to know.

But Anna's happier predictions all came true, for the family grew by three and filled up the rooms of the little white house. She called her children Landon, Esther, and George Robert, finding in them a surprisingly merry little crew. The three of them were more than just funny, they were downright entertaining in both music and humor. Anna wondered where in the world all this banter was coming from, for neither she nor George ever so much as cracked a joke.

The Great Depression eventually came, of course, but did not wreak such frightful havoc upon the Wests as it had so many others. George guarded over their prospects as a hen would her chicks, as one by one the surrounding farms faced difficulties and, in some cases, collapse. Time and again, the West farm held fast.

"And how are we faring today, George?" Anna would occasionally ask while stirring the gravy. Her husband would pause, and say, "We're holding our own."

"Thanks be to God," Anna said, for she knew that only the Almighty could lend success.

Anna had once planned to be a missionary in a land far from home. But shepherding her little flock of three had become, in a thousand ways, much the better choice. She doubted whether a foreign mission field could have kept her any busier than their home grown one.

Through her window, the sun hovered low along the horizon and brightened the wheat growing there. From the midst of that golden grain she saw three little heads bouncing, shouting, laughing, the tallest one in the lead. Behind them walked George, now in his fifties but as strong as he'd ever been, bringing the little flock of Wests home to their suppers.

CHAPTER EIGHT

She Had An Inkling

1940

Pennie saw the new boy one day in the school hallway, and thought instantly that he liked himself. It was silly, really, that he should feel that way, and that the people around him should so obviously agree. A group of girls walking past glanced back, giggling over the dreamy, dark-headed Senior whom they would practically die to get to know. Pennie felt embarrassed for them. She and her friends would know better; they would never make such ninnies of themselves on account of a boy.

But many such "ninnies" populated the hallways of McLoughlin High School that year, and a growing number of them began to congregate wherever it was he happened to be.

"Who is that?" whispered one rather silly girl to her friend, as they scurried past Pennie.

"His name is Landon," said the well-informed girl, "and isn't he gorgeous? He's a singer, every bit as good as Frank Sinatra..." The clutch of girls finally turned left down the hallway, and their breathless giggling faded away.

Well, Pennie would pay no attention, however popular he might be. What could she do about it anyway? A boy like that would never be interested in the likes of her. Besides, he liked himself and Pennie really could not tolerate swagger. Hurrying up the stairs toward her next class, she put the new boy, and his dark wavy hair, out of her mind.

Of all the classes at Mac High, Pennie's favorite was Photography. To create something that had never existed, snapping photographs and mixing the chemicals as Mr. Hawke directed, fascinated her. Mr. Hawke had only one strict rule when it came to his Photography class: boys and girls inside the darkroom at the same time was considered off limits.

"If you go into the darkroom and find someone in there who is OFF LIMITS, you must leave at once." Pennie, having a high respect for rules in general, would never dream of breaking this one.

She reached her seat just as the bell rang and Mr. Hawke closed the door. In the resulting silence, they all heard the door opening again. To their surprise, the new boy entered and handed the teacher a slip of paper.

"Mr. West, eh?" said the teacher. "The office said you'd be coming. Please take the empty seat at the front there, next to Pennie."

Landon took the proffered seat, turning his gaze on her as he did. Pennie could not help but notice, up close, how very attractive he was.

"Hello, Pennie," he whispered, with a wink. "I'm Landon."

No boy had ever winked at her before, and Pennie couldn't tell if she liked it or not. She happened to be one of those rare girls who are beautiful, but do not know it. Boys tended to stare at her as she walked by, but she ignored them. Boys were simply there, people with whom one must share the classroom, or the cafeteria, or the universe. She had an inkling that they would one day become more important (Mother, after all, had married Daddy), but until that distant day, her life would remain uncomplicated, sensible, and certainly not silly.

"He's uppity, I think," she said afterward, when the other girls asked. "..and maybe a little bit proud."

"But he winked at you," said one, "in front of everybody!"

"Hmm," Pennie replied. "That was too smooth, don't you think?" She couldn't quite put her finger on it, but it had irked her. She shrugged.

"You can't be so nonchalant about him," another girl said. "A boy like that doesn't pay attention to just anybody."

But Pennie persisted in her nonchalance, simply tossing her head and walking on. Landon probably winked at all the girls, and they probably all giggled. So there was no sense in worrying about it.

"There's no sense in worrying about it," she said, secretly worrying just a little, all the same.

Meanwhile, the subject of all this curiosity sat thoughtfully in his History class. He knew he should be paying attention to the Articles of the Confederation, but however hard he might try, Landon could not take it in. He felt his mind would be forever distracted from anything but that striking girl in his Photography class. Pennie, the teacher had said. Landon had always scoffed at the idea of love at first sight, but wondered now whether there might be something to it.

He thought of this girl now, as would almost any teenaged boy forced to sit through a History class. And what did he see? He saw a tall girl, slender, with brown eyes and the softest brown hair tumbling to her shoulders in the most appealing fashion. Other girls kept their hair somehow more contained (he could not think how) but hers seemed - well, flowing. Carefree. He liked it. And what a coincidence her height fit with his exactly. Not too short, not too tall. This girl was, as the old fairy tale said, just right.

Landon himself stood tall and slender, his hair dark auburn with what his grandmother called a "natural curl". He was strong, as a boxer is strong. He was, in fact, a boxer, winning his matches and finding the most exquisite joy in flailing away at some hapless opponent from another school. His mother refused to watch, declaring it to be "the strangest way to earn a grade".

Yes, he liked this girl. He liked her a lot. Even her name intrigued him. He hadn't known any Pennie's before. But Landon would bide his time. He did not wish to have her startled, as a young colt might be startled.

As all these thoughts were scrambling his brain, someone came into the classroom and handed the teacher a note. He paused in his lecture and said, "Great Scott, the Nazis are bombing London."

The class woke up (for at least this was interesting) and he continued, "They've been bombing the docks all night long and people have gathered in the Underground for protection. There's no place else for them to go. It's horrendous."

Such news sobered them all. The United States had not gotten involved in the European war yet, and many of the young men were anxious to change that. If we did get in, they would go. Landon would go. At least, he would want to, if his father would only let him. They had already had that conversation and intensely disagreed, George insisting upon a deferment. They were farmers, he said, and Landon was needed. But for now, why should they argue? The U.S. would, for now, stay out of it. And at 18, Landon didn't see what his father could do to stop him, if the U.S. did get in. Then everything would change. Absolutely everything.

McLoughlin High School had a reputation for its musicals and dramas, with almost everyone trying for a part. Even the smaller roles had stiff competition. Student auditions filled the hours at the end of each school day, and the auditorium became crowded with observers. They had to remain quiet, for the director did not want even one of his budding actors distracted.

One day these lucky observers saw and heard something they never forgot. During auditions for the comic opera The Mikado, Landon tried for the lead - Nanki Poo. It was a tough part. Indeed, it would be a tough production, an ambitious choice for any high school. But the part suited him down to the ground, and he decided to give it a shot.

When his name was called, Landon made his way to center stage. People were standing around in small groups, whispering quietly, studying lines. After the pianist's short introduction, he began to sing. A hush instantly fell upon the auditorium, as if some kind of spell were being cast. Landon quite literally commanded the stage, singing his heart out and posturing as stated in the show notes.

Mr. White knew Anna Compton and had expected quality from her son, but nothing like this. Landon's vibrato surprised him, being strong and steady. Most high school boys didn't have a memorable voice, let alone a vibrato - and Landon had both! Mr. White had never heard anything like it.

Landon continued on, looking his audience in the eye and giving them access. There was something personal to it that reminded the director of Frank Sinatra, who had not found fame until age 28. Landon at 18 already carried the Sinatra magic. Everyone present felt as if they were looking at, and listening to, a Star.

Unaware of the sensation he had created, Landon kept singing right up to the end and held his position, surrounded by a pin-dropping silence.

"Thank you Landon", said Mr. White, scarcely able to contain his excitement. "We will be posting the results on Friday."

The auditorium burst into applause as Landon stepped from the stage, surrounded by his peers. He looked around but did not see Pennie among them. A hundred people may have been cheering and banging him on the back, but he really only cared about one.

After that, the other Nanki Poo hopefuls fell rather flat, and it surprised no one when Landon's name was posted for the part.

The Mikado was a success, beginning to end. Everyone became so caught up in the production that it was a wonder any actual schoolwork was accomplished. Rehearsals took on the look and feel of performances, complete with applause and cheering until Mr. White finally had to insist upon silence, "...or I will need to ask you all to leave."

The production sold out for every performance. On opening night, Landon couldn't help but feel the significance of it as he waited in the wings for his cue. He wondered if Pennie would be in the audience, and decided to put his all into it just in case she was.

At the stroke of 8:00 pm, he and his entourage leapt to the stage with a grand gesture, and sang as if with one voice:

If you want to know who we are,
We are the gentlemen of Japan.
On many a vase and a jar
On many a screen and fan...

(Gilbert and Sullivan, Public Domain)

From this magnificent beginning, Landon finds himself alone on the stage, performing the solo A Wandering Minstrel, I. In it, he explains how he met Yum-Yum and fell in love at once. She loved him too, but was already betrothed to the scoundrel Ko-Ko, and so, as all good love stories do, this one moved from emptiness, to love, to sorrow, and back to love again. He especially liked the 'love' part, and thought of Pennie as he sang.

The town declared it was the best they had ever seen. They were proud, especially of "that West kid". Landon soon received requests to sing solos for assemblies. He traveled to other towns, representing the school. He sang for the local women's groups and made them all cry. Yet even with the popularity, and girls clustering around him for attention, Landon never acted as though he were special. It came naturally to him and, rather like his boxing, it was the most marvelous fun.

A few days after The Mikado had finished, Pennie and her friend Iris were walking home from school and talking about their shared nemesis, Geometry.

"How many problems do you have finished for tomorrow?" asked Iris. "I've hardly..."

A car approached from behind, but they weren't paying attention. Pennie had turned to cross the road when the car slowed, and pulled alongside them.

"Need a ride?" said a familiar voice, and they turned to see Landon smiling up at them from his little Ford two-seater, one hand on the wheel, the other resting along the back of the seat. Wearing sunglasses and an open-collared shirt, he would not have seemed out of place in a film.

Pennie assumed the ride was meant for Iris, so she stood back. But then Iris all at once climbed into the car, and Landon asked Pennie to get in too. So she squeezed into the seat with them while struggling with her armload of books. She had books and Iris had books. And then there were Landon's books. It became awkwardly crowded. But Landon and Iris chatted amiably as he pulled away from the curb, something about who had beaten whom in baseball. Iris always knew about things like sports. Pennie didn't pay much attention because of her worrisome homework.

She noticed they had passed her street, and were heading toward Iris's. "My house..." she began, pointing. But Iris intervened.

"That's okay, I'll get out at the corner," and in some confusion Pennie let Iris and her books get out. "Thanks for the ride - see you tomorrow, Pennie!"

Feeling a flash of shyness, Pennie climbed back in, her eyes on Iris's departing back. There was something dejected about it. But Landon had already moved on and they circled back, finally drawing up in front of her house.

"Pennie," he said, as she gathered up her books, "there's a game this Saturday."

She stopped gathering, and looked at him. "Hmm?"

"Well, how would you like to go to it? With me, I mean."

Pennie couldn't believe it. The star of The Mikado, this boy who could get any girl he wanted, had just asked her on a date. Would a baseball game be considered a date? She supposed it might be. It must be! She looked out the windshield, and thought about it.

"Well?" he asked. "Would you like to? I could pick you up at 1:00."

She wondered what her parents would say, and whether she should ask for permission. But Pennie already knew Mother and Dad would like him, and that they would say yes. So she felt she could say it first.

"Yes," she said simply. "I'll just run in and check with Mother. Be right back."

But Landon said, "Why don't I come in with you? Seems more friendly that way." So together they walked up to the house, Landon opening the door for her. Ike and Ida looked up from the table where they had been doing some figuring.

"Mother? Dad?" Pennie began. "This is Landon, George West's son. He gave Iris and me a ride home today."

The scene before them immediately clarified itself. They had wondered when a boy would come through that door with Pennie, and now one finally had. Both stood.

"Landon, these are my parents, Ike and Ida Kenoyer."

"Hello, Landon," said Ida. "How do you do?"

"It's nice to meet you both," he replied with a smile.

"Landon has asked me to go to the baseball game on Saturday. Is it alright with you?"

Her parents looked at each other. They knew about Landon, and of course had seen The Mikado. They knew about his mother, and that his father had a working farm. A prosperous working farm. They saw no harm in a baseball game.

"No harm in a baseball game," said Ike.

"Of course you may go," said Ida.

"Alright then Pennie, I'll pick you up at 1:00 Saturday."

As he climbed into his car and drove away, Dorothy came up the porch steps.

"What was he doing here?" she asked. Pennie had never brought a boy home.

"Oh, he gave me a ride home, that's all," Pennie replied dismissively.

"Are you sure?" laughed Dorothy, with a growing perception.

Pennie found herself strangely short of breath. It seemed odd. She hadn't even been running. Without warning, her cheeks began to burn. Dorothy laughed again, but only briefly.

There was a change in the air.

CHAPTER NINE

Getting To Know Him

Landon arrived on Saturday in a different car, not the little two-seater which Pennie had liked and looked forward to riding in again. This time he brought his father's larger, more substantial sedan. Any boy would be proud to take a car like this to a girl's house. Pennie couldn't imagine any family owning two such cars.

Standing at the edge of the window, she watched as he rang the doorbell. He held a flower - a simple white daisy, but perfect. Pennie ran to the door, and as she opened it, he held out the daisy.

"My mother's favorites. She had them planted last year."

"How sweet!" she said. "Come in. I'll run and get a vase."

She went to the kitchen, and saw her mother, who saw the daisy.

"Oh, how sweet..." Ida said, and their eyes met. A flower. Pennie's cheeks were pink. Something was up, Ida thought, and it didn't take much to figure out what.

Pennie came back to the living room where her father and Landon sat chatting easily about the farm. Ike asked questions, and Landon, in his friendly way, answered them. They had found something in common in the few moments it took to find the vase. Both stood as the ladies walked in.

"Thank you," Pennie said shyly, placing it on the table. No boy had ever given her a flower.

"Well," said Landon, "it's time we started. I'll have her back early evening, sir." He shook hands with Ike.

As they drove away in that smart sedan, Pennie looked back toward the house and saw all of her siblings - Dorothy, Barbara, Alan, and Lorinda - grinning at her from the window. They clearly thought the whole thing hilarious. Suddenly the four watchers disappeared, whisked precipitously away by their mother. Pennie laughed, happy to give them at least a little entertainment.

On the way to the game, they stopped at the corner soda fountain where several other high schoolers sat perched on stools at the counter. From the juke box drifted the voice of Frank Sinatra, the words "I Only Have Eyes For You" ringing out as they found an empty table. Pennie didn't actually like Frank Sinatra, even though her friends talked about little else. Sinatra liked himself a bit too much, she thought.

But she remembered having thought the same thing about Landon, at first. He had liked himself too. Maybe singers had that effect upon themselves, or maybe they liked hearing their own voices. Pennie thought Sinatra probably had scads of girlfriends, and wondered uneasily if Landon did.

Then she remembered the daisy resting in its vase back home, and thought, I'm being silly and disloyal. She smiled up at Landon, and gave no further thought to "Ol' Blue Eyes".

Landon and Pennie started out as friends, going for walks and sodas, or sitting on the porch visiting with Ike. But in time, it became known around the high school that the two were "going together". A general moan went up among the boys of her year, none of whom would have a shred of a chance with her now.

"Pennie?" he said one afternoon as they walked from the school to the soda fountain. He calmly reached over to take her hand, and she did not withdraw it. They had never yet held hands, and doing it now made him feel as though he might float away, on a cloud. Elated, he thought. They walked on, both smiling, both apparently elated.

"Did you ever have a boyfriend?" he asked, "before now, I mean?" He'd been wondering about this, and had asked around. But no one knew. Pennie, he could see, had become something of an enigma at the school. None of his friends could adequately explain her, and this intrigued him.

"Well," she hesitated, "there's never been a boyfriend. But there was once a boy." Landon's eyebrows shot up along with his curiosity.

"Oh?" he asked.

Pennie looked up at him. "Do you really want to know?"

"I do, if you really want to tell me."

And so she told Landon about a boy who had been kind, and funny, and carefree. His name was Warren, and they were both 14.

"Mother said we were too young to date, and so we didn't. We walked, instead."

* * *

WARREN

Pennie and Warren enjoyed walking around the town perimeter, talking. They called these walks of theirs "talking walks", where anything could be discussed and nothing discarded. Warren told her about his mother and his sister (their father had died), and the places they had lived. She told him about being the cook last summer at a mountain logging camp, and sleeping in a tent.

"I made three meals a day for the men, using nothing but a rickety old camp stove. There were forty loggers to feed, always hungry! Little Alan came with us too, so I looked after him as well as the cooking."

"Did you see any bears?" asked Warren, who had a holy fear of them. Shaking her head, she laughed and her nonchalance amazed him.

"Weren't you afraid?"

"No, not really," she said. "My father slept outside our tent to block the entrance, so I didn't worry. Even bears would have a hard time of it with Dad. All he'd have to do is say, 'BANG!' and they'd run a mile." Warren believed her. Ike's voice was legend.

"A river ran next to the camp so the men rigged up a rope swing for us to take turns on every Sunday, giving us a mighty push. We usually fell in."

Pennie remembered these fun things, and laughed. "We were so busy that I didn't think even once about the movies I'd been missing back home."

"I've never been to a movie," Warren said matter-of-factly.

Pennie stopped walking. "Never been? Why not?"

He stopped walking too, and laughed.

"Yes, well, I don't go to them because we are Seventh Day Adventists, and Seventh Day Adventists don't believe in movies. I mean, they don't believe in going to them. They believe movies are bad for you." He shrugged.

Pennie couldn't understand how movies could be bad for you when they were such terrific fun. "Even Shirley Temple movies?" she asked. He nodded.

"But what about The Wizard of Oz? It's coming next week, Warren, you can't possibly miss that!"

He continued walking. "And yet, I probably will."

They ambled along the dusty road encircling the town, wary of the occasional car swinging around the bend towards them. After deliberating the pros and cons of movie-going, and much animated talk about that intriguing wizard, Warren suddenly decided he would go. With her. Pennie was thrilled.

"But what about the Adventists?"

"They'll probably get over it."

On opening night, Warren arrived at the theater first and took his place in line. As she approached, Pennie saw him staring up at the life-sized poster of a Scarecrow, a Tin Man, and a Lion. He looked so sweet and so excited that Pennie saw something she had not noticed until now: this friend-boy, her sidekick and unassuming chum, was cute. She stood still, thinking.

Just then, Warren saw her and waved.

"Over here, Pennie! I've got a place in line…"

The excitement of the crowd was palpable as they purchased their tickets and their popcorn. That night Pennie had as much fun watching Warren enjoying the movie as she had watching it herself. He sat mesmerized from beginning to end, in awe as the tornado advanced, as the black and white screen changed miraculously into "living color", and as the Wicked Witch of the West met her treacherous demise. Just as Pennie had predicted, it had all been the most enormous fun.

* * *

Pennie paused in her narration, thinking of the final moment in the final scene when Dorothy had repeated, "There's no place like home."

Landon asked, "But where is he now? I don't know of any Warrens, here."

"My family and I went away again that summer," she continued, remembering the day as if it had been yesterday.

* * *

"Going back to the mountains, are you?" Warren asked.

"Yes, we leave tomorrow. Only I won't be cooking this time. Mother will."

"Well then, I guess it's goodbye for now. Come look me up when you're back, and we'll have ourselves a good long walk." He suddenly reached out and touched her arm, something he hadn't done before. "Take care," he said. And with a smile, he had gone.

Pennie heard nothing from home while they were away, the mountain camp being too remote for telephones or letters. But she thought of Warren, and how fun it would be to tell him she actually had seen a bear this time.

On the day of their return, Pennie hurried to unpack so she could go and find him. The sky was empty of clouds and she felt a slight breeze - a perfect day for walking. As she opened the door to leave, Ida gently said, "My dear." Pennie stopped, and looked up.

"Yes, Mother?" she said.

"I'm sorry, Pennie, but it's Warren," said her mother.

Pennie looked around her. "Warren? What... "Then she took in her mother's concern-filled face. Ida had been speaking with someone on the porch earlier, but Pennie had not known why.

Ida hesitated. "He - while we were in the mountains, Warren was walking along the road toward town. And - I'm sorry, Pennie, but a truck hit him at that corner by the old Johnson place." She paused.

"What happened to him!" Pennie cried, panic in her voice. "What happened to Warren?" But she quickly saw the truth in her mother's face, that the accident had been fatal and Warren... gone. They had often talked about the cars that came around that particular bend almost too quickly to avoid. If only he had been more careful; if only she'd been there to remind him! But now the worst had happened, and there could be no more if's.

* * *

"Oh no..." said Landon, stopping and turning toward her.

"They had the funeral weeks before we knew; before we ever got home. I went right away to his house, and saw his mother. She cried when she saw me standing on the porch; and then I cried. It was dreadful."

They walked on. "He was a good friend," she murmured. "He might have been more than that, if he had lived."

Landon squeezed her hand as they entered the soda fountain and heard the cheerful voices of their friends.

"Come sit with us!" someone called from the corner booth.

There was a sudden flurry of activity as the waitress took their order, and the bustle of life inside a soda fountain surrounded them. But Pennie hardly noticed. Her thoughts were out on a dusty country road where soda fountains, juke boxes, and laughing friends were all still the future, and Warren was the past.

With Landon in it, Pennie's life became sweeter. She now had a boy to walk or to ride with; someone to go to the soda fountain with, along with any number of their friends. The juke box boomed out all the popular songs of that year, and the kids couldn't get enough of them. One day when the box had fallen silent, Landon stood and began singing "I'll Be Seeing You" to Pennie until she fell into helpless giggles and begged him to stop - all the while hoping he wouldn't.

And so, the "new boy" won her heart. She knew he had, long before that first year ended, the year after his mother had died. One day Landon told her about it.

"Mother stayed in the hospital over Christmas that year. She wanted to be with us at home, but the doctors wouldn't let her. I used to sit by her hospital bed and hold her hand, the way she did when I was sick. It felt terrible. The day Dad came home and told us she had died was the worst day of my life. Nothing has ever been the same since."

"When were you sick?" Pennie asked.

"I missed a year of school at age fifteen," he said. "Rheumatic Fever. Mother would sit by the bed and read or sing to me, and we'd play the "Authors" game by the hour. She kept me from going crazy, Pennie. I got used to seeing her there when I woke up. She'd always been a wonderful mother, but we got closer than ever that year."

"And the daisies?" said she.

"Yes. She liked having them around her...my father never speaks of her, Pennie, or of losing her. Whenever my mother's name is mentioned, Dad gets up and leaves the room. More than anything else, this hurts us the most."

Landon suddenly put a hand over his eyes, and Pennie shyly reached for his other hand. They two sat there for a while in the silence.

And then he said, "I think I'm going to kiss you now."

Pennie looked up at him and thought, "It's about time," but said instead, "Okay."

And sitting there, on a park bench in the middle of the town, Landon kissed her. It was gentle, and chaste. No feeling of fear on her part, or of urgency on his, just the first, tentative kiss of two young people on the verge of love. For Pennie, it would be the moment she became certain that this man, in the year of 1941 with war looming and the world uncertain, had become the one, the only one, for her.

For the rest of that year, Landon performed in every musical and drama the school produced. Pennie would slip into the darkened auditorium and watch his rehearsals as a way of seeing him. She sat toward the left near the door, and waited for him to notice her. He always eventually did, and could not resist singing his parts straight at her.

"Landon!" Mr White would shout. "Eyes to the center in this piece!

Eyes to the center." And Landon would obediently sing toward the center, stealing a saucy glance in her direction now and again.

He came often to the house to see her, but not only her. He liked them all, bringing candy for the smaller ones and playing catch out front with Alan. Pennie humbly repented ever thinking of him as "uppity". How could she have come to such a conclusion? Landon simply liked people, and enjoyed it when they liked him back.

He took her to the farm to meet his father, heartily wishing his mother had still been there. George was not the warmest of men, but Landon's mother would have covered this and given Pennie a thorough welcome. It would probably have been unforgettable.

No one could ever forget Anna Compton West. She had impressed everyone, and now it looked as though her children would go on to do the same. Although she had not been there to see The Mikado, she had confided to George her surprise at the performances she did get to see.

"George," she said to her husband one night, near the end, "I am not well, and I regret it. I wanted to be here and see what becomes of these children of ours. I think I know what will become of Landon. He is good, and will likely become great. Bob and Esther probably will too, given time. I am satisfied."

She died three months later.

CHAPTER TEN

The Day That Brought Them War

"Yesterday, December 7th, 1941—a date which will live in infamy—the United States of America was suddenly and deliberately attacked by naval and air forces of the Empire of Japan." -President Franklin Delano Roosevelt

On a Sunday morning in early December, the Kenoyers arrived home from church to find visitors on the porch, concerned and unsmiling.

Ike murmured, "What's this?" They pulled up onto the gravel, got out, and went to investigate.

"Ike, you'd better get inside and turn the radio on," said the normally cheerful Bill Paulson whose family lived next door. The color had gone from his face, and Pennie wondered if he might be ill.

"Why's that?" Ike asked, his face suddenly grim.

"Them Japanese.." began Mr Paulson, following Ike inside. The little group followed, surrounded by the mouth-watering aroma of Ida's Sunday roast. Whatever else might be going on in the world, there would always be the Sunday roast, and it would always be delicious. But Pennie would forever link the smell of that roasting of the beef to the shocking words which followed.

Ike stood at the center of the group, Pennie with her hand on his arm, such a firm and capable arm. Surely whatever they were about to hear about the Japanese could be borne, so long as they had such men as Ike to depend upon.

He switched on the RCA, located a news station, and then they all heard the devastating words none of them would ever forget.

"And now, ladies and gentlemen, the latest. The United States Naval base at Pearl Harbor has this morning sustained a surprise attack by the Japanese. Airplanes, presumably from aircraft carriers, bombed and torpedoed the great Naval Base on the island of Oahu in the Hawaiian Islands." They all stared at the radio in horror, as if it were somehow at fault.

"Oh dear," said Mrs. Paulson. "I suppose we'll be at war now, too." Such a possibility had loomed for a long time, but an act of aggression like this, on Pearl Harbor on a Sunday morning, came as a shock. The announcer went on to state that a number of U.S. battleships had been destroyed and capsized, with hundreds of sailors trapped at that moment, below.

"God help those poor, poor men," said Ida, coming to stand by her husband. "Stay and have lunch with us," she said to the Paulsons. "We must still eat, war or no war." She distractedly dished up the food with the girls' help, setting it all on the long oak dining table.

They gathered together, bowing their heads as Ike prayed over the meal and for God's guidance on this day that had brought them war. A hush fell around the table as the food was passed and the radio continued its commentary. When someone said, "Please pass the gravy," Ida drew in her breath.

"What is it, Mother?" asked Dorothy, concerned.

"I'm so sorry, it's just that - I've forgotten to make the gravy." The girls paused in surprise, and looked at their mother. It was the only Sunday in all of Ida Kenoyer's cooking life that she had ever forgotten to make the gravy.

Landon's Christmas break came soon after that day of infamy, and he headed home from college to the discussion he'd dreaded for months. Pennie heard all about it when he called the next day.

"Let me guess," she said. "Your father still doesn't want you to join the Army."

"Yep," Landon said with annoyance. "And he'd already gotten me an agricultural deferment! I'd planned to join up, but he made it official before I had the chance."

"Oh... well, that would be alright with me," said Pennie, thinking of battlefields. But she knew by the tone of his voice that it would never be alright with him.

The boys in town hooted endlessly over Landon's predicament, and treated it as a grand joke.

"Hey, Nanny, heard about your DEFERMENT. Gonna sit this one out?" It was aggravating, and only grew worse as Army and Navy uniforms began showing up on the streets of the town. Now Landon really was fit to be tied.

But those boys had forgotten that the West kid could box, and pretty soon some of them felt the business end of Landon's right hook. No one could call him a coward, whatever else they might say about him. Not so long as he had his right hook.

While Landon fought his own battles away from the war, Pennie joined her friend Blanche on another front. The two had graduated from high school, moved to Sumner, and wanted to do their 'bit' for the War effort. After all, there were jobs everywhere now, at least if you were a man. They decided to see what the Tacoma shipyards had to say on the subject.

The shipyard clerk peered skeptically over his glasses, first at Pennie, and then at Blanche.

"We've never hired women for these jobs," he said, shaking his head. "Never needed to."

"Yes, Sir," the girls murmured, politely awaiting their fate. Outside the plate glass window, the shipyards of Tacoma were a massive sprawl of boats, ships, and junkets, hardly a place to find women at work. But things were changing now, and everyone wanted to pitch in.

"I've got to hand it to you, you're the first women to apply for it. Tell you what - the men are all going to the Front, and quite frankly, we need you. I might as well give you a try, because there's not much left of the men."

"Yes sir," they said, thinking it didn't sound much like a compliment.

"If you do well, we'll hire more women. If you don't, well, we won't. It's as simple as that." He stood, then they stood. "Can you start today?"

"Anytime you like, sir," said Pennie.

"This afternoon, then. Swing shift, 3:00 to 11:00. Punctuality is imperative. You'll be time-keepers, and it's no use being a time-keeper if you're going to be late."

"We'll be here, sir. We won't be late. And, thank you!" With that, the girls walked serenely out of the door and down the yard, almost floating. Once they were around the corner from that windowed office, they broke the veneer of professionalism and became little girls again.

"We did it, Blanche!" said Pennie as they grasped hands and squealed discreetly. "We're actually going to earn money!" They felt the relentless shadow of the Great Depression finally beginning to lift.

When Pennie told her parents, they sat grinning at her while the children jumped around shouting nonsense.

"You're going to be rich, Pennie!" exclaimed Alan. "Rolling in the dough!" Their obvious joy went straight to the heart of this earnest girl who had found a way to do her "bit".

"What sort of work will you be doing?" asked Ida.

"Time-keeping. We're going to be guinea pigs, Mother."

"Guinea pigs?"

"Yes. They will try us out, and if we do well they'll hire more women. If we don't, they won't. So - guinea pigs." Pennie smiled.

"Of course you'll do well," said loyal Dorothy.

And Dorothy spoke the truth. From the start, the boss found them punctual and hard-working and not inclined to flirt. Other women soon appeared at the clerk's metal desk (Dorothy included), and were hired. The war effort surged ahead everywhere as shipping, munitions, and transportation took off. Looking out over the ships in Tacoma Harbor, Pennie knew one thing for certain: Japan and Germany were going to be in for it now. They had awakened the Giant.

PART THREE

BIND MY WANDERING HEART TO THEE

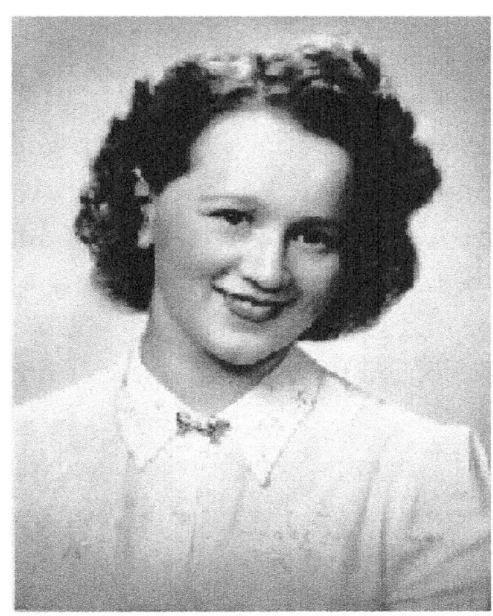

CHAPTER ELEVEN

A Sudden Dash For The Phone

1942

A YEAR HAD COME AND GONE since the attack on Pearl, and Landon wanted in. His friends were now sprinkled around the globe while he sat helplessly shackled to his deferment. His early attempt at college had ended badly (too much easy fun), prompting shouts of outrage from George for the money he had squandered.

"What do you mean, you failed out?" cried George. "You better not have!"

"Well, but I did," said Landon. "And I'm sorry." He bowed his head, looking repentant. But Landon was a pretty good actor, and George became suspicious. He shook a piece of paper in his son's face.

"This transcript says you withdrew months ago. What the Sam Hill?"

Landon cringed. If only colleges could keep such knowledge away from parents! He glanced around for a getaway, but George glared into him.

"I wasn't born yesterday, boy, and you're not too old to thrash. In fact..." The man's hands twitched.

"But I'll be 21 in May!"

While no actual "thrashing" took place, Landon was wounded by this most recent parental squall. His thoughts turned toward Pennie. He loved her, but she was 300 miles away, working at her Shipyard and doing her bit. Why couldn't they be doing their bit together? A daring man might pull it off. A daring man might spring himself loose from the 2-C Deferment, join the Army, and get married.

Galvanized by these compelling thoughts, Landon made a sudden dash for the phone. It might be a long shot, but why not give it a try? He was, after all, a daring man.

It took him all of seven days, a record for any government bureau. Having successfully "sprung" himself into the Army, he called Pennie.

"Can you meet my bus?" he asked. "I'm coming your way tomorrow!"

This surprised her. "You're finished with school already?"

"I guess you could say so," he replied vaguely. "But I'll fill you in later."

Pennie had picked him up from bus stations before, and knew Landon always sat in the back, talking to the other passengers, telling jokes, charming them all. He couldn't help it, she knew. Pennie had herself been charmed.

When he stepped down toward her, Pennie was surprised to see he was holding a cigarette.

"You're smoking now?" she asked, more from curiosity than chagrin, because so many of their friends now smoked. But Landon didn't, because they had decided together not to. It made him look different somehow, sort of like Peter Lawford.

He dropped the cigarette and stepped on it. "Exams were grueling. But I'm planning to quit."

"Okay," she shrugged, grasping his hand and pulling him forward. "Come on, everybody is waiting to see you and we've got a mile to walk!"

As they reached the long grassy lane toward home, she picked up speed. "Wait till you see, Mother has made all of your favorites, and…" But suddenly, unexpectedly, he dropped her hand and said, "Pennie…"

She turned, and saw him bending a knee onto the grass. "I've been wanting to ask you something for ages, Pennie," he said, "and it can't wait another minute."

She caught her breath.

"I love you…" He hesitated.

"Yes?"

"And - will you marry me?" he blurted. "I've joined the Army… in tanks!"

She looked down into his earnest face.

"Tanks? But what about your deferment?" Whereupon explanations were made ("The Army agreed with me!"), leaving Pennie somewhat dazed.

"Your poor father," she said, finding it in her heart to feel sorry for George. "He isn't going to like it."

"No, I don't suppose he is. But he's there and I am here, and my knee is getting awfully wet, Pennie. Will you marry me? Tanks and all?"

Landon looked so hopeful and so sweet that Pennie decided at once, bending forward and holding his face in her hands. "Yes, Landon, I will marry you. Tanks and all!"

Landon pulled a small, dark velvet box from his pocket, gently took her left hand in his, and placed a ring on her finger. Somehow he had gotten the size just right.

"It fits perfectly!"

"A little bird told me.."

Pennie laughed, gazing at her hand in a kind of awe. She had wondered what it would feel like to be given such a ring at such a moment, and now she knew.

Her heart thumped away inside her fit to burst, and she grabbed his hand again, pulling. "Let's go!" she said, starting to run. "We'll tell them!"

Off they flew, pausing along the way for a few dozen kisses. On the porch where Alan had stood watch, the two were quickly seen and surrounded by family, everyone talking at once. In the midst of all the joy, Pennie's eyes met Dorothy's.

"Are you?" whispered her sister, noticing Landon's one damp knee.

"Pennie held up her left hand. "Yes!" she said. Then all at once everybody saw, and everybody knew. The noise level grew as they all trooped inside.

The eating and the celebrating continued long into the evening, as the questions flew thick and fast.

"Where will you be stationed?" ("The Presidio, in San Francisco.").

"Why did you choose tanks?" ("I didn't. They chose me!").

"What will your father say?" ("Nothing very good.").

And, above all, "When will the wedding be?"

At this Landon looked over at Pennie, who looked expectantly back at him. The question had no ready answer, he said. The Army was in charge, and would grant him leave whenever it suited them.

Two days later, Pennie drove Landon back to the station.

"When will I see you again?" she asked, resting her head on his shoulder.

"It's up to the Army. They'll be the Boss, now."

She laughed. "Pretty big Boss…"

As Landon stepped aboard, she thought about this new Boss of theirs, and felt intrigued. It beckoned them out to where the world's great armies had gathered for the fight of their lives. She and Landon would now join this fight, going to wherever they'd be needed the most.

Pennie watched as the bus rolled eastward, away from her. She waved and then he waved, a wisp of cigarette smoke rising above his head as he did.

"I guess he hasn't quit just yet," she sighed, and climbed back into the car.

It occurred to her then that he had not told her how he'd finished the school term so early - and in all the excitement, she had forgotten to ask. Oh, well. Maybe it was best not to know.

The familiar smell of diesel fuel hung in the air as she pulled away once more, and drove herself thoughtfully home.

CHAPTER TWELVE

He Meant Every Last Word

1943

When six months had passed without a wedding date, Pennie began to wonder about her marital status.

"I'll be an Old Maid after all, Mother," she said one day.

But in early July the phone rang, and there was news. The Army had spoken.

"I've got my leave!" Landon said. But the line was crackly and Pennie couldn't hear him.

"Landon? You've what?"

"Got my leave, darling, and we are going to be married in FOUR DAYS!" He was practically shouting now, eager to set things in motion. "Can we pull it off?"

"Of course! But - four days!" She'd have to be quick.

Her dress wasn't purchased yet, and they were at the end of their sugar ration. But Landon would be there, and the preacher could come on a Tuesday. Everything else would be worked out. Her friend Marge had already agreed to act as Matron of Honor, with husband Del driving them to the bus in his shiny new car. Del could hardly wait to show off the maroon Ford convertible coupe with its rumble seat in back, perfect for the newlyweds.

Everything suddenly became a lot more real - real wedding, real vows, real husband. Pennie gulped. She'd better go and fetch Mother.

She hadn't seen Landon in six months, and felt strangely shy. There was so much about marriage she didn't know yet, and little time now in which to learn it. She knew about cooking and running a house, of course, and had helped raise her brother and three sisters. But there were other things, delicate questions she had wanted to ask but didn't know how.

Then on Sunday, when Landon finally strode up the lane looking so incredibly dashing in his uniform, she forgot these uncertainties, and ran. Then everyone else ran, welcoming him so boisterously that the dogs leapt helter-skelter into the crowd, barking their heads off.

Pennie loved her war wedding. A borrowed movie camera captured and preserved the happiness of that day as it was passed from person to person. Twenty years would elapse before Pennie ever got to see the film, and by then life had changed so dramatically that the movie seemed almost to have sprung from a different world.

But on that clear July day in 1943, the joy was palpable. There were beautiful flowers everywhere, flowers the children had "borrowed" from neighboring gardens in the dark of night. It was really very naughty of them, but Alan had been determined and Ida had not scolded.

"Can't have a wedding without some flowers!" he had cheerfully declared.

On the stroke of eleven o'clock, the crowd quietly gathered in Ida's living room. Pennie appeared at the top of the stairs, clutching her new and pretty bridal bouquet. Landon and Ike waited below, looking up at her as if no one else in the world existed. At the minister's signal she stepped slowly down and faced them. A hush descended upon the group.

"Dearly beloved," the minister began, "we are gathered together here in the sight of God and in the face of this company, to join together this man and this woman in holy matrimony, which is commended to be honorable among all men." He looked at Ike, and asked, "Who giveth this woman to be married to this man?"

Ike looked over at Ida, and cleared his throat. "Her mother and I do," he said for the first time in his life, gently placing Pennie's hand in Landon's.

"I now pronounce you husband and wife," concluded the joyous minister. "You may kiss the Bride!" This suggestion Landon instantly obeyed, causing the crowd to erupt into loud applause and shouts of congratulation. From the porch outside, Pennie's dog barked his agreement.

They all poured out onto the lawn where the bride and groom stood laughing, side-by-side.

"Husband and wife," Landon repeated, and "Kiss the bride". For him it had been the highlight of the ceremony, and he carried on doing it at frequent intervals.

Ida's splendid luncheon on the sunny lawn showered them with all manner of food, fun, and laughter, none of which came from a bottle. It was well known that although no Kenoyer took a drop of alcohol, they laughed as if they might have.

Then Del checked his watch and became all business, bustling them and their bags into the rumble seat of his impressive new car.

"Let's make tracks, you two," he said. "Can't have you arriving late for that bus."

From her perch, Pennie looked down at the crowd and felt happy, and sad, and nervous all at the same time. Her eyes began to water.

Seeing this, Landon handed her a handkerchief.

"You alright?" he said, concerned.

She sniffed. "Oh, I'm fine. I always cry when I leave home, that's all. It can't be helped."

Del put the car in gear and drove them once around the circle of the drive. Alan followed them on his bicycle, holding a white bunny and laughing at the old tin cans rattling along behind. The very last thing Pennie saw was Ida, standing arm-in-arm with Dorothy, holding a handkerchief to her face.

Landon slid open the window next to their seat in the big Greyhound. Marge and Del stood outside it, Del smiling and Marge shouting "Goodbye!" vigorously waving her handkerchief. She knew Pennie felt nervous. How could she not? At nineteen, life had never yet tempered her dreams, and Marge fervently hoped it never would. Her own dreams would never be tempered, for the simple reason that she had never indulged in dreaming. She hadn't seen the need to, and so Del's feelings at any given moment didn't seem to matter. If he was sad, he'd get glad again, that was her doctrine.

But Marge knew that Pennie did not share this doctrine. And so she stood watching the face of the young bride, deciding, at the very least, to be there for her should the need arise. Pennie thrust her hand out of the window toward her friend, who instantly grasped it and said, "It'll all be fine, you know. It'll all be just fine."

The bus pulled away, and with a final wave out the window, they were finally alone. That is, as alone as you can be on a Greyhound bus filled with strangers. Landon gently put his arm around Pennie and kissed the top of her head. It was such nice head, he thought admiringly.

"Well, we finally did it," he said. Pennie leaned into his shoulder and suddenly yawned.

"Oh, so sorry. I'm just .... sleepy..." It had been a long day, and she could not stay awake for another minute. As Pennie dozed, Landon sat looking over her head toward the passing landscape. I'm a married man now, he reflected, feeling the importance of it. As the bus lumbered along the tree-lined highway, Landon felt a momentary attack of nerves, as if he stood on a precipice with Pennie and might fall off, taking her with him. What if...

But there he stopped - or tried to stop. A vision he had wished a thousand times to eradicate from his memory snaked back in, as insidious as a slow, relentless flood. Landon rather liked the vision, but knew he shouldn't. His past had presented circumstances a woman could never be expected to understand, and he would make sure Pennie never had to try. She was the most wonderful girl he had ever met, and if anyone could make him good, it would be her. Little did he know that the prospect of any woman making any man "good", if he were not good already, stood a small chance of succeeding.

But he kissed the top of her head again and pushed these thoughts away. Today would be a new beginning, the beginning of a future he must guard with every fiber of his being. He looked at his sleeping wife, and remembered his vows.

"Landon," the minister had asked, "wilt thou have this woman to be your wife; to live together after God's holy ordinance in the holy estate of Matrimony? Wilt thou love her, comfort her, honor and keep her, in sickness and in health; and, forsaking all others, keep thyself only unto her as long as ye both shall live?"

"I will," Landon had said.

And he meant every last word of it.

CHAPTER THIRTEEN

With Scarcely A Dime

It was the last full day of their honeymoon on the farm, and Landon did not want to see it end. Three days had not been nearly enough. But the Army did not know this, and even if it had known, it would not have cared.

His father had again been impressed by the tall, gracious brunette his son had so proudly brought home. George may have been a stern man, and not exactly what a new daughter-in-law might think of as "warm". But in his chair at the kitchen table, he spent some very happy moments visiting with her. Pennie could cook like the dickens, in contrast to Aunt Lilly who kept house for him and did not over-burden herself with the details. Besides, Pennie knew how to listen and to laugh at his stories, which went far with an inveterate storyteller such as himself. His son had certainly struck gold. George wondered how the young scalawag had managed it.

This Pennie-girl would have fit in well here if only his son hadn't gone and gotten himself signed up. George's thoughts went drifting back to this, his greatest peeve. He was a strong man and a determined one, but even George West could not compete with the United States Army.

The three days slipped by, finally taking Landon and Pennie away to San Francisco and the war. George sighed, wondering what it might do to those two hopeful young people, as obviously happy as he and Anna had been.

But there was no time to think about that right now, and George got up out of his chair. War or no war, he still had a harvest to work. And at the grand age of sixty-four, it wouldn't get any easier.

The two hopeful young people finally arrived in San Francisco at sunrise. Pennie caught her breath. "Marvelous," she murmured. She had been married for less than a week, and was really quite deliriously happy.

Marriage had turned out to be both surprising and satisfying. It was surprising, because she found it suited her and she needn't have worried. Once she had gotten over the strangeness (after all, she had never spent lengths of time alone with any man), she stopped being afraid. And it was satisfying because Landon had been so endlessly funny and kind, and good at conversation. This helped immensely on their long and tedious bus trip south, during which time he entertained not only Pennie, but the other passengers. Landon made it clear to her and everyone else that he not only loved her, he appeared also to like her.

She hadn't in fact known what to expect upon getting married. In 1943, the facts of life were mostly hinted at, not heavily discussed. Pennie had soon discovered you just had to find your way and make the most of it. This she had done, without the help of any but their family doctor. That kindly gentleman, when Pennie had gone in for the obligatory blood tests, presented her with something vaguely unsettling which he called a "diaphragm".

"A diaphragm…" she repeated, looking curiously at it. Something about the device, along with his explanation of it, made her face turn pink. Pennie decided not to press the point, and the doctor murmured that Landon would "probably take care of it anyway". In the end, Pennie determined to try and not make a hash of it.

She laughed, thinking how naive she had been (a whole week ago). The truth was that whatever else may have happened, a "hash" had certainly not been made.

"What are you laughing about?" asked Landon from his window seat.

"Oh, myself, mostly…" she murmured.

Landon's first day back on the post came as a shock. The poor man had had a wedding, a honeymoon, been given delicious meals, and woke up each morning next to a beautiful woman. Now, a Sergeant was shouting in his ear. Landon tried to visualize Pennie standing on the porch of the peaceful West farm, but failed.

There was a war to fight, and "Fortress San Francisco" had fully mobilized. Everyone pitched in, ready to conquer the Hitlerite threat by all necessary. The west coast gleamed out as a target for the Japanese, with the San Francisco shipyards their prime objective. The Presidio had been placed on alert, and rang out with the sounds of men marching, men at rifle practice, and men, including Landon, training in tank operations. No one took for granted the Allies would win this war, but everyone worked as though they must.

Landon's battalion, preparing for duty in northern Africa, underwent the routine battery of medical tests. It was in the midst of these tests that one of the doctors discovered Landon had Asthma.

"Asthma?" Landon said, with surprise. "I don't feel it, Sir, except just a twinge of a wheeze now and then."

"I'm afraid it's more than just a twinge, Private," said the doctor. "Fighting in an African desert would turn your 'twinge' into something irreparable. You're lucky they let you into the Army!"

Landon was disappointed. To serve with General Patton while driving a tank into battle would have been a terrific privilege. But now he'd been removed from the battalion. He was offered a position as bar tender at the Officer's Club until they found another place for him.

"Bar tender?" he said, again taken aback. He had not expected to hand out martinis during a war.

"I've never mixed a drink in my life."

"Doesn't matter," said the Sergeant, shrugging. "You'll be taught. And it's an extra ten dollars a month."

Landon went home and gave Pennie the news.

"Asthma?" she said. "I never suspected."

"What do you think I should do?" he asked, a little embarrassed about the bar tending job.

"The extra money would help out a little, I guess," she said. Landon agreed, fully aware of the fact that they, between the pair of them, had scarcely a dime.

They decided he would take it. In spite of his initial hesitation Landon was a quick learner, soon becoming skilled at mixing the right amounts of liquor with the right amounts of water, or juice, or soda. As for socializing, Landon excelled at it, telling jokes, learning the officers' names, and remembering their favorite drinks. They loved him.

In the new battalion, there had been hints about an assignment to the island of Curacao, located someplace near the equator.

"Never heard of it," said one soldier upon hearing this news. "Where in the world is Curacao?"

"Don't know," said another. "Sarge says it's some Caribbean place, whatever that means. But I heard it's hot. Hot, hot, hot."

"Hmm. Don't mind hot, as long as it has women."

"It'll have women alright. Wherever American soldiers are, there'll be women. Lots and lots of women."

Landon overheard this banter and inwardly scorned their lack of geography. At the same time, he liked their description of the place. Warm, Caribbean island with lots of women? Intriguing, he thought, then quickly repented it. He couldn't think like that now, he was a married man.

Still, the pretty idea of Curacao had been planted.

The newlyweds had a tiny place on 32nd Street, a room with kitchen privileges. With only the two of them in it, they did not need much. As soon as she saw the space, Pennie began to make it into a home, for Ida had been a living example of genteel frugality. Landon noticed the cozy touches she added, and approved.

"We're as snug as two bugs in a rug!" he declared.

Their landlady, Mrs. Hanson, took to Pennie from the start and did everything she could to pave the way for her. Pennie seemed so sweet, so nearly angelic, that Mrs. Hanson felt compelled to protect her as best she might in this vast and unknown city.

"Mrs. West," she said one day, "Let us take ourselves off to the bank and get your account settled in there. I'll introduce you to the bank manager."

"But why would a bank manager want to meet me?" asked Pennie, who had never so much as seen a bank manager before.

"Why, a person doesn't just walk into a bank willy-nilly and sign up. You must know someone with an account there to recommend you." Mrs. Hanson winked. "And that someone will be me!" Pennie laughed. She had never heard of such things, not in small towns such as Sumner, nor even the slightly more respectable Puyallup. Clearly, Pennie had a lot to learn about this big city.

The two ladies donned their dresses, heels, hats, and gloves, and took a trolly downtown to the bank. It felt strange, being nineteen years old and meeting a bank manager. But the bank manager didn't seem to think it strange at all. It was just a part of life in San Francisco.

San Francisco. Both Landon and Pennie fell instantly in love with it. They figured out the cable cars and went everywhere on them. They searched until they found Lombard Street, and walked all the way down it and back up again, multiple times. On the steps of the City Hall a kindly passerby snapped their picture in the sunshine. They made simple picnics and ate them on Fisherman's Wharf, strolling home at sunset hand-in-hand. The fact that they had so little money didn't seem to matter. Each only had eyes for the other.

"Mother. You'll never guess what I got to do last night," she wrote Ida in late July. "I heard Army wives can go to the Fort for dinner and a movie for next to nothing. Landon was at work and so I decided to try it by myself. I had a huge steak, Mother, with vegetables, a salad, dessert and coffee. Delicious. And it only cost sixty-five cents! Then I saw the movie Stormy Weather starring Lena Horne, for fifteen cents. I had a wonderful time alone. Lots of other young people were there, and so I wasn't lonely. Everything is cheap like that at the Fort and Landon says that's because it is 'subsidized'. I think I'm going to like being subsidized."

Pennie soon found a job at the San Francisco shipyards, happy to do her bit again for the war effort. Everyone in the city wanted to do their bit.

"Look, Landon - the Chronicle says even people in prison are volunteering to take on war work. Imagine that. Prisoners!" They were shocked to hear of inmates at San Quentin and Alcatraz getting early release in order to help, if they showed themselves trustworthy. Crime rates declined, surprising even the criminals.

In all the excitement, only one thing rankled. Pennie's day shift meant he would be alone every morning, and she, every evening. He had to make the most of it, though, because it wasn't as though they had a choice. Landon read lots of books during his down time, but this eventually lost its appeal and he became restless.

He took to going for walks or seeing the city on a cable car, seeking places to wile away the hours. It was all in good fun, he told himself as he got to know other soldiers with the same dilemma. The places he visited with these new friends happened to be further afield than the ones Pennie knew about. He thought it best not to mention them to her, and assured himself again that there was no harm in it.

In the meantime, Pennie felt happier than she had ever been, and this contentment spilled over into everything she did. She was nineteen, a newlywed, and had met the bank manager. She could hardly wait to see what might happen next.

CHAPTER FOURTEEN

Bambino

On a cold, early morning in mid-December, Pennie awoke with a sense that something had gone drastically wrong. She'd been just fine the night before, but now, she...she had to dash to the bathroom, and very nearly didn't make it.

Oh, not stomach flu, she thought. I don't think I could bear stomach flu. She rinsed out a wash cloth, placing it on her forehead and lying back down. In a while she felt marginally better, so maybe it would be alright. But she would have to pull herself together soon in order to get to work.

"Pennie?" said her husband.

She lay as still as possible. Lying still sometimes helped her to concentrate her way out of being sick, and she hoped it would work this time. It wouldn't, though, not if she had to talk. "Hmm?"

"Are you going to be alright?" Landon repeated.

"I hope so," she whispered. "But I'd best not talk..."

Landon knew of this small ritual, and did not wish to disturb it. He slowly, quietly got up out of bed, and tiptoed toward the bathroom.

"Landon - wait!" Pennie said, and ran past him in a panic.

He stood stock still in the tiny hallway. Uh-oh, poor Penn, he thought. Maybe he'd better go down to the Post and get ready there.

Pennie finally made her way to the shipyards, feeling as if all the world was spinning. Part of her job as time-keeper was to watch as the men clocked in for their shift. When the nausea came, she discreetly rested her face on the cool metal cabinet next to her, and briefly closed her eyes. Two kindly Italian brothers, standing nearby, noticed.

"Bambino," whispered one brother, indicating Pennie.

"Eh?" whispered the other, and looked. "Ahh, Bambino!" Pennie overheard this exchange, but didn't understand what it meant. The following week, she decided to ask her friend Evelyn.

"Evelyn?" she whispered, at break time.

"Hmm?" the girl replied.

"What is a 'Bambino'?"

Evelyn laughed. "Bambino is the Italian word for "baby", you silly goose. Why do you ask?"

But Pennie sat still, dazed in the midst of the busy break room.

"A baby..." she whispered, as the conversations bubbled around her.

Pennie couldn't think why, in all this time, a baby hadn't occurred to her. She thought back to the device the doctor had given her, along with the expectation that it would do its job. Clearly it had not, at least not for very long; and now, surprisingly, wonderfully, her life was about to change. But she blushed to realize the Italians knew about her "bambino" before she did!

She wasted no time in getting to the Army doctor, who soon confirmed her hopes and talked about where she should have the baby.

"It might be easiest to deliver it here," he said. "I would be the attending physician, and nothing could be simpler." But Pennie privately longed for Sumner, and Mother. She didn't want to be left alone once Landon shipped out, and immediately began thinking of plans.

"Landon," Pennie said next morning as they sat down to breakfast. "I haven't felt very well lately."

He lowered his fork and looked at her. "I've been worried about that. How are you doing now?"

"A little better, at the moment. But I saw the doctor..."

"The doctor! What..."

"...and Landon, we're going to have a baby!" she blurted, suddenly in floods of tears.

"My dear girl..." he said, pulling out his handkerchief. "Are you alright?" She gratefully took and utilized it.

"Yes, yes I'm fine. It's just that I'm so happy!"

"Well, of course it's a baby!" he laughed. "I should have thought of that myself."

"But what should we do?" she asked. "I'm working now, but in a while I'll have to quit. And where should I have the baby? And where will we live? This apartment is awfully small…" She poured it all out, and then looked at him sheepishly.

"Ok, darling," he said, "let's think of one thing at a time. At this moment we are going to celebrate, and that is all. There will be plenty of time to organize everything else." So they sat at their tiny table, breakfast forgotten, and thought of the adventure out ahead of them.

As predicted, their lives began to change, altered by the presence of one tiny and much-anticipated human. She bought a baby book and memorized the instructions on everything from sleep habits to feeding schedules.

"I hope the baby will follow these instructions. What if it doesn't?"

Landon laughed from behind his newspaper. "You'll figure it out, Pennie; just think of all the siblings you've already raised."

After talking through the possibilities, they reluctantly decided Pennie should have the baby in Sumner.

"After all, Mother will be able to watch over me."

"But I'll miss you."

"I know, and I will miss you."

"What will I do, rattling around this big city without you?"

"You won't be rattling around, silly, you'll be going to Curacao."

"Maybe…"

When the decision was made, Pennie felt both happy and sad. There might be any number of regrettable things about leaving him behind. On the other hand, the Army could transfer him any day (nobody ever seemed to know when), and they wanted Pennie settled beforehand.

"I'm sorry you're going," said Landon woefully on the day he took her to the station. "This'll be a lonely old town."

The train pulled in and Landon went into action.

"Well, it's now or never," he said, picking up her suitcases.

"Oh Landon," Pennie said, momentarily quailing. "I don't know…"

The thought of having a baby so far from her husband now filled her with confusion. It mightn't have been the right decision. But it was obviously too late to change course now as the conductor, ringing his deafening bell, shouted "All aboard!", and Landon helped her up the steps.

CHAPTER FIFTEEN

He'd Never Felt So At Home

At 2:55 p.m. Landon arrived at the Officer's Club and got dressed for duty, gliding effortlessly behind the bar. The drinks were all there the way they should be, neatly organized, looking too gorgeous for words. The sight of them comforted him: row upon row of bottles in colors as bright as gemstones; glasses hanging from the rich wooden ceiling above him; and the attractively muted lights surrounding them as a kind of shroud, a concealment of all that was done there and all that was said. These things filled him with a curious pleasure as he stood surveying his domain, reaching for a towel.

"Well now Mr. West, how are things?" came a call as he wiped down the bar.

Landon smiled and launched into an Australian accent, one of many he conjured up as he worked: "Well, the wife's gone walkabout, Sir, getting ready to have the baby. So here I am. What'll it be?"

He had only to hear an accent once to mimic it flawlessly. This was one of the talents Pennie did not quite appreciate in her husband. She found it embarrassing and begged him not to "talk silly" around her. But the officers loved it, gathering around, munching peanuts, shouting orders.

"I'm thinking about that Brandy Sour of yours," said the Lieutenant. "Isn't that your finest? Hit me with it!"

"Right you are, Sir. Coming right up..."

Once again, Landon had an audience. He reached for the Brandy bottle, tossing it into the air with his right hand and catching it with his left. He'd never felt so at home. Women didn't understand this sort of thing. They could never be made to see that when a man had the right drink in his hand, everything else fell easily into place.

HARBOR DEFENSE
OFFICER'S CLUB

He grabbed a highball glass and broke into the song, "Waltzing Matilda" while mixing the Brandy Sour.

Once a jolly swagman camped by a billabong
Under the shade of a coolish tree...

In went a couple of drops of Bitters, some carbonated water, and one part lemon squash to two parts Brandy. He poured this concoction over ice, and handed it to the officer with a flourish.

And he sang as he watched and waited till his "Billy" boiled,
"You'll come a-waltzing Matilda, with me!"

The officers loved this song, and joined loudly in the chorus:

Waltzing Matilda, waltzing Matilda,
She'll come a'waltzing Matilda with me...

Used by Permission

"Here she is, Mate," he said, still sounding very Australian. "Brandy Sour with lemon garnish."

It looked good. It looked very good. The man took a drink, savoring the taste and feel of the mixture as it went down. "Ah, but that hits the spot!"

Landon reached for another highball glass. *Might as well mix one for myself,* he thought as he poured out the Brandy. He shouldn't really be drinking on the job, but told himself he could handle it. Besides, it didn't hurt to practice. And with Pennie away, he needn't worry about the smell of alcohol on his breath.

Landon considered himself to be one of the lucky fellows, to whom the ordinary rules might not apply. He did not take rules too seriously, for why should he? The face in his mirror was the face of privilege, and things tended to go his way. Because of this, there was a swing in his step and a smile on his face.

A popular song, Going My Way, had recently hit the radio waves. The words described him perfectly, something about "Rainbowville" and happiness up on Blue Bird Hill. He had sung it to Pennie one day as they'd wandered along toward the wharf.

It was a popular song from a popular movie, and Pennie had laughed to hear it sung just for her. But now she was gone and he found himself, as predicted, "rattling around" in that big city with nothing at all to do.

On his first day off without Pennie, Landon really had no plan. Fancy free and getting hungry, a sudden idea propelled him south along Presidio Avenue. He could smell the donuts long before he saw them.

The donut shop was famous, not just for the taste but for the price of a nickel. For a long time the owner had worked the shop by himself, both frying and serving. But the place became so busy that he finally hired a waitress. Mary soon became popular, drawing a crowd of soldiers who liked her humor and her blond hair. It was this girl who instantly set her cap for the tall wavy-haired soldier who had started dropping by most mornings. She thought him "dishy".

On his first two visits after Pennie left, Landon had been circumspect, without a glance in Mary's direction. But on the third, she greeted him demurely and was surprised when he responded with a thick Irish brogue.

"Top o' the mornin' to ye'!" he said with a flourishing bow. From that moment Mary was captivated, begging him to teach her how to "talk Irish".

"Such a thing can't be taught," he said. "You've either got it, or you don't. And I've got it."

"You certainly have," she replied, with a slow wink.

He was wearing his wedding band, but Mary didn't seem to notice. From the first, her gum-chewing "Hey, Soldier, what can I get ya'?" had him intrigued. No doubt about it, he was tempted and felt his resolve slipping as if the girl presented a temptation against which he had no armor. Within a week, he turned up at the address she had scrawled on a napkin, *56 Cortland Avenue*. "Why don't you stop by sometime?" she had said, handing it to him. "It's always a party, and six o'clock is always a good time."

The streets of San Francisco are legend. Its hills run steep as they twist and turn, snakelike, around gardens and trees, making them a favorite of bicyclists and anyone else on wheels. From The Presidio, Cortland Avenue was an uphill climb. When Landon finally reached it and Mary pulled him in, it was all downhill from there. And downhill was a whole lot easier.

When Ida called him on the morning of September 1st to say, "You have a daughter!", Landon immediately requested leave to go see her. Being "Dad" suddenly woke him up. He had been ignoring his conscience, but now it pinched him wickedly and he wanted to soothe it again. Well, he was done with that now, and from this day forward, he would be a "good boy".

He poured all of this out to Mary, who listened cautiously but said little. She knew how to bide her time and felt unworried that "her soldier" didn't turn up for her wares. He would, and it wouldn't be long in coming, either. In her experience, the thing Mary wanted generally became the thing she got. It was all simply a matter of waiting her turn.

CHAPTER SIXTEEN

What She Didn't Know

1944

Landon arrived in Sumner unexpectedly the following week, having hitch-hiked nearly 800 miles from the Presidio.

"I couldn't get leave," he told Pennie when they were alone.

Pennie stared. "What do you mean, couldn't? You can't even be here without it!"

Landon laughed, but looked serious enough.

"Well yes, you are supposed to. But they wouldn't let me go, so I just headed down to the highway, put my thumb out and - went." He seemed rather proud of this feat. "Took me 24 hours, too! More rides than I cared to count."

"But will they come and get you?" she whispered, as if someone might be listening at keyholes.

"Maybe, but I don't think so. I'm heading back tomorrow."

"You just got here!"

"All true," he laughed. "But I had to see her, Pennie, and this was the only way to do that and stay out of the Brig." He leaned over to pick the baby up.

"May I?" he asked.

"Of course. She's yours, remember."

"Pennie. She's beautiful," Landon said, his head bent towards the infant in fatherly pride. His smile was just as it had been the day they rode together in his little two-seater. Eager, and searching.

"She looks like you," he said, glancing up.

"Maybe.."

Landon returned to his post before anyone knew he'd left it. In time,

Pennie went back to her shipyard while Ida tended to Ann. But Landon didn't like it. Now that he had seen his daughter, he wanted to go on seeing her. The subject came up whenever he called.

"Let's bring you back down here, Pennie," he would say. "We need to be together."

"But what if they ship you out right after we come back?" she would ask. "Who knows how long you'll be away, and we would have to come back up here anyway." They talked and talked, and finally, when no news of Curacao came through and Landon didn't think he could stand it any longer, they made their decision. Pennie told her boss, and bought herself a one-way ticket to San Francisco.

In great excitement, Landon found a small apartment on 29th Avenue, just right for the three of them. It even had the bay window Pennie had always wanted. Everything was going according to plan, right up until the moment he picked up the phone to call Mary.

"They're coming back," he said.

"Who's coming back?" asked Mary, sounding petulant.

"Well, Pennie and the baby. Ann. I told you they would."

She had known it, but that didn't mean she had to like it.

"What are you going to do?" she said, the flint rising into her voice.

"I'll manage."

"Manage! What does that mean?" The flint became harder and louder.

"Just let me handle it, okay? Please stay out of it and don't, whatever you do, go anywhere near my wife. What she doesn't know won't hurt her."

But even as he spoke the words, Landon held out little hope. Mary wasn't exactly a woman to obey commands. She wasn't what you would call principled, either, and seemed to have a penchant for giving out secrets. This baffled him. She told her friends, she told her mother, she just could not stop all of this telling.

On his next visit to Cortland Avenue, Mary voiced the brilliant idea of telling Pennie herself, hoping she would leave him and give Mary a chance. This idea appalled Landon.

"She would never leave, I tell you," he said. "We have Ann now."

"There's a first time for everything," she said, pulling out a stick of her favorite Wrigley's gum. As there didn't seem to be anything to say to this, Landon merely sat there and watched her chewing, rather like a cow. He wondered why he liked her when whatever she did, it was sure to be the wrong thing. But he could never quite bring himself to send her packing. She was the fatal flaw, the transgression ready to happen, always waiting for him up on Blue Bird Hill. And no matter where he went, she was certain to be going his way.

CHAPTER SEVENTEEN

As Life Crumbled Down

1945

The day after Pennie and Ann arrived back, their doorbell rang for the first time. Who, she wondered, could possibly want to visit already? She had only just begun to unpack, pulling out the few things that would fit. Landon had found the place, brilliant man, and Pennie looked forward to putting it all together.

She opened the door and saw a woman leaning nonchalantly on the doorpost, one hand resting on her hip. The woman was chewing gum.

"Hi-ya honey," she said. "You must be Pennie."

For the first time in living memory, Pennie could think of nothing to say. She had no idea who the woman could be, all brassy blondness, brightly made up, and wearing a purple dress with matching shoes.

"I *said*, you must be Pennie," she repeated.

"That is my name," Pennie said, making no move to invite the woman in. From the porch, she had a magnificent view of the San Francisco Bay, but Pennie saw none of that now. She wanted only for this repugnant person to go away and never come back.

"Well Pennie, my name is Mary, and I'm a favorite of your husband's. I know all about you."

When Pennie still did not respond, Mary added, "I'm the lady who serves him donuts." Another pause. "He loves donuts."

Pennie froze. She cast back to the last time they had visited the donut shop. A flirty sort of waitress had been serving the customers, and Pennie thought her uncouth. Landon hadn't seemed to notice her.

Pennie's tone became frosty. "I'm sorry, ma'am, but you must have the wrong person. Goodbye." She began to shut the door.

“Oh, but you need to listen to me, Pennie,” said Mary, thrusting a spike-heeled foot in the door frame. “That husband of yours is a real cutie pie, and I aim to have him. You see, we had ourselves a fling while you were away having that baby of yours.”

“Don’t you dare to say a word to me about my baby!” Pennie said, and slammed the door as hard as she could, barely missing the woman’s foot. It was a wonder the frame didn’t crack. The noise it made awakened Ann, who began to cry.

Pennie lost all interest in her kitchen, her dishes, the table cloth she had just been laying for the dinner tonight. She was furious. Furious and horribly frightened, her future suddenly hanging by a thread when just moments before, it had been filled with such happy plans.

It was hideously risky for him to do this kind of thing, if what that woman said was true. And yet - what if it wasn’t, and Mary had simply made the whole thing up? Pennie grasped at this lifeline, this hope against all hope, that her baby’s father would never betray her in such a shameful way.

But of course the story was true. It came to her in a moment of clarity that made her wonder why she hadn’t seen it coming. Something in Landon’s demeanor had changed. With the long train ride, and the baby, and the exhaustion, Pennie just hadn’t taken it in.

She held Ann while waiting for him to come home, wandering from room to room, searching for a way out of this botch. What she wanted more than anything was to take Ann with her and get back on the train north, toward the safety of home and Mother. But going home would mean *telling them*, and she didn’t want any of the family to know that the man they all loved and trusted could fail so completely. No, she could not go home. It had to be worked out, by her, right here in San Francisco.

Ann had fallen asleep again by the time his key turned in the lock. As he came in, Pennie looked at him and saw, not the Landon she had laughed with just that morning, but some kind of stranger. He walked over to hug her, but felt her stiffen, and hesitated.

“What is it?” he asked.

"What is it? It's this, Landon. Somebody called Mary came to see me today." Pennie looked hard at him.

He stared at her blankly. "Mary… came? Here?"

"Oh yes she came, and stood on our porch telling me you two had yourselves a fling while I was away 'having that baby'. A FLING!"

The last words were a shout, and her voice cracked. "Whatever did you think you were doing? You went with that woman while I had your daughter, and had an *affair* with her?" She became angrier with each word and had to check herself.

Landon stared, shocked by her anger and by the word she had used - *affair*. It couldn't have been an affair, because an affair meant infatuation; feeling; something worth risking the loss of one's family. He now saw that Mary would never be worth those risks. In the grand balance of such things, she was low, and Pennie, he knew, was high. Mary would never achieve the caliber that came so naturally to his wife. Landon's face prickled with shame, and he dropped his gaze.

"Well, I wouldn't call it an affair, exactly…" he stammered.

"What else could it possibly be?" she shot back. "How could you do this to us now, Landon, when I have this baby and you know I can't leave? Ann and I are dependent on you, and yet you go and mess around with someone hideous like this MARY!"

Pennie heard a movement from the crib in the living room, and modulated her tone.

"We mustn't wake…" Landon stammered.

"Good grief, Landon, do you expect me to be quiet when this person claims she will have you?" Pennie peeked into the room with the pretty bay window - the window which up until an hour ago she had adored. Ann's frightened eyes looked straight into her mother's, as if she knew exactly what her parents were saying.

Pennie took the baby into the kitchen, and Landon followed, all mortification and chagrin.

"I'm sorry, Pennie, I'll stay away from her. Of course I'm going to be a father to Ann. I could never leave either of you!" The short sob accompanying these words rang true; but there could be no getting around it.

Pennie was trapped. She saw no solution, only anguish in the midst of the U.S. Army and a world at war, her mother a thousand miles away.

She looked at her husband as if she did not know him. Landon saw this, and finally realized how close he had come to losing everything. It might have worked, if only Mary hadn't gone and made such a shambles of it. You just couldn't control such a woman.

There was a minuscule sofa in the sitting room, upon which Landon found himself that night, and the next. Pennie herself scarcely slept, waking at 3:00 a.m. and watching helplessly as life crumbled down around her.

By the third day Landon seemed so miserable and contrite that Pennie decided to put the devastation behind her, and for the sake of small Ann, try to forget it had ever happened. What other option was there? Any thought of divorce, with its inevitably painful explanations, mortified her. Above all, the thing must be kept quiet.

"What will become of us?" she asked as they sat down to dinner a few nights later. Her face was pale, empty of the joy she had known such a short time before.

Landon set down his fork. "Nothing will. Because I won't do it again, Pennie. I've already promised."

She looked at him in confusion. "You promised I wouldn't marry a smoking man, and yet there's that pack of cigarettes in your pocket."

Landon's face grew red at this, but he did not reply. Things could have been worse after all. She could have tossed him out on his head.

It seemed almost a deliverance when Landon's battalion finally shipped out. Pennie felt a little disloyal for her relief, but it would be good for Landon to be away from this city, and that person. She hadn't seen Mary again, and as far as Pennie knew, neither had he. But the possibility remained, and each time Landon left the house, she sensed something, some subtle fear or dread she never quite managed to shake.

Having waited so long for his transfer, Landon felt almost light-hearted as he prepared to go, singing the rather funny, rather silly song from the first War as he filled his bag.

"Pack up your troubles in your old kit-bag, and smile, smile, smile," he sang, using such a believable Cockney accent that Pennie had to smile in spite of herself. Grabbing some socks, he juggled them into the air and continued,

"What's the use of worrying?
It never was worth while!
So pack up your troubles in your old kit bag and
Smile, smile, smile!"

George Henry Powell, Public Domain

He gave Pennie a broad wink, and Ann stood up in her bed, clapping and giggling. Her daddy kissed the top of her soft little head, and took up the old kit bag.

"Well, girls," he said, "it's time we made tracks. I need to be at the Post in an hour."

As they proceeded down the street toward the cable car, a blond woman watched them from the corner. Pennie recognized her, only now the dress and heels were red, as if she hoped to be picked up. Landon didn't appear to see her, but Pennie stared, and could not stop staring, try as she might. Mary stared back, and the two women did not break their gaze until the cable car rounded the bend and was lost to sight.

The appearance of Mary took all the wind out of Pennie's sails. She could hardly bring herself to speak as she and Landon said their goodbyes.

"Write to me?" she said, looking him in the eye.

"Of course! Haven't I always?" And she had to admit he had. There existed a box filled with these letters, a box that came with her everywhere she went. It contained more than mere words; it held memories.

Once Landon had gone, there was no longer any reason for Pennie to stay. In a few days she turned in their house keys, said goodbye to the city, and took Ann back to the train station. She had loved San Francisco, once. It had been, for her, a romantic and exciting city. Now she could hardly wait to be out of it.

"Well, Ann," she said with a smile. "We're going back to your Grandma's house! Won't that be fun? And you will probably be spoiled by the end of it."

But Ann was not spoiled, unless a child can be spoiled by love. For they all loved her, calling her "Pet" and playing games with her in the big back yard. Ann grew strong on Ida's cooking, and spent hours sitting on her grandfather's lap, babbling at him with her hands on his face. Something about his whiskers fascinated her.

Ida, for her part, kept an eye on her eldest daughter. She sensed a change, since they had last seen her; something that had taken the sparkle out of her. Pennie did not reveal it, and Ida would never ask. But she prayed long and hard for guidance and wisdom, and the peace that had gone so strangely missing in so brief a time.

CHAPTER EIGHTEEN

A World Without Hitler

Day after day the War news improved, bringing fresh rumors of defeat for the Axis and triumph on the side of the Allies. Then the month of April brought the most delicious rumor of all, something about Adolf Hitler, and his mistress, and his gun. They almost couldn't believe it, because it seemed almost too good to be true. To think even for a moment of a world without Hitler filled them all with hope.

One day, a broad flat box arrived at the farmhouse.

"Pennie, this is for you, and I think it's from Landon!" said Barbara, bearing it in as if it were a trophy. The package had plain wrappings and held only a US Army Postal Code. Pennie picked away at the tightly bound strings, finally fetching some scissors.

"I can't think what he..." she murmured, and suddenly, out onto the table rolled a record album. "A record?" she said, snatching it up before it reached the edge. "What..." But Dorothy knew. "It's a vocal recording, Pennie! He's recorded himself and sent you a message. Let's put it on! Unless - do you mind if we all listen?"

"Of course not. Set it up!" They all trouped over to the phonograph, turned it on, and set the needle carefully onto the record. They waited in anticipation, until... "Hello, Pennie! Hello Ann!" came Landon's scratchy voice from the speaker.

They laughed and clapped with excitement.

"Listen, Ann, it's your daddy!" Pennie whispered. But the baby only blinked up at her from the confines of the crib, maneuvering a small dimpled thumb toward her mouth.

"I am sending this to you from Curacao, because I work in the communications shop where they handle messages. It's fun to play with. This is one hot place, I can tell you that. Hot, hot, hot!" Ann suddenly stared up at the phonograph, the most comical look on her face, and said, "Hot! Hot!"

"And say, what do you think of old Hitler?" he went on. "Ever since he blasted himself out of the picture, we've been perched here on the verge of the end. All of us are working hard, but my thoughts are with you dear ones in Sumner. I'll be home soon. My love to you all..." The needle reached the silent center where it circled on, until Pennie lifted it carefully away.

"Well that's that," she said.

There came three more recordings from Landon in the following weeks, two of them filled with Landon's usual banter and gossipy news.

"It's so much more exciting than a letter!" Pennie said to Ida one day. "How clever of him to think of it."

Upon the arrival of his fourth recording, the family gathered again to be entertained. Landon's messages were a welcome distraction from life on the home front, and they liked hearing about that strange part of the world called Curacao.

"Ready?" said Pennie, as she lowered the needle. There came the usual noise of static, followed by, "Well, here I am again, reporting to you from the heat and humidity of Curacao, the most desolate spot on the planet!" They laughed.

"Last night I went to the Enlisted Club and had just a terrific time. Lots of food, fun, drinking, and - well, heh-heh, I can't exactly say I was *alone...*" Landon's voice was heavy with connotation, as if he were making a confession in a bar.

Pennie blinked, suddenly acutely aware of his ridiculous hint - "*I can't exactly say...*" Her face burned. The folks around her didn't seem to notice, and either out of pity or genuine innocence, ignored it absolutely.

When on May 8, 1945, "Victory in Europe" came gloriously across the wires, the world-wide celebrations were tempered by the opening of Nazi-held concentration camps. All the world reeled with outrage for the millions of slaughtered innocents. Yet only with the surrender of the Japanese would the victory be complete.

In far away Curacao, Landon himself had plans; he lay awake nights visualizing his little family together again, starting over. He would take Pennie and Ann back to Weston and work the farm with his father, as good a beginning as any young veteran could hope to have. But he must first be released from the Army, and the Army didn't seem to be in any hurry to release him.

At the Tacoma shipyards on a warm August evening, the sound of sudden shouting exploded all down the yards.

"Victory in Japan!" someone whooped. "They've dropped the A-bomb. It's finally over!"

"The A-bomb?" someone else asked. "Where'd they drop it?"

"Hiroshima," replied the first man. "Biggest explosion of the war. How about that!?"

Pandemonium broke forth as Pennie and Blanche came outside to join the revelers. They looked at each other, and clasped hands.

"What should we do?" Blanche shouted over the din.

"What do you mean, do? Our shift isn't over yet," said Pennie, responsible to the last. The Allies had just won World War Two, and Pennie was going to finish her shift. But no one else had any thought of working. The celebrations in downtown Tacoma were already in full swing, and everyone was wild to go. The boss's voice boomed out over the intercom.

"If we can have a volunteer skeleton crew to stay on and finish, the rest of you may go. See me to volunteer." It seemed no one wanted to volunteer, and everyone wanted to leave.

"Come on, Pennie. Let's go!" Blanche cried, pulling her arm.

"You go, Blanche. I'll stay and finish up here." So Blanche shrugged, grabbed her bag, and disappeared into the crowd.

The evening of work dragged on, as the skeleton crew consisted only of Pennie and one other person. But she finally finished, and caught the late bus downtown to see it all for herself. As the bus neared the station, an electrifying scene unfolded around her: people, thousands of them, danced in the streets, music blaring from the radios of scattered cars as the headlights blazed.

She would forever remember this moment, especially the ceaseless ringing of church bells which had for so long stood silent. On and on they rang, above and around her as grateful men, women, and children stood in the streets of Tacoma, letting the joyful tears fall.

For a time, Pennie hadn't thought very hard about the future. She sensed it out there waiting for her, but had avoided facing it. It hadn't been real, until now. Tonight's celebrations meant Landon would be coming back, probably soon, and the three of them would begin again. But in order for any of these things to happen, in order to properly start over and give Ann a happy home, there was something Pennie would have to do, something difficult and strangely demanding. She was going to have to forgive Landon. She hadn't yet, not really; the thing had been put off, left for later as the war raged on. Pennie wasn't entirely certain she *could* do it, now that she came down to cases.

But she looked up at the ringing bells, and vocalized perhaps the most difficult message in the English language: "I forgive you, Landon. Maybe you haven't asked me to, but for the sake of our future and Ann's happiness, my forgiveness is yours." The noisy revelers surrounding Pennie did not hear, or notice; but these heartfelt words brought the beginnings of peace to her weary soul.

The Kenoyers had thought Landon would be home soon after V-J Day but they had reckoned without the US Army, whose gears grind ever slowly. Month after long month the men in Curacao toiled on in the heat, the oil refineries needing an Allied presence even with victory achieved. By the end of the year, the soldiers had begun to wonder if the rest of the Army had forgotten them.

One warm afternoon a few days after the new year, word came through at last: they were going to be demobilized, and posted home. No definite date had been set but it would be soon, their battalion commander assured them.

One lanky British soldier stood when he heard this news, doffed his cap, and spoke for them all.

"Well, Sir," he said, with something of an edge, "if you don't mind my sayin' so, it's about bloody time."

PART FOUR

THE HOUSE BY THE SIDE OF THE ROAD

CHAPTER NINETEEN

The Matthew West Farm

1946

As George had desired at the beginning of the war, the two hopeful young people came back at the end of it. Introducing his first grandchild to the farm thrilled the older man, who liked watching her run through the acres as if she personally owned them.

"A thriving first born, Pennie," said he, with obvious pride.

"And not the last," murmured Landon as his wife assembled their lunch. George always came for lunch.

"Eh?" he replied, pricking up his ears. "How's that?"

"Oh, you'll find out come May, most likely."

George grinned, and felt the years-long grievance toward his son finally slipping away. He had to admit that the Army had turned out alright in the end. Landon had been matured by it. He worked hard and did more than his share of the farming, easing his father's load. This, along with the calming presence of Pennie on the farm and another child on the way, contrived to soften the rougher edges of George's soul.

There were other changes, too, chief among them his own remarriage at the end of the war. Clara Byall, a diminutive widow on a visit to Milton, had quietly caught his eye (although from the viewpoint of Landon's youth, he couldn't quite work out how). Landon's young brother Bob was not made happy by the marriage, and took an instant disliking to poor Clara.

"You're getting married?" he had said, shocked when his father told him.

"Yes," said George, "and that's that," squelching any discussion.

Bob considered her to be ancient, and said so. His own mother,

Anna, had been twelve years younger than George, and everything Bob thought a mother should be - fun, talented, and although she expected a lot from him, she'd understood his shortcomings. Clara, on the other hand, was elderly and possessed "false teeth", which began to go mysteriously missing.

"George, my teeth..." Clara would say, making Bob collapse in silent laughter from the other room. The situation became untenable. When Landon returned from the war, Bob was dispatched to live with him and Pennie, while Clara and George moved into town. Bob took to the arrangement, for Pennie liked him and liked feeding him. With no elder stepmother to torment and no more false teeth to scavenge, they all settled into a happy routine.

Pennie loved every square inch of her little white house, so carefully built and maintained by her father-in-law. It had limited space, but the space it had was useful. There were only three things about it she might have liked to change: the outhouse in their back yard (hard on an expectant mother), the deep and dangerous gully in their front yard (small children might fall in), and the old kitchen stove. It had been installed when George had married Anna, and was clearly past its prime.

Soon after they moved in, she came upon the cardboard box filled with Landon's letters. It had gone with her everywhere, and represented just about everything she knew about her husband. The letters were funny. They were newsy. They said what he thought, conveying his personality and humor as nothing else could. She was about to return them to the back shed, when a thought occurred: *I have the real thing now; I don't actually need these anymore.* The kitchen stove was hot with ready coals, so Pennie slowly lifted out the most recent letter, Landon's last from Curacao. The envelope read, *To Mrs. Landon R. West, P.O. Box 12, Sumner, Washington.*

All at once she remembered Mary standing on the porch, claiming she would "have" Landon. Pennie's face grew hot from both the flames and the memory, and she dropped the letter in, watching it burn.

One by one, the other letters disappeared into the fiery depths, an occasional bit of ash escaping out and upwards. The process took a long time, almost all of Ann's afternoon nap.

Then Pennie looked down. The box was empty, and so was she.

In early May when the beauty of Oregon in spring reached its zenith, Pennie got her dearest wish. A boy. He was a funny little thing, dark and inquisitive with large, well-shaped hands. Pennie studied him.

"Maybe he'll be an artist," she mused.

"More likely a farmer," said her husband.

"Artists can be farmers, but I suppose the eldest West boy will be expected to farm. What should we name him? Shall he be George? Or maybe Landon the second?"

"Isaac, perhaps?" he countered.

But in the end, they decided to call him Matthew.

"The Matthew West Farm," Pennie pondered, thinking ahead. He was, after all, the firstborn son of the firstborn son.

"Maybe… one day." Landon smiled, liking the idea.

Months earlier, when she'd told him a baby was coming, Landon had issued a declaration.

"Any woman who gives birth to a child deserves a reward," he had said, with a twinkle in his eye. "And you shall have yours."

"The child *is* the reward," said Pennie. But she was intrigued, and wondered from time to time what kind of reward he had in mind.

Landon had been true to his promise, as Pennie saw when she came home from the hospital. To her surprise, the old black wood stove had disappeared. In its place stood the most beautiful apparatus Pennie thought she had ever seen: a new white Norge kitchen range.

"A range?" she cried. "I don't believe it! Oh, Landon…" The whole kitchen gleamed the brighter for it.

Pennie marched straight over and gave him the hugs and kisses he so clearly deserved. "I thought we would never get rid of that old thing!"

Landon felt extremely pleased with himself and thought his surprise had come off rather well.

"And what would you like next time, Dear?" he asked, rather saucily.

"Very funny," she said, gently pushing him away. "Don't you have something to do? I want to get my hands on this fascinating stove."

CHAPTER TWENTY

When Time Stopped

1948

Landon stepped through the kitchen door, late for breakfast again. Pennie's breakfasts were delectable, and he did not wish to be late for any of them. But the farm contrived to delay his arrival just when it was time to eat. It couldn't be helped.

"I'm sorry to hold you up," he said kindly, taking off his boots and washing his hands at the sink. Landon was always being kind. In fact, Pennie did not think there had ever been a mean bone in his body. There were other things about him she might have complained about, but what with the cooking, cleaning, laundry, gardening and animal care, she never had the time.

"I'll be out singing tonight, remember," he said. "Athena Baptist is having an evangelist in to preach, some kind of foreigner. They say he's sensational."

Pennie remembered, but a week on her own at night didn't sound sensational, at least not to her. The farm was lovely, and welcoming, and dear - during the day. But at night, and night after night, she did not quite yearn to be alone in it.

She sighed, and then repented of it. "I'm sorry Landon, it's just that the evenings here can be long without you."

"You could come too," he said tentatively. But they both knew that finding a sitter at such short notice bordered on the impossible. Besides, Pennie didn't think she felt up to hearing an evangelist every night, either foreign or domestic.

"No, but thank you," she said. "…you go on without me."

And he did, leaving the house right after dinner. Pennie listened as his car pulled out toward the white steepled church four miles away. She had been there. It seemed livelier than other churches she'd visited, and somehow more personal. She and Landon were members of the Methodist church - mild, predictable, and perhaps a little dull. Sometimes she couldn't remember why they went.

Landon's speed increased now as he left the town, checking his watch. His foot pressed the gas pedal a little harder as he ran through the songs the quartet would sing. It would be just one more performance, something he could almost do in his sleep. Landon often wondered at this thing inside him which came so easily, so effortlessly - a "piece of cake", he called it. Well, tonight would be no different, he thought, and smiled. Just another piece of cake.

Hours later, after putting the children to bed, tidying the kitchen, and writing to her mother, Pennie woke to the sound of Landon's car, which was clearly in a hurry. He jumped out, slammed the door and - was he running? Yes, he was actually running, across the wobbly bridge and up onto the porch. She propped herself up in the bed and waited. Soon he thrust his head in through their bedroom door. "Pennie..." he said in an excited whisper.

"Yes? I'm awake," she answered. "But don't wake the children..."

"I'll try not to," he said, coming to sit on the side of the big bed. He hugged her with enthusiasm, strangely animated.

"What is it?" she asked.

"It was wonderful, Pennie - the whole thing was just wonderful!" He tried to speak in a whisper, but could not.

"What whole thing?" she asked, pulling away to get a better view of his face. It shone brightly at her in the moonlight from their window, as his eyes beamed into hers.

"What on earth...?" Pennie faltered. She had never seen him looking anything like this.

"Well," he said, "Here's what happened. I met the guys at the back of the church, you know? Like we always do. And we saw right away that it would be a full house. We love a full house, it always makes us sing better. Over to the side, the preacher stood next to a big man I guessed to be the Scot. I'll never forget him. Archie McNeill. He has thick red hair that looked as if someone had mussed it up every which way." As if to illustrate, Landon ran his fingers through his own wavy hair until it stuck out in all directions.

"Oh, Landon, surely it didn't look like *that...*" said Pennie, laughing and trying to smooth it back into place.

"Well, maybe not," he chuckled. "But nearly. And then the service started. There were two hymns, and by golly you should have heard those people singing. I've never witnessed anything like it. It would have been worth the cost of a sitter for that moment alone!" He stopped, still thinking about this marvelous thing, and wondering at it.

"Go on," Pennie prompted, reaching up to smooth the rest of his hair down from its wildness.

"Well, the four of us got up to sing our first number, and the crowd loved it. They clapped and cheered, and someone toward the back shouted, 'Amen!' We could have gone on all night!"

Landon took a restoring breath. "When we finished, Dr. McNeill got up to preach. And that right there was when time stopped for me, Pennie. Completely stopped."

Pennie waited cautiously. "Stopped? Time stopped?"

"From his first words I felt as though the sermon had been meant for me, and no one else. He talked about the struggle. You know, the struggle like we have had, you and I, trying to be good, and failing."

Pennie knew. There was a cycle to it that seemed, for her, never to end. She went from sin and guilt to asking for forgiveness, and then back again. All her life she had battled this one thing, and had found no answer for it. So she'd given up trying.

"And anyway, Pennie," he said, "you've got to come back with me tomorrow night. We'll get a sitter and go. How about it?"

Pennie hesitated. If she did go, well, anything might happen; they might get involved. But Landon had already become involved, and seemed so strangely elated. By nature a happy man, there were dark corners in his life Pennie felt excluded from, and even darker ones she wanted to be excluded from. Now, those hidden things seemed to have been replaced by something she did not understand. Maybe she ought to go with him, and find out.

"Alright," she said slowly. "I guess we can at least try."

Landon smiled and hugged her enthusiastically. "That's my girl! We can at least try." He seemed light as air, and years younger. What could one simple preacher have said to touch Landon in this dramatic way?

"But Landon, what could be so different about this meeting that we haven't heard before?" she asked sleepily, yawning. "We've listened to so many sermons."

Landon looked out the window, stopping to think. "It was more than just a sermon," he finally said. "Archie says the difference is Grace."

"Grace," she repeated. She had heard about it in Sunday School, something religious about God's mercy given and not earned. Still, she didn't understand how something like that would, or could, bring about the difference she now saw in her husband.

Pennie lay awake long into the night, well after Landon's breathing had become steady. She felt, down deep where there had been melancholy, a sensation she had not felt in a long time; something she had not expected to feel again. It might be, she pondered now in amazement, a tiny flicker of hope.

Pennie awoke the next morning wondering if she had merely dreamed their conversation in the moonlight. She heard her husband getting ready for the fields, got up, and padded quietly into the kitchen.

"Landon?"

He stood at the sink, and turned at the sound of her voice. She saw then that it had been no dream. Landon smiled a different kind of smile, a real smile.

"How are you?" she asked.

"Me? Oh, I'm fine - finer than fine!" he said, chuckling. "And I'm getting us a babysitter first thing this morning. I can't wait for you to hear Dr. McNeill and meet Evangeline."

He was as good as his word, making arrangements for a sitter not only that night but the remaining nights of the revival. Such a thing had never happened to them before. While the children napped, he came in search of her. Pennie wasn't difficult to find, for she had set her bread to baking and the smell of it drove him half distracted.

"Any of that ready yet, by chance?" he asked hopefully.

She peered into the oven. "Almost."

"Well, what do you think, Pennie? It's all settled. Every night this week you get to come out with me. Won't that be fine? Just like the old days!"

"But Landon, the expense!" she exclaimed in alarm.

"Worth every penny," he said.

Landon impulsively held out his arms toward her, and she just as impulsively walked into them. They stood together on that quiet afternoon, as if on a brink waiting for something to happen. In a few moments, something did. Matt clawed himself up into a standing position and looked at them through the bars of his crib.

The afternoon sun beamed in through the westward window, casting its soft light onto the baby's head.

"Dada.." he said, using his first word.

"Smart kid," said his dada.

CHAPTER TWENTY-ONE

Almost A Giant Of A Man

The excitement was palpable that evening as they stepped inside the little church, looking for the other members of the quartet. They had been hard put to find parking, as cars jockeyed for position up and down both sides of 5th Street.

"It's an even bigger crowd than last night!" said Landon.

They sat near the organ as the prelude began. Pennie had heard lots of church preludes, which were typically soft and restrained. But this was not a "churchy" prelude. This one sounded vibrant and lively, a real toe-tapper. Pennie sat listening and curious, somewhat on her guard.

Presently, a tall man dressed in blue stood to introduce the first hymn, 'To God Be The Glory'. The organ burst forth - full throttled, upbeat, instantly catching everyone's attention. The congregation rose to their feet and sang at the tops of their voices:

To God be the glory, great things He hath done!
So loved He the world that He gave us His Son.
Who yielded His life an atonement for sin,
And opened the life gates that all may go in!

The people surrounding her sang in a way that moved Pennie deeply, as if she were part of something bigger than herself, something permanent. Her eyes began to sting, so she felt in her pocket for a tissue just in case. Landon's hand closed around hers, and squeezed.

The quartet's songs, cheerful and upbeat, raised the roof as the congregation joined them in the choruses. Pennie found herself laughing, and saw that she wasn't the only one. The four men returned to their seats grinning as the applause and the 'Amen's thundered around them.

As they sat, Dr. McNeill rose, stepped to the pulpit, and the delighted congregation fell silent.

He was huge, almost a giant of a man, with a broad neck and wide, strong hands. A massive Bible sat on the pulpit, which he now lifted and opened. Pennie would forever remember that image of Archie, standing and holding it while speaking to them in his thick accent.

"My friends, being with you here tonight is a tremendous privilege. From where I stand, every last one of you looks happy, healthy, and perfectly respectable. Look around - do you see it? We've dressed ourselves up so nicely, no-one could ever guess at what lies behind our respectability.

"But back behind there, from the kindest parishioner to the most wretched prisoner, we all stand in need. We all have a burden of sin, needing to be forgiven. Who do you know that is strong enough to forgive every cruel deed we have ever done, every shrill word we have ever spoken, or every brutish thought we have ever entertained? Who?"

He spoke of the "twin struggles" facing all humanity: the first being Sin, and the other its alarming sequel, Death. Pennie knew quite a bit about those two things, and feared them both. Her sins seemed to be inside ones that showed up on the outside; especially anger, which simmered and burst into harsh words.

Archie went on, "'For God So loved the world that He gave His only begotten Son, that whosoever believeth in Him should not perish, but have everlasting life...' Jesus came here as a man, my friends, to free us. We are not required to free ourselves, for He has done it for us already on the cross, the only place forgiveness may be found."

Pennie had heard about the cross from other preachers, but had never fully understood its significance. Their rather dry sermons had come to her as words in a fog, and now all at once that fog began to clear. The nails and the hammer had become personal.

At the end of the service, Archie and Evangeline quietly slipped into the pew next to her. Evangeline took Pennie's hand in hers.

"Hello, Pennie?" said Archie. "Landon told us he would bring you tonight and we are so glad to meet you!" Evangeline's lively face smiled in kindness.

"Would the two of you like to come to the farm for dinner tomorrow night?" Landon asked, "since it's a free evening. Maybe it would give us time to ask you some questions and straighten out the things that have confused us."

Archie laughed. "Well, I can't promise to clear all of your confusions. But certainly we would love to come and confirm the faith I think you have begun to understand tonight."

The church by now had emptied, but Pennie glanced down and saw that her hand still held Evangeline's. She was reluctant to let it go. As they walked together toward the car, Pennie realized she had met a true friend - one who would remain a friend from now until the end of their days. And she no longer feared becoming involved. They were involved already.

The next day Pennie surveyed her living room, deciding to use the drop-leaf table there for the dinner. They would have pork chops, she thought, and pie. Something about Archie told her he'd be a great fan of pie.

She was nervous. It wasn't about the cooking, she had cooked for so long that it was second nature. Her nerves were more about the significance of the evening. After last night, Pennie decided that the two McNeills must be perfect - or as near to perfection as a human can be. But Pennie was not perfect, and might even be irredeemable. Surely the two of them would notice.

She glanced at the clock. Heavens! No time left to worry, her hair was still a mess. Evangeline would look lovely. Last night the woman had been wearing a beautiful green suit with matching shoes.

Pennie dashed to the bedroom, and went straight to her closet. There were dresses and skirts hanging neatly inside, but all of a sudden she hadn't a thing to wear.

Ann stood in her favorite spot by the window, watching for their visitors.

"When will they come, Mama?" she asked, and not hearing a reply, she went in search. "Mama?" she called quietly, so as not to wake Matthew. Waking a baby always mysteriously complicated things, she had noticed. It was one of the first lessons she had learned about being a big sister.

She went into the kitchen, but it stood empty so she trailed along toward the french doors, and peered in. Her mother sat brushing her hair. She looked elegant, so slender and stately with such thick brown hair. Ann's own hair didn't please her in the same way her mother's did, because Ann's had an off-putting reddish tint to it. But she loved to watch Pennie's glossy tresses bouncing as the brush strokes smoothed them into perfection.

"Mama?"

Pennie looked up and saw Ann watching her through the mirror. "Yes?" she replied.

"When will they be here?" She watched as her mother applied scent to both sides of her neck, just behind the ears. Her mother never over-applied her scent. A woman wants to be noticed just enough, she had said, but never over-noticed.

"Any minute now, Archie and Evangeline will drive up to our little house, and you will meet them."

Ann stared. "I've never known an Evangeline before."

Pennie finished with her brush and her scent, ready at last.

"Well, you are about to now. Off you go to your own room and brush that mop of curls before they get here." Pennie looked down and touched her daughter's head. "Evangeline's hair is red, did I tell you?" and she smiled as her daughter's eyes opened wide in surprise.

"No. I didn't know it was red." Ann looked forward to meeting a grown lady with red hair. "Does Mrs. McNeill like it?" she asked.

"I don't know," said Pennie. "But Mrs. McNeill doesn't seem to be unhappy about much of anything. You'll soon see."

CHAPTER TWENTY-TWO

When The Vows Were Spoken

Dusk was descending upon the fields when a car finally approached, stopping at the edge of their foot bridge. Landon hurried out to help Evangeline across, as there was scarcely a hand hold to steady her. Pennie cringed, watching from the porch. Often she had requested this frail bit of wood be strengthened, or the gully below it (created by a long-ago flood) filled in. But Landon, Bob, and George had agreed amongst themselves that both gully and bridge were perfectly fine, so Evangeline now picked her way across it as Archie followed. The bridge sagged noticeably beneath his feet, but he showed no alarm. His deep voice rang with laughter as he reached the other side.

"You're a lucky man, Landon," he shouted. "That foot bridge of yours must be blessed!"

Ann stood in the doorway and regarded him solemnly. From her height, Dr. McNeill's towering form stretched upwards, his kindly face beaming down at her from the top.

"How do you do?" he said, bending to shake her hand in greeting. "You must be Ann."

And with that, the little group made their way through the front door, talking and laughing together in the most companionable way. Dusky sunlight rendered the surrounding wheat fields the most deliciously golden yellow.

"Just look at those fields, Archie," said Evangeline. "Marvelous.."

Pennie needn't have worried about any part of the visit, for both the McNeills were naturally friendly, and really quite funny. Evangeline's dress was lovely, but no lovelier than Pennie's, who soon forgot the comparison. They ate and enjoyed the delicious dinner and pie, all the while

speaking openly about their own discovery of the Savior. Archie and Evangeline clearly did not consider themselves perfect human beings.

"We were both brought up in church, but discovered we needed to make our own decision as to whether we, too, would follow Christ. We had to choose Him on our own, for no one is ever 'grandfathered in'."

Landon and Pennie listened intently, but as the discussion went on, only Landon seemed to be asking any questions. Pennie wanted to ask them, for her heart was filled with questions. But her tongue felt strangely thick and dry, and she thought, *I will just die if I ask my questions...but I will just die if I don't!*

When she could no longer bear it, Pennie finally said, "How can I be saved, and stay saved from my sins?"

She had finally done it, vocalizing her deepest fear that she could not keep herself saved, and might be lost forever. She remembered the picture on the front cover of *Inferno*, and shuddered.

Archie said, "Pennie, do you believe the Bible is the Word of God?"

"Yes, I do," she said.

"Well, these are words of great importance: John 3:16. 'For God so loved the world that He gave His only begotten Son, that whosoever believes in Him should not perish, but have everlasting life.'" KJV.

"Now I would like you to read it, placing your name into the verse, because it applies to you."

So Pennie read, "For God so loved Pennie that He gave His only begotten Son, so that if Pennie believes in Him she shall not perish but shall have everlasting life."

A hush settled around the table. Landon leaned in, his eyes glued to the verse his wife had just read. This simple truth included him, regardless of the things he had done. A great weight began to lift from his shoulders.

"What if I don't feel saved?" Pennie asked. "And what if I do something so bad, God lets go of me and I am lost?"

"Pennie," Archie said, "when you and Landon got married and the vows were said, did you feel any different after you said 'I do' than before you said it?"

"No, I didn't," she said. She felt Landon's arm around her shoulders, remembering that day five years before.

"You were still just as married, weren't you?" he continued.

"Yes."

"It was settled legally, and your feelings before or after were not what married you. When you make a covenant with God, it is settled."

Archie handed her a card, and asked her to read it for them. She took it and read, "My sheep hear My voice, and I know them; and they follow Me, and I give them eternal life, and they shall never perish; neither shall anyone snatch them out of My hand." John 10:27-29, KJV.

Pennie repeated the line, "... neither shall anyone snatch them out of My hand," and sensed the burden of her own sins lifting. She would never forget the moment. The baby slept on, so there were just the five of them, Ann hearing everything alongside her parents. Her little face and innocent expression were all a part of what Pennie knew she would never forget.

Together they prayed, Landon, Pennie and Ann offering up the prayer of their hearts, asking outright for His forgiveness. For the first time, they knew the irrefutable presence of God, the Father almighty, whom they could not see, but in whom they believed.

Pennie awoke with the dawn, and whispered, "The Lord is my Shepherd." She lay quietly as a new happiness suffused her, rather like tea leaves when the hot water is tipped in. It becomes tea, and then never goes back to being water.

How young she felt. And how healthy! She was young, only twenty-four, but had stopped feeling it. Youth could too easily shrivel on a remote farm surrounded by chores and little money, day upon day. But with a newfound energy, Pennie fairly ached to go out and find something that needed doing!

"Landon…" she said quietly. He slept on, but she persisted.

"Landon?"

He stirred. "Hmm?" came his sleepy reply.

"I don't know what to do."

"Do?" Landon asked, turning towards her.

"I mean, what to do *first.* Surely God means for us to *do* something now."

"Well," said Landon with a yawn. "Archie said not to think of that, yet." He could just see her pale face in the early dawn, and reached over to touch her tousled hair. "He thinks it is right to go to church - we might even consider switching to the Athena Baptist - and read the Bible, and pray. But he said none of these things are the uppermost thing." Landon leaned his head over to rest it next to hers. "Jesus is the uppermost thing."

Ann stepped in through the French doors.

"Mama? Daddy?" she ventured.

"Yes, my dear?" said Landon. The little girl padded over to their big bed, standing where she could see their faces as they turned kindly toward her.

"What happened?" she asked.

Her parents laughed. "What makes you think something has happened?" asked her father.

"It feels different," she said. "It's happy in here." They laughed again.

"Well let's get up, then, shall we?" said Landon. "We're going to have the first ever West breakfast Bible study. Ann, run and get the big Bible and take it to my chair in the kitchen."

"Wait," said Pennie. "Let's eat at the living room table. Like last night." So special had last night been that she did not want anything about it to change.

"Alright, the living room it is!" Landon said, ruffling Ann's hair.

She brought his Bible, and a daily tradition began. They had to get up earlier than usual, as farm chores wait for no man. But from the moment they became Christians, Landon and Pennie clung to their Bible readings as a drowning man would to a lifeboat. Day after day, the tradition held until Ann became convinced it would never end.

The living room table took up extra space in their little house, but two weeks passed before Pennie could bring herself to fold it down and out of the way. She loved to look at it, at the place she had been sitting when her freedom began. Pennie's spiritual life would never again be the guilty, terrifying thing it had been.

Landon declared one morning at breakfast that he felt "light as a feather".

"But men are heavy, Daddy," said Ann.

"Yes they are, my dear, on the outside. What I mean is something that happens to them on the *inside.*" He smiled at her. "Before being a Christian, it felt like I was carrying a bag of heavy bricks on my back, and those bricks were my sins. They'd burdened me for years, until God came along and took them."

"Where did He put them?"

"He put them 'as far as the east is from the west'", he said, quoting a Psalm he knew.

"What made you lighter?"

"God did that for me," he replied. "He forgave all of that heavy sin, so much heavier than a brick, or even thousands of bricks." He gestured from floor to ceiling. "They are mine no longer. And that, my dear, is why I am feeling light as a feather."

Landon felt a sudden lump in his throat as he said this, and put a hand up to his eyes.

Pennie, listening from the doorway, came and sat next to him. She held his hand, her face so marvelously cleared of the worry he had watched develop over the years. The things he had put her through... he did not like to think of them now. But then he remembered: the things he had put her through were all part of the sin now forgiven. The thousands upon millions of bricks. All of them, every last one, had gone.

CHAPTER TWENTY-THREE

A Worker-Man's Smell

1949

"Daddy has on his worker-man boots," said Ann, looking out the window. Her father made his way purposely toward the house, waving and smiling, wearing his straw hat. "Mattie, get ready! He's almost *here!*"

They stood side-by-side and watched the door, ready for the moment it would open and they could pounce. They heard a noise. "Clump. Clump. Clump," came the boots. "Clump-slide," came the sound they made when he scraped the mud from the bottom. Their grandfather had installed the mud-scraper long ago when he had lived in this house with Grandma Anna. She had once been a famous singer, and could never bear to have mud in the house, farm or no farm. Matt and Ann loved the mud-scraper, because it was the very last sound they heard before their father arrived.

Suddenly the door opened, and the head of their father peeked around it. "Daddy!" cried Ann. "Da!" squeaked Matt. Their father's big smile beamed over at them to signal that it was time to pounce.

They sped toward him, and *bang!*, with a thud they careened into his legs. Then *bump!* as he pretended to fall backwards and into his chair. Then they attacked his boots.

It had become their favorite time of their day, the time when they were allowed to help him pull his boots off. They had no end of trouble doing this, for the boots were big and heavy, and he almost always had to help them a little. But eventually, the boots would come off with a 'Swoosh!', and clatter to the floor.

"Eww!" Ann would cry.

"Uck!" Matt would intone.

"The smell, the smell!" they hollered together.

"What smell?" Landon would respond, pretending not to notice.

Their father's feet did smell, but not with a bad sort of smell. They called it a "worker-man's smell", and decided they liked it. He came in from the fields every day to have his lunch with them, and they always wondered what he might do or say to put them into "stitches".

Pennie served up the lunch quietly, and took her seat at the table with nothing but a few saltines on her own plate. This could mean only one thing.

"Saltines?" Landon said, his eyebrows arching upward into comical question marks.

"Saltines," she said, rather weakly. "I'm not sure yet, but - I'm probably pregnant."

Landon leaned over and squeezed her.

"Well done, Pennie!" he said. "When is it due?"

"Late October, I think."

"October! Then Cannon Beach in August is still a player."

She bit into her cracker thoughtfully, and remembered Cannon Beach. Archie and Evangeline had opened a conference center on the Oregon coast, welcoming families to come and "vacation with a purpose". More than just a holiday, the conference provided lodging, meals, and Bible teaching morning and evening, with beach time in between. They had gone last year, and found those seven unforgettable days to be everything a young family could dream of in a vacation.

Evangeline had asked them back again this summer, and of course they would go. They had worried about the expense last time, for they quite literally had no money to spare. But it had been so important that they'd held their breath and written the check.

On the last day of the conference, Evangeline came trotting up to their table in the dining room and discreetly handed it back. "We won't be needing this, my dear," she said to Pennie. "But you might." Then she turned and trotted back out again. They watched her departing back in stunned silence.

"Thank you..." Pennie stammered, finding the precious check in her hand, torn into two pieces. She looked at Landon.

"Praise the Lord," he said, eyebrows shooting up.

The appearance of the crackers on Pennie's plate had been a true prophecy, for soon the whole family began to speak openly about their "October baby".

"What project will you do this time, Daddy?" Ann wanted to know. "Another stove?"

But Landon looked mysterious. He had a plan that could only be carried out once Pennie had gone to the hospital, so he would have to be quick. Seven days would be cutting it mighty close.

CHAPTER TWENTY-FOUR

Bits Of Paper And Tobacco

1949

Cannon Beach Conference Center

The month of August in Weston became so hot that the Wests could hardly wait to escape it. The children dozed in the back seat as they made their way due west along the Columbia River Gorge, through Portland, and straight into the forested beauty of the Sunset Highway. Their parents in the front looked like a couple of teenagers, smiling and laughing with the sheer freedom of getting away.

Nearing the turn into Cannon Beach, they saw the Crab Broiler restaurant sitting proudly to the right. Ann, now awake, stared at it in wonder. The Crab Broiler was famous and enviable, and Landon said they would go there one day when their "ship" came in. Ann asked what the ship looked like and when it might arrive, but her parents only laughed.

She turned to her brother lounging two feet away.

"Mattie, you are about to see Haystack Rock."

Matt sat up. "Wock?"

"Yes! It's a great huge boulder standing on the beach, shaped just exactly like a haystack." She made a rough sketch of it for him in midair. "Like the ones on Daddy's farm. You know." Ann leaned forward.

"Will we climb it this time, Daddy?" she asked.

"Not really, my dear. Haystack is much too big to climb. But we will certainly look at it."

Landon reached for a cigarette, and then paused. He had smoked since starting college, but didn't feel as sure about it now. Maybe he should quit. But what if he quit one day and wanted a cigarette the next? He had once asked Archie about this, and heard the reply, "Give it all to God, Landon. He'll tell you what to do!"

Then all of a sudden, just before they reached the town, Landon quit. He was no longer a smoking man. The couple in the car behind them saw a small white package come shooting out the window, scattering bits of paper and tobacco along the road.

"Those are the last cigarettes I'll ever buy!" he declared with feeling. Pennie's eyes stung. She had not nagged, but had most certainly prayed. And what a marvelous answer.

That evening as they entered the chapel, Ann noticed a magnificent harp sitting on the stage, waiting for someone to come along and play it. The instrument was over six feet tall and imposing with its walnut sheen and delicate stool. To Ann's surprise, it was Evangeline who stepped up to the stage and began to play, smiling sweetly and making it sound as if angels were singing. Pennie thought for a moment that they really might be.

When the song had finished, they all stood for the first hymn.

Come Thou Fount of every blessing,
Tune my ears to sing Thy grace.
Streams of mercy, never ceasing
Call for songs of loudest praise!

Pennie knew what was about to happen, because it always happened. From the midst of the crowd came Landon's voice ringing out clear and powerful, and quite possibly perfect. The people near them heard it, and looked discretely around for the source. Landon never seemed to notice people's jaws dropping in amazement. His growing popularity around the grounds and elsewhere bounced off him as if it were some other man, and not him drawing a crowd. Pennie understood the charm.

It was a dream of a week. Besides making new friends and eating three marvelous daily meals, they found the candy store and devoured copious amounts of taffy. They entered the cafe on Hemlock Street, and ordered (oh, unheard of luxury) a chocolate coke. They even drove to the famous Haystack Rock and parked, legally, with the other cars along that sandy shore. As the children played in the tide pools, their parents dozed, until -

"Mommy, the water..."

It was Ann, standing suddenly knee-deep in surf as Matt waved a plastic shovel at them from his water-soaked perch.

"Wet!"

"Landon, wake up!" Pennie said, putting a hand on his shoulder.

"What on earth..!" he exclaimed. All of them were wet by now. They quickly gathered up children, blankets, shovels and pails, and got the car out just in time. Everyone who heard the story agreed that the quick-thinking Ann had saved the day.

Cannon Beach had become for them more than just a place-name; it was somewhere they would always want to go, and never want to leave. Wherever they went during that dream week, the highlight was coming back for the most astonishing evening services, where truth, and kindness, and music were poured out for them in abundance.

As all good things must, the week at Cannon Beach finally came to an end. Matt protested ingloriously the moment he walked in from breakfast and saw his suitcase out and opened.

"Me no go!" he implored, tears wetting his cheeks. Yet it must be done, and soon everything, even some of the sand, had been packed neatly away for the long drive home.

While Landon carried their bags to the car, the McNeills came to watch and say goodbye. Pennie wondered again why someone so important seemed to care so much about them. In time, she would understand the McNeills did not see themselves as any more important than anybody else. In fact, they treated others as if others were more important. It was surprising. It was humility.

Pennie rolled down her window and Evangeline reached for her hand. Archie and Landon chatted about plans for the grounds, so Evangeline leaned toward Pennie and gently said, "I know you will have a nice time getting back to that lovely farm of yours." Pennie nodded.

"But it's hard to leave this place," Pennie choked out.

"Yes, I know. We all feel that way about the conference. It is blessed. But its purpose is to prepare us for going back, you know. Those who come here soon learn that the truth they found here will not change, there."

The car started up, and Archie reached in to shake hands with Landon.

"You must come back to the farm," said Pennie. "Anytime. We don't need warning."

The two McNeills stood arm in arm, the Irish lady and the Scottish preacher, waving, smiling, calling out, "God be with you!" until the car finally rounded the bend and they were lost to sight.

Landon drove slowly over the bridge, passing the A-framed fisherman's shop and on toward the highway. Pine trees loomed tall above them, slender and aromatic.

"Mama?" came a voice from the back.

"Yes, Ann?" Pennie answered.

"Mrs. McNeill is nice."

Pennie turned again and looked at her daughter. "She certainly is. I don't know of anyone, really, who is any nicer than Mrs. McNeill."

They sat thinking, for a while. Then Pennie felt something, some bits of paper sitting on her lap. She looked down, and saw their check, torn into two pieces. Evangeline had done it again.

CHAPTER TWENTY-FIVE

An Unexpected Conversation

"What's happened to Landon?" asked Betty.

The question was posed during Saturday Afternoon Club with fifteen other women, all sipping tea. Saturday Afternoon Club was a monthly gathering for the women in the area, by invitation only. Pennie had always wanted to be invited, and finally, a few years after the war, she had been.

"Happened?" she asked.

"Well, yes - Bill came home the other day and said Landon had some sort of 'experience'. Said he'd never seen such a change in a man. He mentioned a Scottish preacher, or maybe the man was Irish…"

Pennie laughed. "He did meet a Scottish preacher. We both did. And actually, both of us had the same experience." The woman's question surprised her, but did not put her off. More than a few of their friends had heard, and been wanting to know. "Landon sang at a revival meeting, and that is where we found out about becoming Christians."

"Well, we're all Christians, aren't we?" said Betty. "I mean, we're Americans, which is just about the same thing." Pennie understood this because for such a long time, she had held that view. They chatted, while two other ladies leaned in.

"We learned that the Bible says no one is righteous, and that everyone has sinned. Landon and I knew this, but kept trying to fix ourselves, to become good all on our own, and always failing. Anyway, you probably don't want a long explanation, but…"

"I wouldn't mind one," said a rather timid lady sitting nearby.

So they talked on as others came and went. An unexpected topic of conversation for Saturday Afternoon Club! But Pennie found it nice to talk about. Talking about it made her more certain, not less.

She saw hope in the eyes of especially one of the ladies, and wanted to help her.

That night, she told Landon about it.

"At Club today, Betty told me Bill noticed you were different because you had met a 'Scottish preacher'. I guess that's Archie all over! So I told her about our conversion." She looked over at her husband. "Some other ladies wandered over and started listening. It surprised me."

Landon became thoughtful. "Bill asked me about it last week when we were handling his cattle. I didn't realize anything showed."

They both had lots of friends, for the Wests were young and fun to be around. One day Pennie said, "Our friends aren't Christians, Landon. Should we keep on seeing them, now that we are? Or are we supposed to get different ones?"

"I'm not completely sure, but it seems like we shouldn't forget the ones we have. Let's ask the Pastor."

They were forever asking the Pastor about things, and he had become accustomed to their frequent forays into what they should and should not do "now that we are Christians". He answered simply.

"Absolutely. You stick with those friends of yours, Landon. And don't you be afraid to talk about God with them, either, or to tell them what's happened to you. They'll see it anyway, and be asking. You don't want to hide this thing under a bushel."

"What about politics?" Landon asked.

"What do you mean, politics?"

"Pennie and I have always talked politics around the table, and our friends like that sort of thing. Should we change that now, and talk about God instead?"

But here, the Pastor didn't have a sure answer. "Landon, I just don't know about that. Politics sometimes gets people awfully hot and bothered, and it can hurt things rather than help them. But if you stick to the truth, I suppose it wouldn't hurt." Still, he hesitated.

The Wests determined there would be no hiding their new faith under a bushel. They kept having their friends in for dinner, and the table conversations were spirited, with or without politics. The children were smack in the middle of it, too, for Landon didn't hold with the "seen and not heard" mentality when it came to the table. His children should be polite and respectful, but they were also expected to have a mind, and to use it.

As for politics, they tried talking with their friends about it the way they always had. But in time, the topic itself quit coming up. Landon had always been a dyed-in-the-wool Democrat, and Pennie, like her father, a firm Republican. This did not change, even after their conversion, and they concluded that more often than not, the subject of politics would be best left alone.

CHAPTER TWENTY-SIX

The House By The Side Of The Road

"**Look at this, Landon,**" Pennie said one evening, as she sat with her book. "It's a poem by Sam Walter Foss."

"Foss?" Landon said. "I've heard of him. Let's have a look at it." He held the book and read the poem, aloud, to his wife:

The House by the Side of the Road

Let me live in a house by the side of the road,
Where the race of men go by,
The men who are good and the men who are bad,
As good and as bad as I.

But I turn not away from their smiles nor their tears,
Both parts of an infinite plan;
Let me live in my house by the side of the road
And be a friend to man.

I see from my house by the side of the road,
By the side of the highway of life,
The men who press with the ardor of hope,
The men who are faint with the strife.

But still I rejoice when the travelers rejoice,
And weep with the strangers that moan,
Nor live in my house by the side of the road
Like a man who dwells alone.

Let me live in my house by the side of the road
Where the race of men go by,

They are good, they are bad, they are weak, they are strong,
Wise, foolish- so am I.

Then why should I sit in the scorner's seat
Or hurl the cynic's ban?
Let me live in my house by the side of the road,
And be a friend to man.

He seemed lost in thought.

"The house in this poem is our house, Pennie," he said. "It's what we've always wanted."

His wife nodded. "It is, especially now that we are Christians. I don't need to go out and blaze any trails, but I want to be here for those who do blaze them. Especially our children."

"I like this Foss fellow," he said, with growing interest in Pennie's Library book.

"There's more," she said. "I particularly liked..." but she may as well have been speaking to the moon, for Landon was already adrift. His powers of concentration were legend. It was a favorite story that as a fifteen-year-old, he'd become too engrossed in "A Tale of Two Cities" to notice when his brother and sister came in from school.

"Hey," whispered Bob, "just look at him sitting there, as lost as a goose in a snowstorm."

Esther tiptoed over and waved a hand in front of Landon's face. Nothing. The only movements she saw were two eyes tracing sentences across the page.

"I bet he wouldn't even notice if we stacked chairs up around him."

Esther turned, and their eyes met. Without another word they went into action, dashing from room to room for the chairs. The stack had reached ceiling height when they heard a noise coming from the porch.

"Ye gads, it's the folks already!" cried Esther. "Help me get these chairs down, you big Galoot...!" But it was too late. The door opened, and Anna took center stage.

"What on *earth!?*", she shouted, and Landon jerked, perpetuating an avalanche onto his head. When at last the dust settled, Anna calmly said, "George, do go and get me my switch.."

It was Pennie's favorite Landon-as-a-child story.

On a late windy evening when Landon was out, Pennie heard a knock at the door. She opened it, and saw two small blond boys peering up at her from the porch.

"Oh - hello," she said. "Are you lost?"

They shook their heads, but said nothing.

"Well then, why don't you come in and tell me about it."

The boys did as she asked. Besides their sneakers, they wore only white t-shirts and Levi's, and both were shivering.

"You must be freezing! Come to the stove and take the chill off." She brought them a blanket, and they had just begun getting warm when Landon returned. He was surprised to see the two anxious boys looking at him as if he might toss them out.

"Boys," said Pennie, "this is my husband, Landon."

He pretended surprise. "Oh-ho, and whom have we here?" he said, in his best Irish brogue. They looked at Pennie quizzically.

"He wants to know your names," she prompted.

"Oh. I'm Billy, and this here is Mike."

"I don't know, Pennie," Landon continued, "I'm surprised to see you sittin' with a couple of gunslingers out on a cold winter's night lookin' fer loot!" He winked broadly. "By the looks of 'em, I'd say they just busted outa' jail and are makin' hey for Mexico (only Landon pronounced it "Meh-hee-ko").

Their eyes grew wide. "No, sir, we couldn't possibly be highwaymen, we're only boys!"

Landon smiled. "Oh. Well then, how do you do?" He took a low bow, shaking their hands respectfully. Both giggled.

"And why are you out in the country so late on this night?" he asked, forgetting his accent. "Shall we go find your parents?"

"Oh no, sir, our parents don't know we come out like this. We're runnin' away."

"You are?" Landon exclaimed. "At your age? That's a harsh thing for a body to do, my boys. You might not like it much."

"Landon?" Pennie interposed. "Let's let them warm up, have a bite to eat, and then maybe you can give them a ride."

The boys brightened at the prospect of food, and Billy (who did all the talking) said, "Yes, please."

As Pennie assembled their supper, Billy told Landon about his father.

"Our Pa said 'no' to us yesterday when we wanted to go and visit our cousin in Tolgate," said Billy.

"Is that why you are running away?" he asked.

"Well, yes - sort of. Pa's always telling us no about things, and we jus' got fed up."

"How old are you?"

"I'm ten, and Mikey here is nine. We live back in Milton."

Landon was surprised. "You mean you've walked seven miles out here in the dark of night?"

"Well, we rode our bikes." The boy looked rather proud of this achievement.

Pennie, bringing in the food, murmured, "If I were your mother I'd be terribly upset and worried..." The boys looked at each other as if they had not considered this.

As they ate, Landon remembered when he was a boy, feeling as if his only choice was to run. In his case, he ran because his father spanked him every day, whether he needed it or not. Landon tasted the bitter humiliation of it for years, and often wondered why his mother hadn't come to his rescue.

"I ran away once when I was about your age," Landon said. "Right from this very house, and that very door.."

"You did?" said Billy, looking up from his supper. Mike looked up too.

"I sure did. Maybe every boy has at some time or other. My dad was harsh, and I didn't like it much.."

He reached over and picked up the Bible.

"Ever hear the story of the Prodigal Son?"

The boys looked uncertain.

"It's a story in the Bible, here, about a boy who got itchy feet and wanted to get away, see the sights, play a little. He didn't like his father telling him 'no' to things. So he up and left."

Landon read aloud the story, stopping now and again to see if the boys were following. They were.

"When things got real bad, when he was hungry and destitute and somebody beat him up, the boy saw his mistake. He reckoned even his father's servants had a good life, compared with his. So he turned and went on home."

Landon closed the Bible. "And do you know what his father did?"

Billy said, "He whopped him good?"

"No, not that. Not that at all. His father saw him coming from a long way off. He'd been waiting for the boy, and watched that hill every day until he finally saw the familiar figure, limping along toward him."

It grew quiet around the table.

"Well," said Landon, "finish up your dinners, and we'll head out. Is it to the cousin's house you want to go?"

But the boys said they'd just as well go home, it being so late and their mother likely worrying.

"There's an outhouse at the back, if you need it," said Landon, pulling on his coat. The boys looked at each other and laughed.

"Our big brother pushed over an outhouse last week and got into trouble." Billy's eyes danced with fun. "Someone was still in it."

"I feel for the poor sitter!" said Landon, who seemed shocked. "Just imagine.."

"Now you know perfectly well you did the same thing when you were a boy," teased Pennie.

As the laughter rolled, Landon got the boys and their bicycles into the car and eased out onto the highway toward town.

I see from my house by the side of the road,
By the side of the highway of life,
The men who press with the ardor of hope,
The men who are faint with the strife.

But still I rejoice when the travelers rejoice,
And weep with the strangers that moan,
Nor live in my house by the side of the road
Like a man who dwells alone.

"Come again!", Pennie called, waving, hoping they would. If they did, she would be waiting for them right here, by her side of the highway of Life.

PART FIVE

JESUS SOUGHT ME WHEN A STRANGER

CHAPTER TWENTY-SEVEN

The White Wicker Basket

1949

Kathleen West arrived safely on the 26th, surprising everyone with her dark and striking beauty. In the hospital room Pennie stared at the small, sleeping face, utterly charmed.

"Ours is by far the prettiest baby in the nursery," she said when Landon came in. "I feel sorry for the rest."

Landon laughed. "That's kind of hard on the other mothers, honey. What about what they think?"

"No, but it's true. Even strangers say it. I've heard them."

They studied her together.

"Hmm. I see what you mean," he said, and received a kiss in reward.

When Landon arrived at home, he found Ann and Aunt Jeannie waiting for him at the window. Aunt Jeannie, young and slender, wore jeans and had two dark braids that made Ann think of Elizabeth Taylor. Jeannie had married Bob when she was just seventeen, and they lived in the little white house George had once occupied. She loved Bob, in large part because his sense of humor matched hers. The pair had scarcely stopped laughing ever since.

Seeing no baby, Ann asked, "But where is Kathleen?"

"Oh, she's still at the hospital, getting used to the world a little bit. It takes time to bring a baby home." Landon wanted them home too, but he had a promise to keep. This time the project required actual work, and with two small children and farm chores to cope with, it would be a close thing.

The children watched with curious interest all week as their daddy's project took shape. He finished it only moments before leaving to collect baby Kathleen for her ride home from the hospital.

But hospitals seem to take a long time to let the people who are inside of them, back out again. Pennie had been ready all day, but the doctors were not ready, and the administrators were not ready. She did not know what they all had to be ready for, since it was she who would be leaving.

Home at last, Landon guided Pennie carefully across the wobbly bridge to where Ann and Matt waited. Aunt Jeannie watched from the doorway.

"Children," Pennie said, bending a little so they could see, "here is your baby sister." Matt, on tip toes, examined the tiny face.

"Mine.." he whispered, reaching a small brown paw toward the baby's head.

"She belongs to us all," said their mother, kindly. Matt trotted off to the kitchen, where there was a strong smell of paint.

"Mommy..." said he, pointing.

Pennie smelled it too, and with great curiosity followed him in. There, she stopped. Built into the wall near her range were three shelves set into a graceful arch, offering new and necessary storage space. On them, he had placed a few kitchen items he thought looked rather spiffy.

"Oh Landon, built-ins? I never even dreamed of such a thing!" Pennie recognized the time and effort it had taken while she had been resting all week at the hospital.

She sat down, putting a hand to her eyes.

"Mommy cwying," said Matt with a frown.

"Don't worry Mattie, it's only because she is happy," said Ann.

Landon bent to hug his wife, and asked, "How do you like the new shelves, dear?"

"I love them, and you know it!" she said, sniffing.

From the doorway, Aunt Jeannie cleared her throat. "Well, I'd best be off home, then. Bob will be wanting his supper."

"Oh, thank you so much, Jeannie," said Pennie, wiping tears with Landon's handkerchief.

That little Kathleen is a kick, Jeannie thought, making her way up the lane to her own little abode. *Never seen anything so pretty.* Jeannie wouldn't mind having one just like her, and wished it would hurry up and happen. She'd been seventeen when Bob married her five years before, and now here she was practically ancient.

Little Kathleen came into the world charming it, and then never stopped. She soon recognized the faces above her crib: Ann's look of proud possession; Matt's curious gaze and quiet repetition of the name, '*Kaff-ween...*'; Pennie's watchful scrutiny; and Landon's...well, Landon's seemed the more puzzling of these looks: searching, loving... rattled.

The little family grew in wisdom and in stature in that year of 1949, with many reasons to be grateful. Landon knew he should be, and certainly did try. But there was an undeniable pinch to his life: the brick wall of near poverty. Other farmers in this position leaned upon banks for relief, and now, with Landon's family growing and his bank account shrinking, he finally decided to do the same.

The day after Kathleen came home from the hospital, Landon took out a loan. It was surprisingly easy. The bank manager simply wrote out a check, which Landon promptly signed and deposited. Money in the bank! The relief he felt was immediate and almost physical. He saw no reason to burden Pennie with it, so the loan's particulars became lost in the bustle of family life, to be discovered some distant day.

CHAPTER TWENTY-EIGHT

Nothing Could Be Simpler

1950

The sudden flush of loan money slipped away almost as quickly as it had come. Their checkbook sat on the kitchen table, the numbers inside dipping into the negatives again. The children had to go without new shoes in the fall, which brought on a disagreeable squeeze for some little feet.

Pennie slept poorly. A memory of her Shipyard with its lovely and regular pay packet awakened her, and set her to wondering about pay packets in general. Could she find another? Should she? Working away from home seemed out of the question, but Pennie began to wonder if she had a choice.

When the opening for a school bus driver was announced, she pounced on it. Here at last was a job she could do without a babysitter.

"I'm going to bid for the rural bus run," she told Landon that night, waving the announcement in her hand.

"Really?" Landon said, lowering his newspaper. Any prospect of income deserved his attention. "But - the children?" The baby was only a year old.

"I've worked that out. They'll ride on the bus with me, and when it snows they'll stay here with you." Their eyes met, and he recognized the look of sheer Kenoyer determination.

"Now about the lowest bid, Landon," she continued. "What would be appropriate? I really haven't any idea."

They sat down and talked about the income they would need to make the effort worthwhile. Then they considered what other bidders might submit. The trouble was, they simply did not know. So they prayed.

"If the Lord wants you to get it, Pennie, you'll get it. I certainly won't stand in your way."

Pennie submitted her best guess, and settled in for the wait. When an official looking an envelope arrived in their mailbox the following week, she found she had won the bid! It felt to her as if a door had opened, and a hand was beckoning her through it.

"Well, well, children," she said at dinner that night. "What do you think? Your mommy is going to be a school bus driver!"

"You are?" asked Ann, who would begin first grade in the fall. "Will I be riding to school with you?"

"Yes, and so will Matt and Kathleen. We'll be quite a nice little group, won't we?"

The only real wrinkle involved providing their own station wagon. Their old Ford was too small for a bus run, and as Pennie mulled it over with Landon, she was surprised by his easy answer.

"I'll go down and get a bank loan," he said. "Nothing could be simpler!"

She hesitated, thinking about the Kenoyer Way and how borrowing like this might be a departure from it. But there didn't seem to be any alternative, so she finally agreed.

The next day, Landon came home filled with excitement and said, "Pennie - I've got the loan!"

She looked up from the sink.

"Goodness, that was quick," she said. "Well then, let's go on down tomorrow and pick out the car! I've been thinking of something in a light blue, Landon. I wonder.."

"*And* the car," he interrupted.

Pennie paused, uncertain what she was hearing.

"The car? You've gotten the car? Where is it?" She walked to the window, and peered out.

"It's, ah, behind the house..." He seemed a bit sheepish now that the truth was out, and didn't quite meet her gaze.

She quietly followed him around the yard, and there it was. The new station wagon, gleaming white (he hadn't thought of blue), large enough to seat a driver and eight passengers. Above the rear bumpers its modest wings stood out on either side. Pennie touched one of the wings.

"It's beautiful, Landon. Truly. But I thought we would be choosing it together." He was too distracted to notice the disappointment on her face, as he ran his fingers across the hood.

"No need!" he said. "It was easy as pie, Pennie, and you're all set now. That's what matters, isn't it?"

It would have been futile to say more, so Pennie didn't. But it felt as though something in her plan had gone missing.

On the first day of school, the girls on Pennie's bus route looked relieved to see her. Apparently their previous driver had trouble with the boys, who teased the girls relentlessly.

"She's so pretty," whispered one girl. "And she doesn't have to yell at us. She just *looks*."

This turned out to be true for the girls, who viewed their new driver with something akin to worship. The boys started out well enough, subdued by the presence of a new driver and her new car. But as the novelty wore off and the girls *would* wear pigtails, the boys were tempted.

"Mrs. *West*, someone back there is yanking on my braids. It hurts!"

"Pull your braids to the front, Jennifer, then no one will be able to yank them."

"Oh." It was quiet for a few minutes.

"Mrs. *West*, Johnny just said something mean about my mother," said another girl, beginning to cry. "And she doesn't even *wear* boots. I'm gonna tell on him!"

"You are telling on him, dear, you're telling me." Pennie quietly sighed, and pulled to the side of the road.

"Johnny." She turned around to look at him.

"Yes, Mrs. West?" he said, dripping with charm. The other boys giggled.

"Have you ever met Sarah's mother?"

"Well, no, not as I remember..."

"Then you're in no position to make pronouncements. Stop it."

She pulled back onto the road and caught a glimpse of her hands on the steering wheel. All the knuckles were white.

The girls said "Mrs. *West!*" so many times that Pennie thought she would scream. She talked about it with Landon.

"The boys on my route are a puzzle, Landon. Tommy pulls the pigtails of whoever is in front of him, and Larry talks back shamefully. They also like to bounce from seat to seat, whenever the mood strikes. I want to nip it in the bud."

"Were you using the car radio?"

"No-o, for fear of arguments about what to listen to."

"Just tune in to the *Haven Of Rest* program, Pennie, and keep it there. No arguments. Make an experiment of it this week and let me know what happens. I've a feeling those boys won't know what hit them."

It was a good idea. The *Haven Of Rest* hour, with First Mate Bob and the crew of the Good Ship Grace, always opened with, "Eight bells, and all is well!" This, along with the songs and stories from First Mate Bob, instantly captured their collective attention. They'd never heard of a "haven" before, and felt curious.

That afternoon, she looked at her group of riders and announced, "Beginning today, we will have assigned seating."

"What's that mean?" asked Tommy, who had inspired most of the "bouncing".

"It means you will sit in the same place, every day. No exceptions."

"But..." muttered Larry.

"Nope. No buts." Pennie gave him her 'look'. "Every month you will receive a new seating assignment - if you are good." They looked so relieved at this that Pennie almost laughed.

Her experiments worked wonders. To the boys' surprise, Mrs. West and First Mate Bob made them feel nice, and not naughty. Soon they started actually being nice, and never got out of the habit.

One morning, Pennie "forgot" to turn on the radio.

"Mrs. West?" said Tommy earnestly from his assigned seat, "could we have First Mate Bob, please? I wanna know what happens next."

It was every bit as rewarding as a pay packet during World War Two.

CHAPTER TWENTY-NINE

Everybody Has A Job

"**Mother...**" Ann murmured, as she gazed out the window.

"Yes?"They were standing together at the sink, canning pickles. Pennie concentrated, as one must when boiling large pots of water with small children nearby. The endeavor involved placing large, fat cucumbers from the garden into jars of briny liquid, then boiling them until the lids had sealed. Ann loved canning pickles for the simple reason that she loved pickles. Her mother held that children ought to be allowed to eat as many pickles as they wanted. It was just about the only kind of food they could eat with complete abandon.

"Mother, that bull..." She handed over the next cucumber. Her grandfather's barn, with its brilliant red paint against the stark, blue sky, fascinated her, being filled with activity morning, noon and night. But the barn was considered dangerous, and off limits to children. The bull now standing inside its fence, looking ominously in their direction, was one of the reasons why.

They had brought in this special bull the spring before, her father had said, to "improve the herd". He did not say why the herd needed improving, nor what a bull might do to improve it, so Ann was curious. But whenever she expressed interest in it, her mother said, "That is a dangerous animal and if you ever go out to its pen, I cannot be responsible for what might happen." Whenever Pennie said this, she sounded cross. So Ann and Matt never went near the bull's pen.

Pennie placed the next cucumber inside a sterilized jar.

"That bull is *mean*," Ann clarified.

Pennie looked up now, and out. The bull had situated himself behind one of their cows, and placidly climbed aboard.

"Oh, that. Well, Ann, that cow you see there? She's getting ready to have a calf." A small silence ensued.

"A calf? What does the bull have to do with that?"

"He is just doing his job, dear. Everybody has their job on a farm." And since her mother went no further, Ann stopped asking, but went on looking.

One day Ann found herself standing near the barn, talking to Jimmy. Jimmy was Pennie's much younger brother, who sometimes came to stay when he got to be too much for Ida. There were times when Pennie thought he might be too much for her as well, but she wanted to keep him, for her mother's sake.

Jimmy had the unique advantage of being Ann's uncle, though only a year older than she. He liked to lord it over her and tell her to call him "Uncle". But when she wouldn't say it, he would try to wrestle her until she did, and then Pennie would holler and tell them to "STOP!" It happened like this almost every time Jimmy came for a visit.

He had just come off the bus in Milton and was wearing his best suit and tie. The day was so hot that his face had a red, boiled look about it. This put him into a bad temper.

"Let's go inside the barn," he said. "It would be cool in there."

Ann stared at him. "We can't go inside the barn, silly. We're not allowed, remember?"

"I don't see why not," he demanded. "Why shouldn't we go?"

"It's a dangerous place and the bull is in it," quoted Ann. "Mother said." They had all heard of the small boy who ventured inside his father's barn and fallen through the hay trap. He had not died, but it had been a very close thing.

"Scaredy-cat," he said, changing tact.

"I am *not*!" She stomped her foot.

"Well I'm going in, even if you're not," he said, and went.

Ann hesitated, but didn't want him to get into trouble. She took a step.

"Ann," came her mother's clear and unmistakeable voice from behind. Ann stopped, slowly turning.

"Yes…?" she replied, trying to determine her mother's whereabouts. She could see the house, but not inside it.

"What have I told you about that barn?"

"We aren't allowed into it." Ann replied, wondering about Jimmy, who had slipped away.

"Where were you going, then?" the voice continued.

"To the barn."

"Was Jimmy going to the barn?"

"Yes, he was. I mean, he did…"

"Go find your father," said Pennie, "and ask him to come here."

She knew Pennie did not like bothering Landon in the fields. It delayed his work, which delayed other important things. So Ann went reluctantly in search of him, finally running him to ground in the north wheat field.

"Mother says, can you please come see her?"

"Oh? What's the trouble?" said Landon, removing his farm gloves.

"It's about Jimmy. He is - well, he wanted to go into the barn. He might be in it by now."

A look came over her father's face he didn't often get, because he didn't like being cross. But if they couldn't trust Jimmy, they couldn't have him here.

"Go back to the house now," said Landon, heading toward the barn.

As she approached the house, Ann heard voices from behind the woodshed. Then she heard a sharp *thwack*, followed by a silence, then more and louder *thwacks*. She waited.

In a while Jimmy came walking up to the porch, red faced and somber. His shirt and his tie were loose.

"Oh Jimmy, what happened?" she cried as he came in. But he just kept walking. "Jimmy? What happened, I said!"

He turned slowly, and pointed at Ann. "We are *never* allowed to go inside of that barn." He stood at the window, rubbing his sore backsides as Landon walked wearily back toward the fields, putting on his belt.

"Was it very awful?" asked Ann, kindly. Jimmy nodded.

"I reckon I can handle Pennie alright," he said, "she's only my sister. But I'd better lay it low with that Landon for awhile. He can thwack about as good as my dad."

No one could have guessed that Jimmy would one day grow up to become a Washington State police officer. Brave and strong, he would wrestle any number of bad guys, becoming a member of the SWAT team along the way.

"I always knew he would uphold the law one day," his mother sweetly said.

But on this day, Jimmy wanted only to defy the law, not defend it.

CHAPTER THIRTY

So Very Small and So Very Quiet

1951

July 3

It was the hottest day of the hottest summer on record, and for Pennie there was no escape. She could have gone to the Athena pool if only she weren't in labor and giving birth for the FOURTH TIME. But all thoughts of pools and comforts faded with the arrival of the next contraction.

Landon drove her to St. Mary's, still in his farming clothes. He'd had no time to change them, because the day had been a disaster from the start. The heat pounded down, and every farmer's pea crop was burning.

"Are you alright?" he asked every few minutes, and of course she wasn't, but of course she didn't say so. Upon their arrival, she stood tall and serene, almost gliding toward the entrance. You might have thought she was approaching the White House, not a hospital revolving door. Stately to the last.

Once Landon had signed her in, a nurse waved him toward the waiting room and wheeled his wife away. The room was filled with other expectant fathers, and Landon would have liked to join them. But he couldn't, not today. Not with his pea crop crisping away beneath the sun.

He walked out onto the sizzling sidewalk, climbed into his sizzling car, and left.

In eastern Oregon, peas were known as "dry" crops because they used no man-made irrigation. Driving past field after field on the way to his own, Landon realized that none of them would survive. He would have to turn around and go tell his dad.

At George and Clara's house on Main Street, Landon rang the bell. His step-mother's face beamed out at him from behind the screen, as her face always did beam. Crop or no crop, George's second wife was never one to lose her smile.

"Hello, Mother," Landon said. "Is Dad in?"

"Oh yes, he's here," she said, "waiting for you. Come along in."

The tall, gaunt figure of George West stepped slowly in from the kitchen, and looked at his son. George might have been seventy-two, but his face still reflected the keen interest it always held when it came to his crop.

"Well?" His face was gray with the strain and the heat.

Landon shook his head. "I'm sorry, Dad, but it's real bad out there and everyone's losing. I'm headed home now to see if we can salvage even an acre before it's too late."

He paused. "And the baby's coming."

At this, Clara's face beamed brighter. "Oh, the Lord bless you both! Do give our love to Pennie." She walked with him to the door. Watching them from the living room, George stood morosely absorbing his loss and remembering the first time he'd lost a crop.

Landon felt sorry for his father, but his thoughts turned eagerly to Pennie bringing another West child into the world. The joy of this made it impossible for him to despair.

He said goodbye and walked back to the car, hurrying to his task.

As he sailed up and over Milton hill he heard the distant sound of a siren, possibly that of a patrol car stopping some poor speeding unfortunate. Landon maintained that he was a safe driver, but it didn't hurt to have a knack for seeing the cops before they saw him.

He felt rather smug about this, right up until the moment he saw the red lights in his rear view mirror. Surely they weren't aiming for him, but...were they, though? He pulled his foot off the gas just in case. Nearer and nearer the lights came, until there could no longer be any doubt. The patrol car was aiming for him.

The officer slowly approached as Landon opened his window to the dry, blazing heat.

"License and Registration, please."

Landon handed them over.

"In a hurry, were you?" said the officer

"Well, yes sir, my wife is having a baby, back there at St Mary's. And our pea crop is burning..." His voice trailed off as he watched the officer signing the ticket.

"I'm sorry about the pea crop, sir. But do you want to see that new baby of yours?"

"Oh yes sir, I certainly do."

"You might not see it if you keep up the speeds you hit back there. More than 80 miles per hour. That's flying mighty close to the edge, Mr. West." He handed Landon the ticket.

"Yes, sir. I'm sorry sir," said Landon, looking rather hangdog. The officer shook his head, got back into the patrol car, and drove away.

By the time Landon reached the farm, their entire pea crop, every last inch of every last acre of it, was beyond salvage. They were back to square one.

There were now four children in their house by the side of the road, and it really should have felt more crowded. But this littlest angel-girl seemed in fact so very small and so very quiet that sometimes they did not notice her at all. Pennie held her close, and considered the two of them an island of peace in a sea of activity.

Only one thing more needs to be said regarding the baby born on the hottest day of 1951. Landon remained true to his promise, and presented his wife with her well-earned reward: a brand new red kitchen table with six red, padded chairs rimmed with chrome.

When Pennie came into the kitchen and saw them, she almost couldn't believe her eyes. "I've been looking at these in the catalog!" she gasped.

"I thought so," Landon laughed. "That page was pretty well dog-eared." He wrapped his arms around her, kissing her cheek. "Welcome back, honey."

But Pennie unexpectedly squirmed and pushed him away. "Don't muss me," she said. "It's too hot."

Landon looked surprised, but drew back. Ann, who had caught the exchange, felt a little bit sorry for her father. He hadn't been thinking of the weather at all.

CHAPTER THIRTY-ONE

Along The Sunset Highway

March 1, 1952

Dear Folks,

We've been so busy this past week, and one of the reasons is something nice. On Wednesday, Archie McNeill and his brother-in-law Walter were here and spent the night with us. We were all so excited when they drove up. Ann saw them first, and when she said, "Mother, Mr. McNeill is on the porch," I didn't believe her.

Of course we stayed up late, and talked. It's impossible to go to bed early with someone like Archie McNeill in the house. Even the children stayed up with us until they could no longer keep from yawning. Much later, I noticed Ann standing just inside the bedroom door, still listening.

We hope to see both Archie and Evangeline here again soon. I missed her this time around.

With lots of love,
Pennie

Landon liked to catch up on the latest news when he went into town. He heard it because the working farmers (whenever they weren't working) liked to gather, and to gossip, and to gripe. The hardware store provided all these things, and no one ever left without an earful.

But on August 6, Landon heard something he didn't like.

A number of farmers leaned against the counter, comparing problems and advice. The talk went from despair to cheerfulness and back again, as the mood struck. They saw Landon pulling up to the curb, and turned to watch as he came through the door.

"Hey there, Landon!" somebody called. "How's business?"

"Oh, normal I'd say. Not too bad, not too good. How about you, Russ?"

"Well, about t' same as you. Say," the man continued, "didn't you know that Scottish preacher from over Portland way? McNeill?" A silence fell upon the little group.

Of course Landon knew him. "You mean Archie?" he asked, suddenly aware of the past tense the man had used.

"Yes, that's the one. Terrible bad accident yesterday. Was driving into the sun and run smack-dab into some truck at heaven knows what speed. Here's the account, right here, front page..." The look on Landon's face made the man regret having told. He gently handed over his copy of the daily news. "...and I'm sorry..."

"Surely not..." Landon began, and faltered. He was having trouble focusing, his mind wholly rejecting this absolutely desperate news. It couldn't be Archie, he reasoned. Archie would be safely back at the conference grounds today, tending to the many details that were his daily share, laughing and cheerful and - *there*. But Landon reluctantly took the newspaper and finally saw it all: Archie's photograph on the front page, bottom right hand side, *Sunset Highway Crash Fatal to Cannon Beach Man* emblazoned above it. Oh no. How would he ever break such news to Pennie?

"Was he alone?" Landon asked, his thoughts wending their way now toward Evangeline, who always went with him on the grocery run.

"Nope, by himself. Nobody else there but him and the truck driver." But Landon could listen no more, and turned to go.

"I'm awful sorry about this, Landon. I knew you and him were friends..."

The farmers watched as he made his way out the door, his heart heavy with the news. Five people waited at home, unaware, innocent yet on this still innocent Wednesday. He drove slowly, letting his thoughts wander back to the first time Archie and Evangeline had come, bringing Life to their house by the side of the road. So alive, and so vital. Landon's eyes stung.

Pennie saw him crossing the bridge and sensed that something was wrong. Coming in through the front door, Landon said, "Oh Pennie, I'm so sorry."

"Sorry?" she said. "What are you sorry about? Is it Mother?" Her face was a mask.

"No, not Ida," he said. "It's Archie."

"Archie. Landon, what's happened?" Pennie began to steady herself, because the children were watching and she didn't wish to frighten them.

"Let's sit down," he said, handing her the newspaper with its picture of a young and smiling Archie McNeill at the bottom; and then she saw the headline, and then she knew. Archie McNeill had gone, beyond the reach of those who would now be left without him, gone to his "Long Home", as he had always called Heaven.

"Don't you worry about Heaven!" he often said. "Heaven is where *He* is. No worries there!"

The children stood in a solemn little group, waiting as their mother read the strange words beneath Archie's happy photograph.

"What is it, Mother?" asked Ann.

But Pennie could not speak. She looked mutely at Landon, who finally, quietly said, "It's Archie, kids. There's been an accident."

"Is he okay?" Ann whispered.

Her father shook his head. "No, my dear. Archie is gone."

The room fell silent.

"But where did he go?" said Matt, a stricken look on his small face.

"He went to Heaven, my dear. Heaven is where Jesus lives, and because Archie loved Jesus, he went to be with Him."

Pennie thought of the day in March when Archie had been right here, sitting where she now sat. He laughed at something Landon said, throwing his great head back in the joy of it, and then everyone else had laughed too.

A picture of Heaven sprang to her mind, with its Pearly Gates, its Throne, and its gleaming golden streets. And now into that picture came Archie, walking humbly through that Gate and toward that Throne. His face shone bright, and smiling, and calm, and it was this that brought the tears.

The children drew closer, gathering around their mother for comfort in this, the first significant death they had experienced. Landon reached for their big family Bible, the sustenance they had all learned to rally around; and turning the pages to John 14, he read:

"In My Father's house are many mansions; if it were not so, I would have told you; for I go to prepare a place for you. And if I go and prepare a place for you, I will come again and receive you to Myself; that where I am, there you may be also."

John 14:2-4 August 7, 1952

Dearest Mother and Dad,

We've had such terrible news, I still can't believe it. Archie McNeill was driving by himself from Portland to Cannon Beach after a grocery run, when he died in an accident. I have always disliked that part of the drive because there are so many hair-pin turns, and Landon doesn't always take them slowly. The sun was so bright, Archie didn't see a truck coming around a bend and they hit head-on.

The driver of the truck escaped injury except for a cut on his cheek. He bore no blame for it. The highway patrol called it just one of those unfortunate accidents.

I can't imagine what Evangeline must be going through. She has their girls as well as the conference center to run, and none of this is going to be easy. We are scheduled to go there on Saturday, so I'm sure we'll learn more about what happened.

Love to you,
Pennie

CHAPTER THIRTY-TWO

All Now Mysterious

August 9

Driving toward Cannon Beach on Saturday sobered them. Landon applied more prudence than usual, careful on the hairpin turns and waiting until it he could safely pass. Knowing Archie had died this week and on this road had the effect of dampening the venturesome Landon. Neither he nor Pennie would feel quite the same about the lovely Sunset Highway.

Arriving at the conference grounds, they saw clusters of people milling about on the lawns, some weeping, others dazed, having only just heard the news.

"Oh dear Lord, it can't be true!" one woman cried. "What on earth happened?" They heard the details over and again, staff members there to comfort and explain. The Wests received their room keys and, with heavy hearts, left to get settled in. The two older children had bunks while Kathleen and Jenny each had a "cot". Into these cots the girls were placed so Pennie could begin unpacking. As she did, they heard a gentle knock at the door, which Pennie opened. It was Evangeline.

"Hello Pennie, are you finding everything you need?" she asked with her kind smile and accented voice.

Pennie took her friend's hand and said, "Yes, we are, Evangeline, but it is you we are concerned about."

Evangeline exuded an inward peace Pennie had not expected. She later learned that Evangeline had suffered a near breakdown from the shock, but gave it all, each agonizing moment of her survival, to the Lord.

Evangeline smiled and said, "His will be done," but hugged Pennie hard.

"I am so terribly sorry," said Landon. "We couldn't believe it when we heard. It will never be the same here without him."

"No, it won't, and that's a fact," said Evangeline. "But this place has never been about any one person, you know. It will stand or fall as God wills, for He is no less present now than He was a week ago." She turned and stood looking out the window toward the freshly mown lawns. "In fact, His presence seems more obvious now, since…"

She stayed a moment longer, then turned toward her many tasks, most especially the newer task of comforting and supporting those in need.

"Goodbye, my dears," she said, moving down the hallway. "I shall see you at dinner…" Both the little girls had fallen asleep, but the rest of them clustered at the door, watching as Evangeline made her way to the end of the hallway, and disappeared.

The week at Cannon Beach offered them comfort, and sadness, and honesty. Laughter too, of course, for any story about Archie McNeill must contain some element of humor. Pennie's longest lasting memory of that week took place before the first evening session. She had gone to the chapel a little early, to pray and to ready herself for whatever they might hear. An enlarged photograph of Archie stood at the front which made Pennie take in her breath. It all seemed overwhelming, and so she sat, the only person there, bowing her head. "Oh, dear Lord…" she began.

Presently she heard the soft tread of another worshipper entering the pew, and saw with surprise that it was Evangeline.

"I thought I saw you come in." Evangeline spoke in a voice so gentle and kind, Pennie could not help but cry.

"Oh. I'm sorry…" she said. But Evangeline put an arm around her and took out a delicate, white handkerchief with green stitchery around the edges. Evangeline had always preferred green.

"Here, dear," she said, handing it to Pennie. Together they sat, saying little, meaning much, as others arrived and the organist began her prelude. Hearing it, Evangeline squeezed Pennie's hand. "*Be Still My Soul*", she whispered. The two women sat side by side, taking in the melody and remembering the words, more relevant now than ever:

Be still my soul, the Lord is on thy side.
Bear patiently the cross of grief, or pain.
Leave to thy God to order and provide,
In every change, He faithful will remain.
Be still my soul, thy best, thy Heavenly Friend,
Through thorny ways, leads to a joyful end.
-Catharina von Schlegel, 1752

Evangeline got up to go, leaving her handkerchief behind. Pennie had found comfort in the one person she had herself hoped to comfort.

At the beginning of the service, an unexpected visitor stepped to the platform. On his cheek a bandage covered some kind of injury.

"My name is Alex Getz," he said, his head bowed, "and I was in the accident that took the life of Archie McNeill on Tuesday." He looked back up at the crowd, and continued, "It happened so fast that I didn't know what had hit me. I was not much injured, only shook up, so I got out and ran over to Mr. McNeill. The car had been horribly mangled and I didn't expect to find him alive, but - well, he was. And he seemed to be asking for prayer. Said he was worried about *me,* took my hand and asked if I knew where I would be spending eternity if I died." Mr. Getz paused to steady his voice.

"Well, I didn't know the answer to that, so I said, 'No, sir'. Mr. McNeill told me how I could find out. It was getting harder for him to talk, but he asked if I wanted Christ to be my Savior, and I said I did. He prayed, and then helped me to pray, and - well, he died. I'll never forget it."

Mr. Getz stepped away from the podium and walked to his seat. There was neither a sound, nor a dry eye, in the house. The organist began, and everyone stood to sing,

Be still, my soul; thy God doth undertake
To guide the future as He has the past.
Thy hope, thy confidence, let nothing shake;
All now mysterious shall be bright at last.
Be still, my soul; the waves and winds still know
His voice who ruled them while He dwelt below.

Jean Sebilius, Public Domain

PART SIX

WANDERING FROM THE FOLDS OF GOD

CHAPTER THIRTY-THREE

It Just Isn't Going To Work

1956

Ann could hear the folks talking quietly in the kitchen, sitting at the table. She should have been sleeping, but felt worried by the sounds of their worry. A stack of bills sat on the table between them.

"We can't keep on borrowing, Landon. It just isn't going to work." Pennie said it kindly, but it had bothered her for so long that she just had to say it some more. "Here's the bill for a bank loan from only a few months ago! I didn't even know about it. If we go on like this, we'll never be paid up." Embarrassed about his wife's discoveries in that stack of bills, Landon could not meet her eye.

The next day, he and Pennie and the children got into the car. No one spoke, because the grownups were quiet and the children sensed that they should be quiet too. They drove to Grandpa George's house, parked, and waited while their father went inside to meet with Uncle Bob and Grandpa.

"Let's pray for Daddy, children," said Pennie. "He is making a decision today." Exactly what sort of decision remained a mystery, but no one felt they could ask. While he was gone, Pennie prayed and the littler ones squirmed, until Landon finally came back. Ann thought she noticed a difference in her father's face as he approached the car, and got in.

"Well," he said solemnly from behind the steering wheel, "it's all decided. There just isn't enough income to feed three families, so we're going to break up the West Brothers." He looked at Pennie. "One of us boys has got to go out and get a job."

Ann was surprised. "You already have a job," she said.

"Yes I do, Dear, just like Bob and your Grandpa George. But three farmers is one too many, I'm afraid."

They sat still, even the younger ones who had no earthly idea of the trouble their parents were in. They only knew that their mother looked sad, and whenever that happened everyone else became sad, whatever the reason.

There appeared to be nothing anyone could say to any of this, so Landon started up the engine and drove them all home.

"Mother, are we poor?" Ann asked the next day as they washed the dishes together.

Her mother paused. "I suppose we are, Ann. But life is also rich with things that can't be bought or taken. We have plenty of that." They kept on doing the dishes, Pennie washing and Ann drying, until Ann said, "Grandma Ida says that even though they were poor when you were little, your family didn't have 'poor ways'."

Pennie laughed. "That is true. My mother always made sure we had good posture and our clothes were clean. Oh - and ribbons - she had ribbons for our hair, every day. We had to be careful not to lose them." Pennie looked down at her daughter's unquestioning face. "I trust that is what you will do, Ann, when you have a family of your own."

Ann thought of that far off day, and said, "I don't think I'll ever marry a farmer, though. Farmers work harder than anyone else but their bills never go away." Pennie stiffened. Ann noticed this and regretted her words, for her mother's face had become immeasurably sad.

The following week a visitor from Pendleton stopped by the farm to see Landon. A tall man, he wore a light colored suit with shiny brown brogues on his feet. The children enjoyed Mr. White's visits because they found his ears fascinating. They moved whenever he smiled. He smiled kindly at them now from where he stood on the porch. Jenny giggled.

"I hear you might be needing a job, Landon," he said, turning his attention toward Landon.

"You heard correctly, Don. And the sooner the better." They chatted about the reasons for this dilemma as a golden sunset slowly lit the western horizon. Ah, the beauty of it all, thought Landon. How could he ever leave it? He, who had intended to work these acres for the rest of his life.

Mr. White talked for a while longer, then asked Landon what he thought.

"Well, Don, it almost sounds too good to be true."

"It's promising, Landon, you bet it is," the man said, "and right up your alley. I don't know of any farmer in this whole county who would be better suited to sell Crop Insurance. If I were you I'd take myself down to Pendleton right away - tomorrow, in fact - and apply."

They shook hands, and the man left. After talking it over with Pennie, they decided he ought to at least go on over and talk with the boss. The next day Landon made the drive to Pendleton with some apprehension. He was a good farmer. If things had turned out a little differently, he might have had time to become a great one. Now, he might not be one at all.

The following day, their telephone rang.

"Mr. West?" said a voice.

"Yes, this is he," said Landon.

"Tom Hendricks here, Federal Crop Insurance. Do you have a moment?"

Landon swallowed his surprise and said, "Certainly. What can I do for you, Mr. Hendricks?"

"Well, that's simple. You can come and work for me. Now how does that sound?"

"It sounds terrific, Mr. Hendricks. I would be honored to join you." They talked about the details of his position, which apparently included some considerable travel time. Mr. White hadn't mentioned that.

"When would you like me to start?" Landon asked.

"Three weeks, if you can swing it."

As Mr. Hendricks filled him in on the salary and benefits, Landon's countenance changed from disbelief, to hope, and then to amazement. Maybe that ship of theirs had finally come in.

Pennie stood at the kitchen sink while he enthusiastically spilled the details.

"I've got to be mistaken, Landon - I thought I heard you say $1,000 a month."

"Well, it is $1,000 a month," he said, almost not believing it himself.

"How is such a thing possible?" Pennie said in amazement. "We've scarcely had $100 a month up until now, and only because you were in the farm program!"

"That's the government for you. I'll be selling crop insurance to farmers, and the boss says they'll want to buy from me rather than some bureaucrat they've never seen before."

Pennie listened on as he told her about the benefits package, his pension, and even the use of a company car! The difference for them would be like going from a row boat to a cruise ship. It would mean having to leave the farm and move to town, something Pennie did not want to do. Yet it seemed the only choice. Within a matter of weeks their house by the side of the road stood nearly empty. They had found a house in town, so boxes lay scattered hither and thither, blankets and sheets and towels in stacks. While Mother packed on and on, Ann ironed pillow cases to fit into the box labeled "linens". Matt helped Landon out in the cellar, organizing the masses of canning supplies Pennie had stored there. They would need these things because, farm or no farm, she would never stop canning.

When all had been packed and cleaned, it became time to leave the little white house. The place gleamed with the spotlessness Pennie had thrust upon it, and she walked with Ann from room to room, checking cupboards and corners for some stray bit or piece left behind. They came upon some books.

"Mother, what about these? I've loved these."

Pennie knew this to be true. The green front cover of one showed a picture of the two little British princes who, presumably, had been "done in" by King Richard III. Ann liked to read it and puzzle out the mystery. But these books were in the house when they'd arrived in 1946, and Pennie did not feel as though her family owned them.

"No, Ann, they don't belong to us, you see. So we'll leave them here for Bob and Jeannie's children.

Ann stood silently surveying the treasury of volumes, sensing this would be her last glimpse of them. Finally, they heard Landon's voice drifting in from the wobbly bridge.

"Your chariot awaits!" he called, trying in his way to ease the pain.

The six of them piled into the car and pulled slowly away. They would return to their house by the side of the road, but only to visit and never to live. It was just two miles away, but as a crossroads, there was much more to it than simple distance.

CHAPTER THIRTY-FOUR

Goodbye/Hello

1957

As the station wagon turned slowly onto State Street, the children gazed in silence at their house. It had a neglected look to it, odd bits of lumber scattered about with a nail or two pointing precariously upward, as if on alert. Several booted workmen were already there, clearly hard at it.

"What's happened to the roof, Dad?" asked Matt from the back seat. "There are holes." Matt had decided to study architecture, and dubiously eyed the house.

"Oh, it needs to be replaced. But I'll soon have it patched up, and this spring it'll get a real roof."

Each morning, Matt watched the workmen until the ringing of the school bell a half block away forced him to leave. At the three o'clock bell, back he would run to examine the progress. This effort continued inside and out, for Pennie also had much to do in making her State Street house into a home. She painted, papered, chose fresh carpeting, and marveled in the luxury of an indoor toilet.

The children each had their own interest in discovering this place they would now call home. Jenny took to wandering up and down, peering at the houses and the people who might be inside them. Of particular interest was a certain tall, gray dwelling which stood apart from the rest. Surrounded by large, low-hanging trees, the place appeared to have no discernible occupants or caretakers. It was simply a blank. Although no one actually said it was haunted, Jenny concluded there was something creepy about it. She would have avoided it altogether had it not stood between her house and the McCullough horse pasture.

Passing it alone one afternoon, she noticed the intricate latticework lining the porch. Someone had put a lot of thought into that pretty little detail, and Jenny stepped forward for a closer look. Suddenly, a curtain moved, revealing something strange. A man. He stood in the big window, looking out at her and wearing nothing but a short, dirty t-shirt. She didn't understand what his lack of trousers meant, but sensed that her mother would object. Back down the street Jenny sped as if the man was running behind her, and gaining.

"I thought you were going up to ride Connie's horse," said Pennie as the girl ran past, disappearing into her bedroom. When there was no reply, Pennie shrugged. Jenny must have changed her mind.

When the others were in school and the house was busy with workmen, Jenny liked to watch as Penny made curtains or look over the carpeting samples. Careful not to get in the way or accidentally annoy her mother, the girl was sometimes asked for an opinion, on whether perhaps she thought the blue or the green might be nicest. When this happened, Pennie smiled, making Jenny feel as if they two were close friends and not just mother-daughter.

If her mother was too busy for such confidences, Jenny was allowed to cross the street and play with her best friend. Her name was Emily, who, along with her friend Kim, was already a talented dancer whom everyone thought should go on television.

Tomorrow would be Emily's birthday, and Jenny had been invited to the party. Since Marion was an exceptional party planner, there was certain to be terrific food, games, and gifts for everyone. The only uncertainty Jenny felt was the prospect of spending a night away from home. But as she didn't want to miss her first slumber party, the next day she folded her things into an overnight bag and walked across the street with her mother.

"Hello," said Marion, setting the bag down in the closet. "Everyone's out back hitting the piñata Jack has set up. Go on out and try it." But Jenny slipped over to the front window to watch her mother walking back across the street. Someone came to stand behind her.

"Your mother is very pretty," said Margaret, Kim's mother. Jenny turned to look up at her. The woman's face looked puzzled, as if being pretty might not be a compliment.

Someone said, "Margaret, can you carry out the lemonade?" and she left. Jenny turned back to the window, but her mother had disappeared inside.

The party was a magnificent success. Marion served such nice food the whole evening that Jenny had rather a lot of it. It was the hot dogs, which for some reason her mother rarely served. Thrilled with the opportunity to indulge, Jenny ate more than one. She even ate more than two. She ate *three*. The girl had never before had thirds of any sort of food, and her mother would have been horrified. But it felt so nice to be allowed to say "yes" that she just kept on saying it.

After the gifts, the cake and the ice cream, all the other little girls went home, and it was time for bed.

In the middle of the night Jenny was awakened by a terrible feeling, a more sickening and lonely feeling than almost anything she'd felt before. There had been the time last year when she'd gotten stomach flu, and had nearly been hospitalized. Until then, she had been unaware that what went inside a person might threaten to come back out.

"Emily..." she said. But her friend did not hear her.

"Emily!" she said with more urgency. When again nothing happened, Jenny stumbled out into the hallway and into Marion's bedroom, where the worst happened. Marion and Jack awoke with a start.

"What on earth...!" he cried.

It is best to draw a veil over the next thirty minutes, except to say that no one involved in it ever forgot.

Across the street the phone began to ring. Pennie's bedside table said 3:10 a.m.

"What on earth?" mumbled Landon.

"Hello?" said Pennie into the phone.

"Pennie, it's Marion. I think you'd better come on over here and get Jenny. She wants to go home."

"She does?" said Pennie. "But it's past three in the morning..."

"Yes, and I'm sorry about that. She's been pretty sick. Too many hot dogs, by the look of things."

Hot dogs. Jenny did have a penchant for them. Pennie wished she had warned Marion about this penchant, but it was too late for that now, and so she put on her coat, and went.

A long time passed before Jenny went anywhere else overnight, and years before she could look another hot dog square in the face. Especially one with grill marks along its sides.

CHAPTER THIRTY-FIVE

UNRAVELING

AS HIS FAMILY FOUND their way and made new friends, Landon had a way of his own to find. He had been introduced to the new boss and fellow salesmen, had already done a sales run, and now concluded the job fit him like a glove.

Driving along in his company car, he thought how fine it felt to man a vehicle with government plates. *US Government, 1957. For Official Use Only.* He noticed people noticing him. The car, the paycheck, the status of his new position all produced for Landon an unexpected lift. He marveled to think he'd been a poor farmer such a short time ago.

Approaching the parking lot, he saw a small clutch of men waiting for him.

"How goes it, Landon?" someone called, coming over to shake his hand.

"As good as it gets," Landon smiled, joining in the friendly bonhomie typical of most American salesmen. They all went inside where the boss briefed them, outlining each man's responsibilities. Landon was paired with Jerry, who would complete his training that week. They were to ride together, giving them more time to review the details along the way.

He and Jerry found they already had much in common. Both had served in the war. Both had families at home, with children of similar ages. They spoke of getting their wives together soon, and when Jerry said, "The Crop Insurance business is all about family, you know." Landon smiled, but wondered about the long absences.

"Served in Curacao, you say?" asked Jerry.

"That's right, and San Francisco before that. Both were good places to be, all in all. I even learned to tend a little bar, so it wasn't all work," and immediately wished he hadn't said it. Jerry shot him an excited look.

From his motel room Landon called Pennie, who said, "We miss you already. The children are all standing here, smiling at the phone as if you are in it."

He laughed. "I miss you too. It's going great, though, honey," he enthused. "Everyone is so helpful that I've learned most of the drill already. Jerry couldn't be any more friendly."

After dinner that night Landon went to pay for his meal, but heard Jerry and the others chuckling behind him.

"No, Landon," he said, "just put it on your tab. Government business, remember?" It felt grand to have a boss who took care of the fine details.

"Well, I'm going to turn in," Landon said. "Long day tomorrow."

"Sure," said Jerry. "But wouldn't you rather come down to the lounge with the fellows, and relax? We'll have ourselves a little drink, a little game of pinochle, whatever you like. We'll shoot the breeze! Everyone wants to get to know you."

"Oh - well, I don't drink," put in Landon right away. He wanted to make that clear from the start.

"That's fine, Landon," returned Jerry. "No need! Hey, fellows, we have ourselves a real bartender here! Says he doesn't drink, but that's ok. He can just mix it up for us. Right?"

Landon hesitated, but the others quickly caught Jerry's enthusiasm.

"Hey, that's terrific," said one. "We don't have Jim here this trip, he usually mixes. But you'll do, won't he, fellas?" Landon was swept down the hall with the other men, past his room (number 10), through the door, and spilling out into the lounge. The room had been set up with card tables and a bar, cozy and inviting, lights low, soft music, just the sort of place to make new friends. It looked alarmingly familiar to Landon, who made a quick decision. *I won't drink, I'll just mix.* He walked over, rolling up his sleeves.

"Alright then, Mates, what'll it be?" slipping into an Aussie accent. They laughed, soon bellying up to the bar. "Scotch and soda for me," someone called.

"Right-y Ho," said Landon, with just a tinge of regret. It had been years since he'd been in a place like this, and it felt strange. Sort of nice, sort of not. He could make up for it later, let them know this time would be the last. However, as the evening wore on and his popularity grew with the number of drinks he mixed, and with the sudden and electrifying addition of friendly women into the lounge, later never came.

The women were a surprise, and he wondered for a moment why they were there.

"I'll have a martini," said a soft, feminine voice. Landon looked up and, seeing a brunette strolling towards the bar, he quit wondering.

"Coming right up!" He reached for the gin. After all, martinis had been one of his specialties. He hadn't mixed one in eleven years, but it was all coming back to him now, almost as if he had never left.

The men quickly agreed they'd never had a more entertaining bartender. Landon had such impressive stories to tell, and in such hilarious accents. They had never laughed so hard. Jerry felt ridiculously proud of his protégé, the classic hail-fellow, well-met, the star of their show and an instant success. Landon had found his center stage.

Nobody noticed it when the brunette followed him out the door and down the hallway. Nobody cared. They all fell sooner or later, then watched it happen to the next fellow. They liked it because they could keep one another's secrets, if they all had secrets to keep. Their only surprise with Landon was how quickly it had happened.

The decision not to drink swiftly abandoned him, and that first drink brought it all back - the taste, the smell, the "high" of it. He soon found himself holding a cigarette, slipping along the old familiar cloud, downward and out of control.

Jerry's face floated past him at one juncture, saying with a wink, "You don't drink, eh?" Landon's face burned to think what a fool they must think him. But he didn't care, because all that mattered was that blue-eyed woman standing at the bar.

Walking down the hallway with her, he briefly recalled the brown eyes he should have been thinking of all evening.

Get out! something inside of him urged, *before it's too late!* But Landon didn't get out. He jangled the coins in his pocket and felt for his room key, playing with it a little. Unlocking the door of room 10, he stepped inside.

"Want company?" the woman asked.

"Why not?" he said, as she stepped in and closed the door.

Landon woke to a crashing headache, but couldn't remember why. He'd have to get up and find an aspirin. Standing slowly, he began to recall where he was and what he had done the night before. Lowering himself carefully back onto the bed, he mumbled, "Oh no, not that; anything but that..."

He turned slowly toward the other side of the bed, relieved to find it empty. Maybe...but then he saw it, like some evil omen - a dent in the pillow next to his, the comb and lipstick on the night stand. Bright pink. Impossible!

He thought of Pennie at home with the children, all innocence, and cringed at the possibility of her - of them - ever finding him out. A sickening shame washed over him, enveloped him, as he sat reliving the night in all its hideous clarity.

For the first time in more than a decade, Landon was afraid to go home. What if Pennie noticed something? She was good at noticing things, and he was not very good at hiding them. But he needn't have worried, for they were all so happy to have him back that their joy superseded his concerns. It had been a close call. *Never again,* he promised himself. *I'll never, ever, do that again.*

A few months later, Pennie sat in the kitchen with her coffee, puzzling over their bills. It felt strangely familiar, calling her back to their days of near poverty on the farm. But life should have been different now, with Landon's new income.

She checked their bank statement again and wondered, *where on earth could it have gone?* She didn't have an answer, and Landon was evasive when she brought it up. Maybe it was the remodel with its ever expanding budget, he had suggested.

So Pennie went back to work the figures with the foreman, whom she trusted.

"Well Pennie, it's taking longer than expected," the foreman had said. "But I'll do everything I can to bring it in soon."

After careful thought, Pennie applied for and obtained the full time position as school secretary, reluctantly ending her bus run. Walking to the school on her first day of work, she couldn't help but wonder for the umpteenth time why she was doing this, and what on earth had happened to their windfall.

CHAPTER THIRTY-SIX

When Wishes Became Nightmares

1957

She hadn't really wanted to go, but Landon was a skilled persuader.

As their anniversary approached, he said they should go somewhere nice to celebrate it. The two of them hadn't been anywhere alone together for ages, what with all of the children and all of their activities. So he settled on the Washington Hotel, a place in Portland he'd been to on business.

Pennie had finally agreed, and now stood at her closet, trying to decide what to take with her.

"But where are you *going?*" asked Jenny, sitting on the edge of her mother's bed.

"We are going to Portland, and you are going to stay with Mrs. Crowl. Your father thinks we should go away to celebrate our anniversary. Isn't that nice?"

Not very nice, Jenny thought.

Pennie finished her packing and stood at the picture window, watching for Landon. She felt reticent about the trip, believing it to be a long, unnecessary drive. Why couldn't they stay in Walla Walla? The Washington Hotel seemed ridiculously extravagant, particularly when they were having money problems again. She had a vague idea Landon might be hiding something, and it would probably be up to her to find out what.

When at last he drove up, they all piled in for the short drive to the Crowl's.

"Goodbye!" Pennie waved, as she and Landon pulled away.

"Goodbye, have a nice time!" called Ann, and LaVelle kindly said, "Alright, everyone, come on in the house. I've got something nice for you in the cookie jar."

Turning left out of the Crowl's driveway, Landon reached over to take Pennie's hand.

"Alone at last!" he said, squeezing it gently. "We've been so busy, Pennie, with the move, the house, the new job. It seemed about time you had a break."

Pennie was surprised by this, but kept her hand noncommittally relaxed. Landon continued, "I know you don't like leaving the kids, but LaVelle will take good care of them and feed them well." He smiled. "Shall we let her do that, and have ourselves a good old time? Like the good old days?"

Pennie finally laughed. He was, after all, a charming man. With the laughter, her worried face began to find the smile he'd almost forgotten.

Along the way they talked about their War wedding, with its angel cake and "borrowed" flowers. Pennie remembered her pretty bouquet, from which she had saved one pale rose. The rose still existed somewhere, pressed into a book and preserved. She'd have to find it and show it to Ann when they got home.

The two of them were light-hearted all the way into the city and up to the hotel, where Landon slowed and turned the corner onto 12th Street. There stood the Washington, magnificent and imposing.

"Landon…"

"Yes, Dear?"

"It's bigger than the Benjamin Franklin!"

He laughed. "Only the best for my wife of 14 years!"

Their arrival at the entrance set off a flurry of activity.

"Welcome, Mr. West! Shall we park your car?" the doorman asked, and someone did. The bellhop took their bags, smiling and leading the way. They certainly seemed to know "Mr. West", for the name followed them from registration to the elevator.

Stepping into the vast and mirrored lift, Pennie watched as her husband bantered with the attendant (this time in Scottish). She couldn't help but notice the difference in him. At the Benjamin Franklin, they had both been rather shy and unsure, a little afraid of embarrassing themselves. Here at the Washington, she alone felt shy.

"Your room, sir." The man carried in their bags, received a tip, and left.

Pennie had just opened her bag to hang up her dress when Landon said, "I'll be right back."

"What? But - where are you going?"

He mumbled something she did not catch, and hurried down the hallway. Maybe he had a surprise up his sleeve, something from the gift shop downstairs. It would be just like him to come back with flowers, all smiles and celebration. Finishing her unpacking, she sat down to wait and to wonder.

After nearly an hour, Pennie began to lose her composure. The beauty of their hotel room, the sparkling brightness of the bathroom fixtures, the ornate mirrors all lost their appeal. What could Landon be doing? The thought of their money problems, and the odd fact that everyone here seemed to know his name, disturbed Pennie. She felt that if and when he came through that door, she might just throttle him.

Opening the door, she peered down the hallway to the left, and then to the right. It was an exercise in futility, for the long corridor revealed nothing but the housekeeping lady and her cart. Well, Pennie would go looking for him, as there didn't seem to be any other choice. Taking the elevator down, Pennie had just stepped out onto the eighth floor when she saw them. Landon and someone else had just come from a room to her left. The someone was a woman, and the woman was holding his hand.

Pennie stopped and stared.

"Landon..." He glanced over at her without recognition, as if looking straight through her. Pennie's eyes filled with quick, hot tears as an image of Mary standing on a porch in San Francisco flashed suddenly back. At the thought of what must have been going on in that room for the last hour, a wave of nausea struck.

"Landon," she said again, a hard edge in her tone. "*Who is that?*"

The strange woman looked from Landon to Pennie, and then back again. Her overall appearance was even more loathsome, more disgusting, than Mary's. Older than Landon, she was short with a stocky build, and her teeth had long since lost their gleam. For a moment, Pennie thought her children's father might actually be insane. She turned quickly toward the elevator, Landon in swift pursuit.

"Wait..." he called after her. But Pennie pressed the button.

"I have waited long enough, Landon, and you are going to drive me home."

He said something to the woman, who replied, "Well I told you it wouldn't work, you idiot," as she disappeared into the other elevator.

It was a long and painful trip home. Pennie sat quietly, numb, not knowing what to do or to say. She remembered the green pocket-sized New Testament they kept in the glove compartment, and took it out, pressing it close to her heart. The car was too dark for her to read, but its presence comforted her.

"Lord," she prayed silently, "God, where have we gone wrong? Please give me grace and sustain me. Please take my fears. Help our children; heal us..." All the way home, all through the hours in that wretched car as Landon drove on in the silence, this she prayed over and over again.

She glanced only once at his profile in the darkness, and thought of the years they had given each other. Good years, they were, years that had brought them children, and faith, and possessions; years she had expected would stretch on until the children were married and had children of their own.

"Landon..." she finally said. "This would never have happened if we'd stayed at the farm."

He made no reply, and simply drove on, staring straight ahead.

They arrived back at the Crowl's late in the evening, surprising everyone. Apart from Ann, who was old enough to sense an "atmosphere", the children were ecstatic to see them. LaVelle looked surprised but said nothing, and helped bring the sleepy children out to the car. Pennie could only think of getting them all home. She held Jenny with her in the front, the little girl's spindly arms squeezing her mother's neck.

"You came back, mama," she murmured, in awe that wishes could come true.

Pennie held her close. She might lose her husband, but she would do everything in her power never to lose his children.

The "atmosphere" continued, and Ann noticed. She held a sort of second sight, a perception she wasn't always comfortable with. This inner sense alerted her when people or events were not as they should be, and as it was happening now, Ann wanted to talk to her mother about it. A few days later, she came into her mother's room and sat on the bed.

"Mother, what's the matter with Dad?"

Pennie looked up sharply, making the girl realize these were murky waters. But it was too late to stop now.

"Nothing is the matter," said her mother.

"But something must be wrong, Mom. He isn't like he used to be anymore. He doesn't..."

"I don't know what you're talking about," Pennie interrupted, looking uncomfortable.

Ann finally finished, "Do you think he maybe has a girlfriend, or something?"

"Be quiet!" her mother snapped, alarmed that the girl had veered so near the truth. "I don't want to hear it, and it's none of your concern."

Ann realized then that it was no use, so she stood and fled the room, the house, the block, anything that might remind her of the strange darkness hanging over her family. She ran to the football field, a vast expanse of green green grass which had become for her a personal refuge. It made her feel by contrast utterly tiny, a speck of humanity no one else could possibly notice. She lay down on her back at the very center of the field, and slept.

This marked the first day of a profound and enduring depression.

Pennie now found herself on an almost constant edge of panic. Anxiety pursued her, for she had discovered something she'd not known or noticed until after the weekend of the anniversary. She was pregnant.

Landon had not been told because she didn't know what to do about him. He was a loose cannon, now; untrustworthy. The two of them had discussed neither the hotel nor the woman, leaving Pennie frozen, emptied of all her confidence. She wondered idly if Landon could possibly love such a woman. Pennie could not comprehend being replaced by someone like her.

Burying her desperation as best she could, it began to reveal itself through a loss of appetite. She steadily ate less and less until it seemed to others as if she were eating nothing at all. Normal things no longer appealed, things like Sunday roasts. Pennie made them, of course, and her family ate them heartily, but she herself could not abide them. Just the aroma of savory beef, the potatoes, carrots and peas, not to mention the gravy and the bread, nauseated her. Landon's own appetite and verbal appreciation for the food irritated her. To her it seemed gross.

But she must eat something, so Pennie fell back on her old penchant for dried bread crusts. She saved every end piece from every loaf and ate them roasted, leaving them in the oven long enough to render them crunchy, not quite burnt. She guarded the crusts closely, although the children wouldn't dream of disturbing them. The girls sometimes came upon them in the small side oven, and cringed.

The only other item she cared for were the ice cubes she chewed throughout the day, in between bread crusts. These crusts and cubes, along with numerous pots of coffee, got her through any number of alarming days, so she was never without them. As a result of all this, and although she was pregnant, Pennie became uncommonly thin.

Landon saw these things only at the weekends, so they didn't sink in very far. It never occurred to him that their current troubles might be his fault. A normal man may have wondered, but Landon simply chalked it up to being Pennie's way, and never touched on it. There were too many other worrisome dilemmas to think about without the likes of bread crusts. Best just to keep the peace. Keeping the peace was Landon's way.

CHAPTER THIRTY-SEVEN

The Man He Had Been

Even as a little girl, Ann perceived more than anyone so small ought to, which made her mother edgy. Pennie might be sitting with a cup of coffee or mopping the floor, when she would suddenly feel a Stare emerging from the crib, as though the girl could read her mother's mind. This gave Pennie the uncanny sensation that she and Ann were equals.

When she became a little older, Ann's mother and father experienced a profound change, taking their little daughter and son along with them. Their mother called it a miracle, the difference between night and day. Everything became suddenly better. Her parents sat at the table and talked about faith, and grace, and being forgiven. Just hearing these things made Ann feel happy. Her mother laughed more than she used to, which made Landon and Ann laugh. Even the baby giggled from his high chair, as if such a thing were contagious.

The years of goodness on the farm went on and on, and got better and better. Their father learned the Bible, and taught his children the things he learned. He used to think he already knew the Bible by heart, but it turned out he hadn't known it at all. He had only known about it. It is possible to know about something but not really to know it, he said. Ann listened and grew, just as if she'd been a thirsty plant needing water.

So when things began to change back, back to what they had been before the good times, Ann knew. The family moved away from the farm where those good things had happened. She noticed when her father felt too tired to go to church, and no longer read to them from the Bible. She noticed when her mother laughed less often and worried more. These things frightened her, because they made her father not seem like himself anymore. He seemed like another man, someone whom they no longer recognized.

Ann was twelve. She never saw her father go back to the man he had been. He was only ever the man they no longer recognized.

CHAPTER THIRTY-EIGHT

The Surprise In Their Midst

Sometime during the late Fall, Ann had a notion her mother might be pregnant. The moment of clarity came as Pennie stood on a ladder, painting a wall. When she reached upward, there it was. Ann wouldn't dream of calling attention to this, because it seemed to be a secret, and in the current family climate, secrets were best kept unspoken.

Pennie's labor began several weeks before she was due, during one of Uncle Clarence's visits. Clarence was Grandma Ida's kindly bachelor brother who came for dinner each Saturday. Except for Ann who was out babysitting, the family sat visiting together around the table. Pennie suddenly stood, put on her long coat and said, "I'm going to the hospital now." Clarence stared. The children stared.

"My dear, but whatever for?" he blurted.

"Well...the baby is coming."

These words sent a shock wave through the little group, for none of them had heard so much as a peep about a baby. She and Landon just hadn't mentioned it. Pennie was so tall and willowy, and the weather so cold, that what with all her layers and her coat, no one had noticed.

Clarence, a shy bachelor who would never discuss anything so personal as a pregnancy (he'd never even uttered the word), went suddenly red. But he pulled himself together and said, "Well of course you must go, Pennie. I'll manage everything here, don't you worry about a thing."

So she and Landon left for the hospital. Clarence had never been a babysitter before, and the children instantly sensed fun on the horizon. Everyone ate liberal amounts of his licorice bootlaces and candy cigarettes, while playing cards and listening to old Indian stories. Like any good north-westerner, Uncle Clarence had lots of old Indian stories, enough to last for at least one complete labor, if not more.

They all remembered the night fondly because, when Clarence ran out of candy, he disappeared into the bathroom to wrestle with the "Big Fat Indian" for more. The Big Fat Indian was an immensely popular invention of Clarence's, and the children loved him. They stood outside the door listening to this strange scuffle, cheering Clarence on. The West children enjoyed themselves more on that one evening than anyone, even Clarence himself, had thought possible.

And then, wonder of wonders, into the family came a perfectly darling new West baby: tiny, blond, and practically angelic. Pennie said she had never seen anything so beautiful, which, of course, she had said about all her children. They called her Ellen.

It had been seven years since the last West-baby project, and the children wondered what their father would come up with this time. Would he come up with anything? He was gone so much now that the older ones no longer felt certain about what he would or would not do.

Two days later, trucks and workmen rolled up to the house. Matt recognized the tiles and the nails, and hooted with glee.

"It's the roof!" he shouted. "We're getting the new roof!" He kept an eye on the proceedings with high anticipation until, under protest, he left for school.

All that week, the new roof took shape. The men went about replacing the patched and tattered shingles until Friday, when the last nail finally went in. Landon thanked them profusely as he left for the hospital.

As he drove, Landon thought about the importance of the day ahead. They had little Ellen now. He loved her, and wanted to be worthy of her. Maybe he could be; maybe this baby would keep him true.

He hesitated in the hallway outside the hospital room, and peeked in. Pennie sat holding the baby and for a moment, Landon wondered if he had come to the wrong room. His wife looked years younger, gazing at their fifth child as if it were the first. She said something sweet but undecipherable to the little face, and laughed. He stepped in.

"Hello."

She looked up, and their eyes met; his held a question: *Will we be alright?* Pennie wanted very much to answer it, but she hadn't the power. Landon was the only person in this wide and mystifying world, who could.

CHAPTER THIRTY-NINE

"Remember Me"

1959

During her short life, Jenny had heard much about the Savior, and felt she might like to know Him. He sounded so very kind, ready to forgive a small girl for her bouts of willful disobedience. Granted, her bouts were quiet ones, as she was a quiet girl and did not often use her voice vociferously. In fact, she sometimes did not use her voice at all. But she labored hard under the weight of her cumulative sins, dearly wishing for them to be lifted away, and never return.

In the month of April that year, she came with her family to the evening church service. She liked evening church because everyone who came seemed so much more carefree, and less solemn, than they had been in morning church. The welcome and the songs were that much more upbeat and merry, along with a rousing anthem before the crowd became quiet and the sermon began.

That evening, as she looked up at the minister and heard his words, he seemed to be looking back right at her. At only her. He shared with her the same message her mother and father had heard from Archie McNeill, standing at that same pulpit. He shared that everyone in the world had disobeyed God, and needed a Savior - the President, all the Archbishops, everyone. This included her own small self, disobeying God and needing a Savior. The minister said the most important person in the world held no more importance than she, that all are equally in need.

"All ground is level at the foot of the cross."

When Jenny heard this, she felt a prickle come into her eyes and wondered why.

As the minister explained the cross and its importance, a picture began to form itself within her - a picture of three crosses with three men on them, on a hill. The men on the crosses at either side of His cross were very sad. One was even mad. The mad one said unkind things to Jesus, but the sad one called Him by name, and asked something of Him.

"Jesus, remember me when You come into Your kingdom!"

Jenny wondered what it would feel like to be only a foot or two from the cross of Jesus, and be able to ask Him so important a question. And then the minister said Jesus had answered the question, an answer which had been heard by the people on the ground below Him, and by his holy Mother; by the disciples who had walked with Him, and by the soldiers who had driven the nails into His hands:

"Truly I say to you, today you shall be with Me in Paradise."

Jenny felt she could sit still no longer. When the minister offered an invitation to come forward, she stood to her feet. Her mother saw, and understood, nodding and smiling as her daughter stepped past her and into the aisle.

It felt a little bit scary, for she sensed the people looking at her. But she forgot them as she made her way to the altar. The tears fell, and she felt the sins of her short life falling with them, opening her hands and letting them go once and for all. It was the most freeing, the most wonderfully forgiving moment, of her life.

She would always remember it, just as He would always remember her.

PART SEVEN

PRONE TO WANDER LORD I FEEL IT

CHAPTER FORTY

Rocketing Along The Columbia

1960

Because of her quick intelligence, Ann's name made its way onto every awards list that season. Hard work had gotten her there, but being thought of as smart wasn't always pleasant. Words like "Brainiac", "Bookworm", and "Walking Encyclopedia" came at her from time to time, and the words stung.

"They're probably just jealous, Ann" said her mother. "Not everyone has your gift."

This made her feel a little better, and she could brush off most of the teasing. But for some reason, being called a "Walking Encyclopedia" really got on her nerves.

Today might almost make up for it. She was going to Portland, with her father, to be given a trip to Mexico as a goodwill ambassador. There was nothing like rocketing along the Columbia, straight as an arrow west past Pendleton and Boardman, then into the city itself. The thought of being recognized by the State Superintendent of Schools, and in front of hundreds of people, made her heart race. Most important of all, her father would see it. Even the daughter of an uncertain father hopes for his approval.

She felt pleased and would have been on Cloud Nine, except that this morning there seemed to be something the matter with Mother.

"Is there anything the matter with Mother?" Ann asked as the car pulled away. She had looked back to wave, and caught a look on Pennie's face which gave her pause, as if something important had been lost.

"Nothing I know of," Landon said, staring straight ahead. "She must have things on her mind, what with the baby and all."

The baby and all. Ellen was as good as gold, so Ann didn't think her mother's concern lay there.

Along the way they talked, for when Landon wasn't busy or distracted, he could be a skilled conversationalist. He asked about her studies, which were considerable and heavy, for she aspired to either Valedictorian or Salutatorian her Senior year. Today's award would put her one step closer.

They parked at South Auditorium in Portland and joined the crowds streaming in through the double doors.

"Well, here we are," said Landon, as they entered. "I'll meet you here afterward, and we'll head on over to the hotel." He turned, and soon became swallowed by the crowd.

"But..." Ann began, unsure of where she was meant to go. Searching the crowd, she finally found an official who took her to the student section. The Superintendent of Schools, wearing a blue suit and narrow tie, approached the podium and asked them all to "Please stand for the Pledge of Allegiance."

The crowd rose, pledged, and sat.

"Good morning," he boomed, banging his gavel and smiling benevolently at them. He gestured out across the auditorium and said, "Let us begin by giving each and every one of our outstanding students a great big hand!"

As the applause and cheering thundered around her, Ann wished that her mother had been there to see it.

At his invitation, the students rose and filed onto the stage. Ann searched for her father in the audience, but could see nothing past the bright stage lights.

After his opening remarks, the Superintendent read a paragraph about each student, calling the recipient forward. When at last the name "Ann West" was called, a photographer captured the moment she accepted her award and shook the Superintendent's hand.

Click!

"Congratulations, Miss West!" he enthused, as a fresh round of applause filled the air.

She finally saw Landon in the middle of the parent section, deep in conversation with one of the parents. A mother. The two of them looked like old friends, discussing something fascinating to them both. They were laughing.

He had missed the moment.

As Landon pulled up outside the Washington Hotel, Ann gaped at its size.

"Goodness, Dad. It's huge!" It was, indeed, taking up almost an entire city block. There was a kind of gothic air to its architecture, and she couldn't be sure she liked it.

A man came to park the car, receiving a tip from Landon. At the hotel desk Landon said, "I have a reservation for two rooms, please. Landon R. West."

"Yes of course, Mr. West. Your rooms are ready," said the desk clerk.

"Two rooms?" Ann whispered, as they moved toward the elevators.

"Yes, you'll have your own."

"Isn't it expensive?"

"I'm here on business," he said breezily, "so there's no need to worry about that." They stepped into the elevator.

"Hello, Landon," said a tall, slender lady who slipped in just as the door shut. She wore a tight black sheath dress, and her lips had been painted a bright red. Her badge, engraved in gold, said "Hostess". Landon looked over at her and said, "How are *you* doing?" his eyebrows shooting upwards in a way that made Ann uncomfortable.

A heavy scent of perfume pervaded the elevator, and Ann thought of her mother's words: "*A lady must never over-apply her scent*". This lady's standards were clearly not the same as her mother's.

The Hostess got off at the eighth floor, giving a little wave and wink toward Landon and Ann, who continued up to the ninth.

"Now wasn't that a nice lady?" her father enthused. His comment surprised Ann, who could think of a few words that might describe the lady, but "nice" wasn't one of them.

"Hmm," she said.

When they arrived at Ann's room, Landon showed her through the lovely suite with its tall and ornate ceilings. Mirrors seemed to be everywhere.

"Isn't this fabulous?" he asked, pleased and proud to be showing his daughter such a grand time in the big city.

And it was nice. But Ann didn't like the idea of being alone in it, as if she were from another planet and didn't belong here. If only her mother could have come! If she had, everything would be such fun, would fit together, would feel *safe.*

They had their dinner in the restaurant, which would have been wonderful if not for the strange presence of the Hostess, who drifted into their view every few minutes. Ann couldn't help but think the woman wanted to attract her father's attention. Finally Landon took Ann back up to her room, and said, "I'm in room 824, just below yours. I'll stop by and get you when it's time for breakfast, so wait for me. Alright?"

"Okay, Dad…"

Saying a reluctant good night, she watched him walk toward the bank of elevators. He pressed the button and waited, jangling his change in the way so peculiarly his. When the door opened, he stepped inside without once looking in her direction. Ann felt an isolation, the loneliness of a small town girl left alone in a big city. She finally went inside and shut the door.

In the morning, she was ready early and sat down to wait for her father, reflecting upon her night in the massive hotel bed. Now that it was over, Ann concluded that she much preferred her own little room in Weston with her own little sisters sleeping in it with her. In fact she preferred Weston itself over any other place, even a swanky hotel such as this.

When her father still had not come, Ann decided she would go and get him. So she put the room key into her purse, closed the door, and took the elevator to the eighth floor. There she found room 824, and knocked. Nothing happened, so she waited a bit, then knocked again. There were footsteps.

"It's probably just housekeeping," her father's voice said. He opened the door.

Ann saw, not just her father, but (confusingly) the black-haired Hostess sitting at the foot of the bed behind him. She was clad only in a slip. Ann later remembered the slip had been lacy and white, and the lady had been pulling on silk stockings. Ann had seen her own mother doing this same thing in her bedroom, sitting at the end of the bed as this lady now sat - in front of Landon, in front of Ann. She hardly knew where to look.

"Who is it, Landon?" the woman asked in a dismissive voice.

"It's my daughter," he said, looking back at her.

"What's *she* doing here?" She said this as if Ann had no right to her father; as if Ann must be at fault here, and not him. Not them.

Landon stepped out into the hallway, and closed the door.

"Dad? Why is that lady in there?" Ann whispered. "She didn't have on her *dress!*" The girl had gone white as a sheet, and if Landon had been capable of any human concern, he would have known she was on the brink of shock.

"But why did you come down here?" he deflected. "I told you to wait for me." He went on arguing this ridiculous point while Ann stood overcome by the most appalling disgust. She now thought of the lady as she would a spider, its antennae out and roaming, watching for prey. And her father was the prey. Ann suddenly understood what it might mean to hate someone with a "perfect hatred".

They finally left the lady, and went down to eat a breakfast for which Ann had no appetite. She could hardly consider ordering, but in a surge of loyalty toward her mother, she settled on oatmeal. And right then, the woman in black came over and *sat down at their table.* Ann wondered at her audacity.

"Hiya, honey," she said. "Mind if I sit here with you?" Ann sat silently fuming. This strange lady wasn't nice, she wasn't even pretty. She spoke with Landon in a familiar fashion as he sat so strangely at his ease between her and his teenaged daughter. Ann could not look at them, and Landon later reproached her for being "rude".

It was all a nightmare, and Ann could only feel thankful for one thing: she did not have to ride all that long distance home with him. A friend was taking her back - a friend whose father was apparently normal, and happy, and not some kind of a monstrous hypocrite.

Although her father had not suggested it be kept secret, Ann did not tell her mother about the encounter. She carried it as a millstone upon her heart which became heavier over time. There it lurked as if behind a locked door, hidden away and plastered over, never to be seen, never to be acknowledged. Evidence of it came out only on occasion, at weekends when her father came home; at those times when Ann spoke out coldly toward him.

"Don't be so disrespectful," he would say in rebuke.

"Interesting to hear you saying that to me, Dad," Ann would reply, having the effect of squelching him. But there was no satisfaction for her in doing this. The loss of the man who had once been her father had plundered any happiness, and left her empty.

Several weeks later, the Weston School Superintendent asked Landon and Pennie to come and meet with him.

"There seems to be something bothering Ann," he said. "For the past several weeks her work has fallen off quite drastically. She seems lethargic, even depressed. We wondered if there might be something going on at home that may be the cause?"

The two parents were obviously shocked, as Ann's work had always been exemplary. Landon's usual friendly banter deserted him.

"Ah, no, I can't think of anything that might be causing it. Can you, Pennie?"

"No, everything as far as I'm concerned is fine. Just fine." Her face was hard.

"Well then, with your permission, her teachers and I will begin to crack down on her behavior. We want to nip this thing in the bud, you know, and I suggest you do the same at home."

And so, at home and at school, the "crack down" began.

Ann was not yet sixteen, but she felt hideously old. As old as The Old Man in the Sea; as old as Methuselah, but with so many more years yet to live. Getting through them now was more than she knew how to do.

CHAPTER FORTY-ONE

Right Down To The Wire

Pennie drove past a *Kennedy for President* poster, and uncharacteristically put her tongue out at it.

They were in the midst of the election season, and by all accounts this one promised to be a doozy. The children discussed at great length which of the Presidential candidates might be better suited for the job, landing firmly on Nixon every time. It was no secret which side their parents were on. Landon was still a staunch Democrat, holding the view that big government was better for farmers. Pennie remained unshakably Republican, walking the Kenoyer Way without a helping hand.

On election night, the results went right down to the wire with almost everyone - including Walter Cronkite - thinking it would be Nixon. And then suddenly, it wasn't. Landon was the family's lone Kennedy fan, but at the end of it, his candidate had prevailed. The children were crushed.

"I can't believe Nixon lost," Jenny said as she pulled a poster from the wall. The front room had become a veritable campaign headquarters, with everything from *'Nixon's the One!'* to *'Nixon - For Peace and Prosperity'* plastering the walls. "He mightn't have been as rich or as handsome as Kennedy, but at least he was a Republican." She had grown up during the Eisenhower years, and could hardly be blamed for her views.

"Well, it'll be a Democrat government for a long time to come," said Landon that weekend at the dinner table. "Kennedy is so popular, nothing can stop him now." He smiled, but noticing the sad faces around him, had the good grace to change the subject.

He knew other men whose political leanings were followed by at least some their children. But Landon stood strangely alone. It was tough being the only Democrat in this Republican stronghold.

He looked hopefully at the baby.

"What do you think, Ellen?"

But even that tiny, blond creature simply pointed to the sky and said, "Nixon's the One!"

One afternoon, Pennie came across some old phonograph records she hadn't seen in years. An ancient picture of Bing Crosby beamed up at her from the top of the stack, whom she remembered listening to in the early years. Suddenly nostalgic, she carried the box to the living room.

"Look at these, Landon," she said. "I found them deep in the girls' closet..."

"Hey!" he said. "I wondered where that box had got to. Let's have a listen."

Pennie sifted through the stack, hoping for Doris Day's "Sentimental Journey", a favorite. Instead of this, she noticed four plain-looking record albums with "US Army" stamped onto the sleeves. She stared at them...and then remembered.

"Kids, come over and see this!"

"What is it, Mom?" asked Ann, as they drifted in.

"Your dad made some vocal recordings for me during the war, when he was in Curacao. Remember, Landon?"

"Those old things? I'm surprised they're still in one piece!"

Pennie placed the needle carefully onto the first one, and they waited. It was scratchy at first, and then:

"Hello, Pennie! Hello Ann! I made this in the communications shop where they handle messages. It's fun to play with. This is one hot place, I can tell you that. Hot, hot, hot!"

The others laughed, but Ann got a strange look on her face.

"I remember this," she said. "I remember Dad saying this.." Pennie looked at her.

"You can't possibly remember, you weren't even a year old." Ann said no more, but looked uncomfortable.

The records seemed to entertain everyone but her as Pennie played them one by one. They finally came to record number four.

"Last night I went to the Enlisted Club and had just a terrific time. Lots of food, fun, drinking, and - well, heh-heh, I can't exactly say I was *alone...*"

Ann looked at her parents, who sat as if frozen to their chairs.

"Pennie..." Landon began, but she suddenly stood, grabbed the record from its console and disappeared into the kitchen. After a pause, they heard a cracking sound.

The younger children hadn't grasped the meaning of their father's old message, but sensing something amiss, they all went quietly back to their rooms.

Left alone now, Landon sat at the table... still frozen.

CHAPTER FORTY-TWO

"You Should Have Thought Of That"

A pot of Maxwell House sat percolating nearly non-stop in the kitchen. The house was never without that aroma, for Pennie made and consumed five pots of it every day. And each pot contained ten cups.

With so much caffeine coursing through her body, it was really no wonder she stayed awake nights, working, vacuuming, unearthing the endless clutter of the girls' bedroom. Together with her broom, she worked away at anything that did not belong under the bed or in the closet. The girls lay feigning sleep during these noisy forays, which irritated their mother. They should have been up and helping.

In the middle of a Sunday night, the bedroom door was thrown suddenly open, crashing loudly against the wall. This, followed by the sound of desperate weeping, awakened them.

"How can you *do* this to your children?" cried Pennie. The girls did not move. They could see her dark silhouette standing in front of the hall light, one arm outstretched and gesturing towards them. The bedside clock read 2:05.

"Shhh, Pennie, you'll wake them," whispered their father, hovering behind her.

"Well, you should have thought of that."

Landon did not reply.

"Did you read that letter?" Pennie asked, harshly.

Landon indicated he hadn't, shaking his head back and forth.

"Well, I read it, and it's a miracle none of your children did."

"But..."

"That woman wanted to let me in on it. And she did, Landon. Every single, humiliating detail!"

The door closed with another loud bang. The girls huddled in silence, shaking with the strangeness of it.

"What's the matter with Mother?" Jenny asked in a choked voice.

"She's just upset," replied Ann, unruffled. "Don't worry about it; try and get back to sleep, now..."

Her voice was comforting, but getting back to sleep would not be easy. What if it happened again? Jenny had never liked loud noises in the dark. Her first living memory, age three, had been a July Fourth celebration where the fireworks were so loud that the terror of them had never left her.

She lay facing the door until dawn, then slept. When they all got up to get ready for school, Pennie stood at the stove making the breakfast while their dad sat reading his paper, as if nothing had happened.

But Landon only pretended to be reading. However much he might be hiding it, last night's episode had shaken him. There were so many women now moving in and out of his orbit that keeping track of them all had become a chore. Worse still, his most recent follower had written to Pennie, the letter which had precipitated last night's outburst. He could only hope there would be no more of them.

For Pennie, it was like witnessing a train wreck - except that a train wreck will eventually end.

CHAPTER FORTY-THREE

When It Is Already Too Late

1962

April

Pennie stood at the door, keys in hand.

"Kids, I'm going to the airport now," she said, "but my casserole is in the oven. Can you bring it with you?"

"Sure," said Matt. "Dad's still coming, right?"

Seeing the hope on his face, Pennie laughed. "Yes, we'll come straight from the airport."

The awards banquet was a year-end highlight, and even Pennie felt light-hearted about it. Landon had been so attentive lately that it had come into her head to meet his plane in Pendleton, as a surprise. She picked up her handbag, checked her lipstick, and headed off.

Half an hour later, she was surprised to see her Aunt Stella approaching the airport revolving doors.

"Stella!" she called. "Is Lee coming in? She must be on Landon's flight."

"Yes! Back home for the summer. How lovely to see you!"

As they hugged, Pennie reflected that her aunt, now age 55, was still one of the loveliest women she knew. Just as blond and blue-eyed as ever, Stella moved through life with a demeanor of sheer joy, whatever else might be happening at any given moment. Walking toward the gate, the two women chatted and laughed. They laughed because you couldn't help it when you were with Aunt Stella. Her merry face simply pulled the laughter out of you. It was she who had ridden her bicycle 11 miles to see the newborn Pennie, thirty-eight years before.

The plane touched down in the midst of a perfect eastern Oregon sunset, lights brightly shining along a tarmac surrounded by wheat fields. When it rolled to a stop, steps were maneuvered and the passengers began to disembark. Pennie and Stella stood, arms linked, watching them stepping out onto the platform almost as if it were a stage. A young woman appeared first, tall, blond and pretty, descending the steps and waving toward Stella.

"Mother!" she called. And then she saw Pennie.

Stella knew instantly that something was wrong, for Lee had gone pale. Then Landon emerged, a briefcase in one hand. With the other, he held the hand of a woman whom Pennie did not know and had never seen. Stella saw the woman too, and felt Pennie stiffen. She tried to think of some way to avoid the inevitable, but it was already too late. They were trapped in the audience as the stage for this drama was set, and the players shuffled into their positions.

"Oh dear..." Pennie murmured.

"Oh *dear*," Stella murmured back.

"Aunt Pennie," said Lee. "Uncle Landon didn't notice me on the plane, but - I noticed him..."

At the bottom of the steps, and in the reflection of the bright lights, Landon turned and kissed the woman. Pennie felt her face redden. Had she not been standing right there and seen it all in living color, she would never have thought that anyone, even her own husband in his current condition, could do such an unbelievably ridiculous thing in front of God and everybody.

"Dear, *dear*," her aunt repeated.

Then Landon turned and saw them, the little trio of horrified women behind the glass doors. His eyes met Pennie's, and he stopped short. The woman with him kept walking until she felt the tug of his hand.

"What is it?" she asked.

"It's my wife," he said, and let go.

Back at the house, Matt and Ann had no idea of the quagmire their father had stepped into. Matt studied the mirror one last time, hoping he had finally gotten his hair right. At 6:20, Ann was ready to go.

"Can you get mom's covered dish?" she said. "You'll need a…" but she was cut off by the sound of tires squealing outside.

"Someone's in an awful hurry," said Matt, going to inspect. "Hey! They're in our driveway." Ann came to join him at the window.

The car screeched to a stop. Two doors slammed, and two voices grew louder as they approached the house.

"It was mortifying, Landon. The whole town will know about it in the morning!"

Neither of them noticed the kids.

"Well I didn't know you were going to be there, did I?" He stuttered, trying to excuse himself, "or Stella…" Or Lee! He couldn't quite believe the extent of his bad luck, coming upon such a gathering at the airport. He would have felt sorry for himself, if he'd had the time.

"Calm down, Pennie," he continued, and immediately regretted it as Pennie's burning face turned toward his.

"Don't you *dare* tell me to calm down!" What wife could tolerate such a phrase at such a time? But Landon could think of nothing else to say as he followed her frantic steps from room to room.

Ann and Matt watched the drama, still unnoticed. Their mother was clearly at her wit's end, saying unspeakable things about something unspeakable their father had done.

She finally blurted, "I'm sick of talking," and grabbed her keys once more, running out to her car and tearing off down the road.

"Dad! What's happening?" asked Matt.

But Landon was searching distractedly for his own car keys, and either ignored or did not hear his son. Finally finding the keys, he drove off and followed Pennie along Kirk Road. Ann and Matt watched as both cars streamed past the baseball diamond, turning right and gathering speed up Weston Mountain.

"What should we do?" asked Matt. "Should we call someone? They're going awfully fast."

They could still see the headlights of both cars, the second one gradually gaining on the first.

"No, we're late already," said Ann. "What we should do is get Mother's covered dish out of the oven. Then we should put on our jackets, get our speeches, and go. Who knows? They might cool off. They might even come back."

Matt couldn't believe how calm his sister looked, unaware that none of this surprised her in the least. In fact, she seemed almost relieved. But Matt had worked on his speech for weeks, anticipating the smile on his dad's face as he delivered it. Now, watching the two cars careening wildly northward, Matt's hopes careened right along with them.

Their parents did not come back - at least not for the banquet, the first High School event their mother had ever missed. But Ann and Matt got through it all: the dinner, the announcements, the awards, and the seemingly endless speeches. Then it was their turn. Both were talented speakers, and her speech that night was true to form, inspiring, with something of an edge that kept the crowd listening.

But Matt thought his own speech, and indeed the evening itself, had fallen strangely flat.

Pennie was so furious she would have divorced him then and there, if only she'd had the money. But in five years, she was no closer to finding the hole through which it had all slipped. As in Alice's book of Wonderland, perhaps only the White Rabbit knew.

CHAPTER FORTY-FOUR

A long And Wearisome Wait

1963

The airport fiasco caused a stir in the household unlike any previous stir. But as everyone behaved as though nothing at all had happened, the episode was allowed to fade. And then on a bright, cold November day, everybody's focus changed.

In the midst of Jenny's seventh grade Science lesson, the principal knocked, leaned in at the door, and said five irretrievable words: "President Kennedy has been shot." He withdrew his head and closed the door.

The substitute teacher shrieked, "Oh, the stock market!" which is, when one considers the sudden shooting of a President, an odd thing to do. The shriek frightened all the students, and some of the girls began to cry. Forbidden transistor radios came out of desks, and were switched on.

"Put those away!" the woman shouted, but changed her mind when she heard the calming voice of Walter Cronkite.

"Here is a bulletin from CBS News: In Dallas, Texas, three shots were fired at President Kennedy's motorcade in downtown Dallas. First reports say that President Kennedy has been seriously wounded by this shooting."

The class waited and listened, hoping against hope that it was a mistake. Then the principal's head came back through the door and, again without preamble, announced, "The President is dead." The class stared at the door through which his head had again disappeared, and wished he would have stayed with them. Anything would have been better than being cooped up with the substitute, who had shrieked again.

Cronkite's voice continued, "From Dallas Texas, the flash, apparently official, President Kennedy - died - at one pm Central Standard

Time, 2:00 Eastern Standard Time, thirty-eight minutes ago..." But there, Cronkite had to pause. It is hard to keep one's composure when announcing horrors.

After an assembly, the students and faculty were dismissed to go home and watch the coverage there, where it went on and on. The President's wife wore the pink Chanel suit stained with his blood, standing next to the Vice President as he took the Oath in front of cameras. It seemed terrible that she must do this thing when only a little while before, she and her husband had been riding together in the sunshine. Her roses were still fresh.

People wanted her to change her clothes, but she said, "No. I want them to see what they have done." And so the suit stayed on. It remains now still preserved in the National Archives, never to be seen again for 90 years.

The horror of it lingered as the news reports continued, as the man named Oswald was found and then arrested; as he was jailed; as he was transferred to another facility only to be shot and killed during the transfer; as Jack Ruby was seized and arrested for Oswald's murder; as numerous television commentators continued the dialogue about what was happening, and would happen; as the somber drums of the funeral march beat, and the flag-draped casket passed by; as the President's young son saluted his late father, before their eyes. It simply went on, and on.

The new President, with his ten gallon hats and his Texas ways, carried on as best he could. He set to work creating a "Great Society", and tried to maintain the vision of his predecessor. But however hard he might try, the new President would never be young and exciting. It would be a long time before the country would see young and exciting again. *Young* might happen, but there would likely be a long and wearisome wait, for *exciting.*

* * *

Pennie arrived at the Post Office before any other family member, and breathed a sigh of relief. She had been receiving regular letters from Landon's followers, and did not want the children to accidentally open one.

As she inserted the key, a familiar voice could be heard from around the corner.

"Hello, Pennie." She turned around. A woman stood behind the long postal counter, her face friendly but curious. "And how are the Wests doing today?"

"Oh hello, Mrs. Gantry," Pennie said. "We're fine, just fine."

Mrs. Gantry was the town's postmistress, keenly interested in the doings of all her customers. She alone knew what came and went from this little corner of Weston, and Pennie sometimes wondered just how much she knew about box 73.

In the stack of mail, there was an envelope with unfamiliar handwriting, addressed to her. The return address bore the name of a federal judge's wife whom Pennie knew of only in passing.

"Did you catch the Ed Sullivan Show last night?" Mrs. Gantry persisted. "We sure did. My girls just had to watch them Beatles, and screamed at 'em, fit to kill."

The Wests had watched it too, only no one had screamed. The girls looked as though they wanted to, but it wasn't the sort of thing Wests did.

"Yes, we saw it. Quite a show, I thought." Pennie moved toward the exit.

"You have girls, don't you?"

"Oh yes, we have girls. Four of them."

"Didn't they scream?" Mrs. Gantry seemed interested in this point.

"Well, no, not exactly." Pennie smiled. "Good bye Mrs. Gantry. See you next time."

She escaped to her car and opened the letter, hoping against hope it had nothing to do with Landon. She read it. It did.

Pennie could hardly believe that for the third time this month alone, some woman was demanding she leave her husband. Had they no shame? She sighed, wondering why she had these thoughts to think on such a gloriously beautiful day as today.

It helped that she was busy. With five children ages five through nineteen, Pennie scarcely had time to think, let alone manage a tragedy.

CHAPTER FORTY-FIVE

Death Make No Plans

1966

Isaac Kenoyer had not been well.

In the fall of '65, Ike and Ida came for a visit to the house on State Street. But there was a noticeable difference in him. The deep voice had weakened, and his stories were less frequent. This frightened the West children, who adored their grandfather and could never imagine life without him. Ida remained watchful.

The West household, especially its female inhabitants, were excited to share with Ida the details of Ann's upcoming wedding. Ida had married off all of her own children and wanted to support the next string of weddings, one after the other, rather like dominoes. On the first evening, they gathered around the photograph of an exquisite wedding cake, tall and creamy, accented in roses. The roses began at the bottom of the cake, winding gently around and up until they reached the top, where stood a cross. The girls were enchanted, wondering if they would ever have so divine a cake. It was then that they heard a sudden gasp.

"Ike?" said Ida, getting up from the table. But Ike sat slumped in Landon's recliner, staring up at her as if he didn't know what to do. "Ike!" she cried, and then everyone else got up. Pennie bent over him, supporting his head.

"Landon, call Doctor Adkisson. Dad, can you hear me? It's Penn - oh, Dad..." He wasn't responding. The girls stood against the wall hand in hand, watching this strange and unnameable thing happening to their granddad.

"Oh no," Kathleen said under her breath, closing her eyes. "Oh please, dear Lord, no..."

When Dr. Adkisson arrived, he gave a name to the unnameable: their grandfather had had a "stroke". Neither Kathleen nor Jenny knew much about strokes, and indeed thought of them mainly in terms of "elderly" people. Their grandpa was only 65.

Ike and Ida eventually went home and as the weeks went by, he became steadily weaker. Ida watched him carefully, wondering if and when their Sword of Damocles might fall. And then on a cold day in January 1966, it finally did.

As Ida was preparing their lunch, Ike's newspaper dropped suddenly to the floor. This seemed odd, as he had only just sat down to read it. Running toward where he sat slumped in his chair, she thought of the strapping man he had been when they were newly married, with all the world in front of them. It had not always been an easy life, but whose life had been easy in those days of Depression and shortage? They had their farm now, and their house, the children and grandchildren, a massive crop which would continue expanding, carrying on the Kenoyer Way. She thanked God for these things as she knelt beside him, patting his hand and saying, "Ike? Oh, Ike..." over and over again.

As for Ike, he could see as if through a mist his wife's worried face. He wanted to reach for her, and tried, but his arm was now beyond all movement. For a brief moment he saw in her the nineteen year old bride laughing up into his face; happy, loving, calm. His very own. A slow tear fell from the corner of his eye, landing on the sleeve of her rosebud blouse.

"Oh Ike!" she cried. But her pleading voice was becoming harder, now, for him to hear, and in its place another caught his attention. It was a Voice impossible to ignore, and imperative to obey.

"Come," It said, inexorably. "Come Home."

And he did.

Earth to earth, ashes to ashes, dust to dust; in sure and certain hope of the Resurrection into eternal life. Amen.

-Book of Common Prayer

With these words the funeral of Isaac Luce Kenoyer ended, and Ida's sisters gathered around her like a small, comforting cloud. Now in their fifties and sixties, they were closer than ever, although each lived miles from the other. Sisterhood trumps distance.

The four of them had varying experiences with husbands, and held strong opinions. Of the four, Ida's views of marriage were the kindest. Stella had had two, neither of which she had favored; Effie's one had produced a comfortable lifestyle, if not a happy one, and they weren't certain about Louise, who lived in California and did not speak of husbands in any number.

"Death makes no plans, dearie, and gives us no warnings," said Effie, shaking her head as if death really ought to be more forthcoming. She had been an immense help to Ida with the funeral, undaunted by the details and saying, "It is all just a part of life."

They all knew, but no longer discussed, how one death in particular had forever changed her. In 1924, Effie's little boy had followed his father out to the fields, where the men were digging post holes. No one noticed him running toward the group. No one saw his new red scarf catching on barbed wire as he scrambled beneath the fence. It wasn't until Frank came in for lunch that the discovery was made. After a frantic search, they found their son hanging by that bright red cloth, in a water-filled post hole, lifeless and still.

It was a heart-breaking accident, and neither they nor the marriage ever truly recovered.

The little white-steepled church gleamed out its welcome on that impeccable March day, as Ann stood hidden in the vestibule. Dotted around the sanctuary sat the bright young collegians she and William counted as friends. Seated and smiling in the West pew were the Norwegians: Effie, Ida, Stella, Louise, Wilbur and Clarence, eyes keen, taking in every word as though it was being spoken to them alone.

The effect of the candlelight service could not have been more perfect. Ann and Landon moved into the aisle, and at the crowning moment, the moment Ann had been waiting for and everyone else anticipated, Pennie stood. This youthful mother-of-the-bride, whose grace and beauty shone from one end of the church to the other, made everyone catch their breath. Then as the organ swelled, the congregation stood with her. All eyes were now on the bride. Ann's was the classic bridal beauty, but with something added in: love...purity...esteem. Her dress, white and gleaming, showed off a waistline so tiny that the middle aged ladies in the congregation stared at it, and wondered if theirs had ever been like that. Their husbands stared at it too, and didn't think so.

But Ann was not thinking of waistlines. Her focus was on William, the man she knew would love her for better or worse. This knowledge was precious to her, for the years of watching her father had filled her with a deep uncertainty. Could a woman ever trust a man enough to believe his vows of commitment? Ann was unsure until she met William, who gradually won her heart by his kindness and patient affection. She was finally able to turn from her parents' pain and trust herself, and William, to live a different way with Christ's help.

"Who giveth this woman to be wedded to this man?" asked the minister. Landon released his daughter's hand, and placed it into William's.

"Her mother and I do," he said.

The flowers, the setting, and the people surrounding them all went unnoticed. In that moment, the two had eyes only for each other.

CHAPTER FORTY-SIX

Along A Country Road

There followed three quiet weeks, as life in the West household became ordinary again. Pennie carefully boxed up the wedding things Ann would want one day when she had a garage of her own to store them. On the evening of April 9, Pennie glanced inside the final box and saw the Infinity candle Ann and William had lit during their vows. The candle was beautiful, but seeing it now made Pennie furious.

The wedding would have been everything they had hoped for, had Landon not spoiled it all. He created a mess behind the scenes that no one else knew about but Pennie. His most recent follower had suggested he and she have a "honeymoon" at the same time Ann took hers. They'd spent ages on the phone making elaborate plans, as giddy as two teenagers. The thing would have gone off like clockwork had Pennie not intercepted a letter about it at the last minute.

She sighed, thinking her husband must finally have cracked.

* * *

And then, into the stillness of that Easter Sunday came the shattering phone call at dawn. Sitting with her coffee at the kitchen table, Pennie jumped at the sound and felt a prick of fear. Who would be calling so early? She picked up the phone and heard her husband's voice on the bedroom extension.

"This is Landon."

"Landon? It's Hank. You'd better get yourself over to the Miller farm, along Gerking Flat on the way to Helix, you know? The ambulance is heading there, and you can just about catch it."

"Ambulance?" Pennie asked. "The girls..."

"Well, Pennie, there's been an accident. They were on their way back from the Cannon's house when the car rolled. I'm sorry. Bob Mayberry came upon the scene on his way to the church, and...well, Kathleen was there on the road. We don't know yet about Jenny."

"You don't know about Jenny? What ..." but Hank had rung off, and so they borrowed Marion's car and drove away toward the unknown. Kathleen and Jenny had left the house in the dark of the morning, making their way to an Easter sunrise breakfast. Pennie had thought how pretty they both looked.

"Take care," she'd said as they left, heading out toward Athena and Gerking Flat.

"Oh do hurry, Landon," Pennie urged, but for once in his life Landon applied prudence.

"We'll be there in a few minutes," he said, keeping his foot light on the gas pedal. The last thing they needed now was another accident.

Turning into the lane, they saw Mr. Miller waiting on his porch. Pennie hurried forward, but stopped at the sight of blood smears on his white front door. Her face lost its color, but Mr. Miller guided her gently inside, and said, "Your daughter ran all the way down here for help. She's plenty shook up, but not much harmed."

"Mom?" came a shaky voice from the sofa. The girl looked small and helpless, her blond hair standing out at all angles, literally caked with dirt.

There was blood on her legs, her hands, and running down her face. Pennie knelt beside her.

"Are you alright?" she asked kindly.

"I hurt..."

"I know. I'm so sorry! The ambulance men have Kathleen, and are coming in to get you now. We will follow behind."

"Can't you come with us?"

"I don't think there's room for everyone, but we'll have our eyes on you all the way." She gently patted the girl's arm. "You were brave to come all this way and find Mr. Miller's." Jenny did not think she had been brave.

"Mother..", she said. "Kathleen was in the road, and she..." But the girl couldn't bear to say any more, about trying to hold on to the dash bar as they swerved and rolled end over end. She later remembered those seconds as though the windshield was a television screen after sign-off; gray spotted, jerking, with frightening bits of dirt surrounding and striking her. Then in one final, cracking smash, she'd been deposited into a field. Unconscious for a time, the radio woke her with some tune Jenny wished she could remember the name of. Barbed wire had somehow become wrapped around the little car, catching at her dress and tearing it as she struggled to get away. In her hurry, she forgot to turn off the radio.

She didn't like to think of her futile search for help as Kathleen lay alone on that road. Back and forth the girl ran, always returning to her sister and the blaring radio.

"Ahhh..." Kathleen said, reaching an arm upward each time her sister came back. Jenny really did not know what to do. The surrounding farmland was flat and pretty, but showed no obvious signs of life. At last she saw a distant farmhouse, just a speck on the horizon, and ran towards it. There, a glossy brown horse watched her from behind the fence, and in her shocked confusion she called out, "Oh please, dear horse. Help me!" But as the horse declined to answer, she gave up and ran on, pounding on the front door of the house, leaving behind bright red blood. No one answered, so she pounded louder, finally opening the door herself. She saw the surprised farmer, running down the hallway and pulling on his trousers.

"What is it?" he cried when he saw her, looking as if she had been in a war. "Good grief! What's happened?"

"We had a wreck - out *there*", she said, pointing in the direction of the car. "My sister is hurt and you've got to get an ambulance!"

"I've got it, Jim," called his wife from the room beyond. "You take care of the girl."

Finally there were Mother and Dad, and the ambulance with its bright flashing lights and men ready to help. At last there was Kathleen, strapped securely in, as pale as the moon.

"I'm sorry," said Jenny, as they lay together side by side.

"No...*I'm* sorry," said her sister.

Then something strange happened as the vehicle pulled away, down the lane toward Pendleton. For reasons unknown to them, the two girls got the giggles. All the way to the hospital they told stories and jokes so entertaining that the ambulance attendants said they should have been on Ed Sullivan. Jenny had never thought such funny thoughts, and wondered where they had come from. The two men just laughed and laughed, and the girls just laughed and laughed, as if this whole thing had been a comedy, not a tragedy.

The Emergency Room in Pendleton was chaotic as the girls were wheeled in. There were other accidents that day, and in the bedlam, Jenny soon lost sight of her sister. She overheard something about a "broken pelvis", and tried to remember from her Science textbook what a pelvis even was.

Landon had gotten a ride to the accident site, but Pennie, curlers still in her hair, hovered watchfully. On her own gurney behind a curtain, Jenny waited. She thought she'd been injured, but none of the doctors had looked at her. If she had been injured, they would look at her, wouldn't they? Anything, even an injury, would be better than lying invisible on a gurney hidden behind a curtain.

Someone finally looked behind her curtain and asked, "Who is this?"

"Oh, that's the sister," said a doctor. "No serious injuries, just some cuts and bruises. Patch her up and send her home."

Send her home. It seemed like forever ago since they had left the house, and all at once she couldn't wait to get back there. After bandaging her cuts, someone led her to the waiting room, where she couldn't help but notice people staring. Admittedly, her hair was a mess of blood and dirt, her dress soiled and torn, the bandages still seeping. Almost worst of all, her glasses had somehow gone missing, and everything around her was a blur.

Pennie finally came out, helped her to the car, and got into the driver's seat.

"We might get in another wreck," Jenny said as they pulled from the parking lot into the street.

"What do you mean?"

Instead of answering, Jenny's body slid downward and onto the floor, where she curled up.

"What are you doing?" asked her mother. "What's the matter?"

But Jenny did not know how to explain that this car, and in fact all cars, had become her enemy.

"There's nothing to be afraid of," said Pennie shortly. "We won't be getting into another wreck." Jenny was convinced they would, but reluctantly climbed back into her seat.

"Let's get you to bed," Pennie said, when they reached the house.

"I'm a filthy mess," said Jenny, seeing herself in the mirror. "Shouldn't I have a bath?"

"Hmm, the doctor said not to get your bandages wet. But I could give you a bed bath."

Jenny paused. "What is a 'bed bath'?"

"Well, a bed bath is done with washcloths and towels while you lay comfortably in your bed. Here - I'll show you."

The girl lay still as her mother made her as clean as she could be after diving into a field of dirt. Because the dirt had become ground into her skin, it took considerable scrubbing. For her mud-caked hair Pennie used a dry shampoo, brushing and re-brushing the tangled blond chaos.

As her mother worked, Jenny lay watching her and pondering. No one in the Emergency Room had noticed her very much, and maybe she wasn't all that noticeable. But she knew there would forever be one person in this world who always did, and who always would.

Kathleen stayed in the hospital for 3 long weeks as her pelvis mended and she gained strength. It was lonely in her private room, and since her father's office was just down the road, she thought he might drop by. When several days had passed and he had not, she asked the nurse to attach a balloon outside her window. Maybe her Dad would see it and wake up to the fact that his daughter was inside, in pain, waiting for him.

Her mother, however, came every day, bringing get well cards, magazines, and chocolates to lift the girl's spirits.

"Why doesn't Dad come, Mom?" Kathleen asked. "I sometimes see his car going past."

Pennie murmured something noncommittal, as the same question plagued her. But she had grown accustomed to her husband's ways, and it seemed almost silly to expect him to do anything other than what he wanted to do.

* * *

It seemed impossible that both Pennie's and Landon's fathers should be taken from them the same year; but they were, by the end of it, both taken. The surprise had been losing Ike at only sixty-six, while George had reached the grand age of eighty-seven.

He had been moved into a care home in Milton, frequently visited by Clara and Bob and Landon. Clara's visits were long and chatty, which George liked, and Bob's were newsy. Landon's visits started out well enough, but usually ended up in the utility closet with one of the nurses. She had discovered she "liked" him, and he, of course, returned the favor.

One morning at the end of November, Clara arrived to find George peacefully sleeping. He had found sleep rather difficult of late, so she refreshed his water glass and tiptoed out. Half an hour later she popped her head in again and saw his position had not changed; a strange stillness filled the room. She spoke softly.

"George?"

When she saw no response and no movement, Clara knew he had gone. She called for the doctor and sat down beside the bed, uttering the prayer for those departed: "I am the Resurrection and the Life," saith the Lord. "He who believeth in Me, though he were dead, yet shall he live. The Lord giveth and the Lord taketh away. Blessed be the name of the Lord."

Watching the still figure in the bed, she felt as if a vacancy had opened up within her. Her life had been a full one, as teacher, nurse, musician, stepmother and wife. Of all these callings (for she had felt personally called to each), she thought this most recent had been her pinnacle, however hard a man George may sometimes have been. And now he had gone away, to be hard no longer. She did not know what she would do.

But these thoughts were interrupted by the arrival of the doctor, who gently pronounced George dead at 8:35 a.m. It was November 30, and so cold, the windows had become frosted over during the night. It was how Clara felt now - frosted over, chilled, numbed by death.

"The Lord giveth, and the Lord taketh away," she repeated, her hand resting upon the still warm head. "Blessed be the name of the Lord."

PART EIGHT

PRONE TO LEAVE THE GOD I LOVE

CHAPTER FORTY-SEVEN

You Can't Control Such A Man

Jenny had to play her French Horn for a panel of judges in a distant city, and Kathleen, her accompanist, could not go. They had practiced for weeks, their father hovering nearby and giving - or rather, bellowing - instructions on style and accuracy.

"No! It's a *B-flat!*"

The girls often resented this as an intrusion, but for once, their father's blusterings were welcomed. The judges would be ruthless, and Landon seemed to know what they wanted.

But the day of their performance arrived, and Kathleen was sick.

"Sick?" Jenny said when her mother gave her the news. "She can't be sick! I'd rather *die* than play *Panis Angelecus* on that stage all by myself. What am I going to do?"

"Do?" said her mother, with a firm look. "I suppose you are going to go on over there and play that piece." She didn't understand all the fuss.

"Without accompaniment? It's impossible!" Jenny was inching perilously close to the edge, and knew it. She was being dramatic, and her mother was no great fan of drama. Tiptoeing to the bedroom, the girl quietly opened the door and looked at the pale face of her sister.

"Can't you please come for just this one song?" she begged, clasping her hands together.

"I'm so sorry," Kathleen said, her voice weakened by the long and harrowing night.

Jenny closed the door and walked back down the hallway, moaning, "I'm about to be made a fool of, this very day..."

Kathleen lay miserably in her bed, imagining how her shy sister would feel, alone in front of those judges. But nothing could be done about it now, except to let it go. She tossed and turned, but finally dozed off.

A sound awakened her, drifting in from the kitchen. Voices, arguing. She tried to ignore them, but couldn't.

"I'm sorry. I'll stop, Pennie, I…"

"That is what you always say. How am I supposed to believe it this time?"

On and on the argument went until Kathleen could bear it no longer. Maybe if she went to the kitchen for some water, they would see her and have to stop. She tottered down the hallway toward that forbidding kitchen, the smell of toasting bread crusts adding to her nausea.

Her parents stopped talking when she came in. But their strange and staring silence unnerved her, and she left as quickly as she had come.

Moments later, she heard a car backing out of the driveway, and then a knock upon her door.

"Kathleen?" It was her father. He opened the door, but did not enter. "I'm sorry we woke you."

"What was it all about, Dad? Mom sounded upset."

He shrugged his shoulders as if he really didn't know. After a pause, it came.

"I guess we were arguing because… I've been having affairs."

She stared at him, and as the silence between them grew, Kathleen absorbed the meaning of that word. The shock and horror of it hit her with an unexpected force.

"I love you, Dad," she said, surprising them both, "but why would you have affairs when you have a wife like Mom?"

"That's what she asked me. And I don't know, Kathleen. I just do not know." Again he looked baffled, as if it were some hapless other person who had done this thing, and not him.

Landon stared at her for a moment longer, then turned, walked out to his car, and drove off.

For the whole of her life, Kathleen had thought stomach flu was the worst possible malady, something to avoid at all costs. But today, looking up at her father leaning nonchalantly against the doorframe, she saw that stomach flu wasn't even in the running.

The house was quiet but for the heavy weeping that came from the back bedroom. For hours Kathleen sobbed, sick at heart as much as in body. What a horrendous thing to be associated with! She felt the splash of its muck upon her, and already feared the shame it would produce.

Having been handed this shocking secret, Kathleen wondered what she was expected to do with it. There seemed to be no one left to ask; at least, no earthly person. There was no one but God. She had known Him a long time, and believed in Him utterly. Why would she carry this burden, when He was fit and able to carry it for her? From her bed of illness, Kathleen pressed her hands together and prayed, shrugging the new knowledge away as if it were a ratty old coat, far too big for her. Then she reached for the water glass, took a refreshing drink, and slept the sleep of the guiltless.

When her mother returned, Kathleen awoke knowing what she had to do. It would be hard, but she had better do her duty now rather than later.

"Mom?" she said, as the bedroom door opened.

"Oh hello, Kathleen. How are you feeling?" her mother asked, placing a cool hand on the girl's forehead. No one's hand was ever as cool and as soothing during an illness. The effect, although temporary, seemed almost miraculous.

"It's not quite as bad, Mom, and I have slept, only - I talked to Dad. Or rather, he came in and talked to me."

"Oh?" Pennie said, a steely tone coming into her voice. Kathleen did not like the sound, but there could be no turning back now.

"Yes. And he - he told me why the two of you had been arguing..." she trailed off.

"He did, did he? Well, I'm sorry you had to hear it. I should never have left the house." Pennie went to the kitchen, poured a cup of coffee and sat at her pretty red table. What would become of them, now that Landon had involved one of the children? She thought of the five young people God had given them; their five little worlds spinning around in this greater world, now in danger of colliding. It was more than she could bear.

In front of the judges, meanwhile, Jenny struggled as best she could through the recital. All of her father's stage training went out the window. "If you act like nothing is wrong," he always said, "the audience will soon believe it." Landon might be past master at pretending, but she certainly wasn't, not with her left leg unaccountably bouncing up and down, interrupting the melody. One of the judges smiled sympathetically up at her, which made matters worse. At the end, it took all her courage to rise gracefully, gather up her things, and leave the stage with her head held high.

Miss Maddy, the band director, stood waiting for her outside the stage door.

"How did it go?" the woman asked in excitement. Jenny had always been a kind of favorite of hers, for whom she had hopes for success.

"It was terrible, and I don't want to talk about it!" cried the miserable girl, running off down the hall.

"What? Where are you going? I have to drive you home!" But Jenny escaped, out the door and down the sidewalk, the heavy horn case banging against the side of her leg. In this moment of humiliation, she despised all French Horns, competitions, and band directors - and never wanted to see any of them, ever again.

On their way to church the next morning, Jenny and Ellen noticed that something seemed to be the matter with their father. He did not talk, and his strange silence made the girls feel equally strange. Their mother and Kathleen had stayed home, and church never felt the same without them. But as the girls had absolutely no control over anything anybody ever did, they simply followed Landon into their pew, and sat down.

Every family in the church had their own pew. Jenny liked the West pew because it sat right at the center, and she could stare around at people during the Reverend's long and thorough prayer. Sometimes she looked across at Ellen (who looked back at her), or at Kathleen (who didn't) and tried to engage them in silent communication. Their mother knew of this tendency, and firmly squelched it; but today she hadn't come and their father was ignoring them, so it didn't seem to matter.

When the sermon finally ended, Landon stood suddenly up and walked to the front. The girls were surprised at this. What was he doing? People didn't just go to the front of the church without being invited.

"Reverend," he said, "I have something to say to the congregation." The minister, who knew of Landon's troubles, hesitated, then nervously nodded his consent and sat back down. All eyes were on Landon. He turned to face them, and bowed his head.

"I came forward this morning because I have something to say to you, our church family." He looked up, out into the congregation, and hesitated. They were good people, people who had loved his family for twenty years and who would have helped, had they been needed and asked. He saw Laura Jean, his secretary, to the left near the piano. She looked surprised, and rather troubled. He swallowed.

"My family and I have been having some...struggles," he began. "These struggles would not be happening if it weren't for me trying to play God and run my own life. I am here to ask for your help and your prayers, that I would be the leader my family needs me to be. Thank you." He bowed his head again, walked down the aisle and out the door. After an uncomfortable pause, the congregation began to stir and, ever so slightly, to whisper.

The girls stood to leave, wondering why their father had gone and embarrassed himself like that. Ellen hadn't understood any part her father's speech, but one thing seemed certain: if their mother ever heard about it, he was going to be in BIG trouble.

When they arrived home, the after-church routines were already in place. Pennie's Sunday roast stood ready to carve, so Landon went ahead and carved it. The girls set the table and Pennie made the gravy. They sat down together, careful to avoid the one subject everyone was thinking about but didn't dare to mention. Pennie had somehow heard about the spectacle Landon had made of himself, and was furious. All she could think of was the dinner tables around which her family would surely now be the topic of conversation.

You just couldn't control such a man.

CHAPTER FORTY-EIGHT

Sad In A Different Way

Kathleen and Jenny stood looking at each other through the bathroom mirror. They often did their hair and makeup here together because in a family this size, no one had their own private bathroom. Not even their parents.

The two girls did in fact almost everything together, from singing to housework to cheerleading. Jenny loved this because her sister provided the spark to her existence, someone whom she could emulate. Whatever Kathleen could do, Jenny figured she could at least try. She hadn't tried singing in front of hundreds of people on a stage, because she would die of excruciating fright. But Kathleen had, and people were just as mesmerized as they had been in the days of Grandma Anna. Kathleen stood with great confidence in her long green gown, singing "The Days of Wine and Roses" with the jazz band behind her. When the crowd went wild and demanded an encore, she gave them "The Talk of the Town". It brought down the house.

But today, Kathleen had on an ordinary dress and ordinary shoes, and was back to being ordinary as they stood looking at each other in the mirror. She looked uncharacteristically somber, which made Jenny feel as if something disagreeable might be coming. She waited, watchful.

"I have something sad to tell you about, Jenny," her sister began.

Jenny looked at her with stricken eyes.

"Is it - *Grandma?*" she whispered. To her, the worst possible thing, the most unspeakably saddening event would be the death of Ida, their hero.

"Oh no, no one has died," her sister quickly said. "Nothing like that - or at least, this is sad in a different way, because Mother and Dad are going to be - well, divorced."

She paused as Jenny stood absorbing this unbelievable news.

"Divorced..."

It was a harsh word, a word every child in every town dreads hearing in relation to their own parents. In 1967, hardly anyone's parents were being divorced. The only divorces she knew of were Emily's parents across the street, which had happened ages ago and carried a strange scandal all its own. Marion and Jack had quarreled and divorced, then Jack had married a different lady, whose ex-husband had surprised them all by proposing to, and marrying, Marion. But these new marriages had not lasted long either, and the whole process of separation and divorce had begun all over again. The gossip had gone on for ages until Marion and Emily had finally upped sticks and moved away.

"But what are they going to do?" Jenny asked.

"Well, they are going to separate. That is what Mother said, anyway. They can't stay here together any more."

"But why are they getting a divorce? Is it Mother who wants to?" She thought Mother might want to because Dad seemed constantly to chase her around the house to get her attention, and she didn't seem terribly anxious to give it.

"No, it isn't Mother. It's Dad. He's got a girlfriend. Or, rather, a number of girlfriends. I don't know how many, or why. But anyway, it isn't just one..." she trailed off, and sighed. "He told me himself about it last week when you were playing for the panel."

"Don't remind me."

"Oh. Sorry." They stood for a silent moment, thinking of Jenny's demise.

"I wish the folks would have told you themselves, but Mom asked me to do it and I said I would."

The girls were shocked at married men having multiple girlfriends or "sexual addictions". They barely knew basic anatomy as taught by the Home Ec teacher.

"When did it happen?" Jenny asked. Their eyes met.

"Well, it wasn't a one-time thing, you see. Mother said it's been going on for... ten years."

"Ten!" The girl grew pale. How had it all gone so wrong without her knowing? And yet - a strange awareness crept into her memory, some knowledge from the past. Knowledge about her father.

"He goes with them..." someone had told her.

"Where does he go?" was her innocent question, then. But when? She could not remember.

"How could Mom stay with him for that long?"

"She forgave him."

"But - every time?"

"Every time."

Jenny checked her watch, and said, "Uh-oh. I'm supposed to play for evening church."

"I'll take you."

The church, unlocked as it always was, stood cool and quiet on that late Sunday afternoon. Jenny walked up to the organ and removed her shoes, climbed onto the tall wooden bench and turned the instrument on. It hummed satisfactorily beneath her fingers as she pressed the keys and set her volume. She and Kathleen were two of several young organ players in the church, carefully trained by Mrs. Whitney in both skill and spiritual devotion.

"You can't have one without the other," she frequently said.

The prelude Jenny had practiced with her sat opened and ready, and would have been a nice, upbeat beginning to the service. But the piece seemed too sweet, now that the world had changed forever. So Jenny laid it aside and chose another, written in a minor key as if it was a funeral march. It may as well have been a funeral march, given the fact that something, if not someone, had died - or soon would. The thought of this made her eyes sting.

As the worshipers entered and her prelude began, she remembered her father singing this song on a Sunday morning. She had been his accompanist. The congregation that day had focussed on him as they took in the meaning of the words. But now, the words she remembered fell flat, for they had been sung by a man who had apparently not meant them. Jenny played, hearing the lyrics in her mind with new meaning:

Flee as a bird to your Mountain,
Thou who art weary of sin.
Go to the clear, flowing fountain,
Where you will wash and be clean.

He will protect thee forever, wipe every falling tear;
He will forsake thee, O never, sheltered so tenderly there.
The Savior will wipe every tear.

Oliver Ditson, Public Domain

At this final line, the line that nearly broke her heart, a tear made its way down her cheek. Mrs. Whitney saw it, and was concerned. Why had the girl changed her prelude? Mrs. Whitney had heard there were hard things happening in the West household, and although she didn't know what those things were, she thought they might be fatal - if not physically, then emotionally.

Jenny somehow made it through the rest of the service, turned off the organ, put on her shoes, and went outside. Mrs. Whitney came to stand on the steps next to her, patting her shoulder.

"Someone picking you up, dear?"

"Yes," said the girl. "Someone..." She hoped Mrs. Whitney wouldn't say anything about the prelude, about her misery, about the world she had known suddenly ending. But Mrs. Whitney, who was the soul of discretion and understood young people, didn't.

"I can wait with you, if you'd like." But Jenny said she would be alright on her own, and Mrs. Whitney left.

The girl stood there, wondering who would be picking her up. Sometimes she got lucky and saw Kathleen behind the wheel of the little car, waving at her and beeping the horn. But this time her luck ran out. This time her father came.

She sighed. As if in tacit agreement, neither of them spoke as he pulled away from the curb, made the obligatory U-turn, and pointed the car toward home.

Sometimes a Volkswagen Beetle just isn't big enough.

CHAPTER FORTY-NINE

Milestone

1967

July 3

Sixteen is an enviable age, and now that day, with all its responsibilities and privileges, had finally come to meet her. For months Jenny had anticipated this milestone, deciding that the highest priority must be getting her driver's license. Some of her classmates had actually put off taking their driving test, but Jenny could never be so slapdash. To drive was to be independent!

Pennie had already taken her on numerous training runs, saying, "The thing is to be always confident and straightforward. Take it up to fifty, now..."

"But I've never taken it up to fifty!"

"No matter, take it slowly on up, yes, that's right. There! You've done it. That wasn't too hard now, was it?" And Jenny had to admit that it wasn't.

The high school required all its students to take Driver's Ed, and the instructor cringed when it came time for them to drive. He secretly pondered a change in careers, if one of those kids didn't kill him first. But Pennie did not cringe and was endlessly optimistic, sprinkling confidence like fairy dust onto her young and inexperienced daughter.

Before Jenny could try for her license, she must pick strawberries in the West fields. Her Uncle Bob ran the operation, and Pennie worked as the Row Boss. She ran a tight ship, letting nothing get past her.

"Mrs. West is a tough cookie," Bob warned his pickers. "If you are caught throwing berries or eating too many, well, I can't be responsible for what she might do..." But there was a twinkle in his eye as he said it.

Pennie had confided to Jenny that it was hard to keep a straight face at some of the antics in the strawberry patch.

"Which antics?"

"Well, yesterday someone opened up a particularly beautiful berry, inserted a spider, and gave it to Jimmy Wells to eat."

"Ew," said Jenny. "Did he eat it?"

"Yes," said her mother. "And a fight broke out." They both laughed.

"Then I heard one of the big boys telling a littler one that his mother wore combat boots. And of course, a fight broke out. I don't know why that particular insult goes so deep. Do you? I can still see his little red face as he pounded away at that much larger boy." Jenny remembered this one, and laughed. She glanced up to where her mother now stood supervising the pickers, spectacular in her wide-brimmed hat and sunglasses, looking prettier than any mother of a sixteen-year-old should. Pennie caught her eye and mouthed the words "Happy Birthday".

After lunch Jenny went up to the farmhouse to sort the berries with her Aunt Jeannie. Aunt Jeannie had never lost her sense of humor, and was always laughing as they stood around the inverted pingpong table in the breezeway, rooting out the bad berries from the good. The screen door opened, and in walked Pennie.

"Well, are you ready to go get your license?" she said with a smile.

"Oh, so that's why you're so happy today," cried her aunt as Jenny went off to wash her hands. "You'll be working the strawberry stand before you know it. In fact, if you do get that license, why don't you drive yourself on out there this afternoon?"

A promotion! This birthday just kept on getting better.

As they got into the car, she could hear Jeannie's voice calling out, "Make sure that Examiner comes out of it alive! Hahaha...."

And off they went, the girl driving her mother into town, accelerating to a little above fifty miles per hour.

"You mustn't worry, you know," her mother said as they went along. "You're already a good driver." Jenny hoped this was true. The accident last year had sobered her, but gave her something of an advantage. She knew the risks now, first hand.

Pennie continued, "…and always remember you are driving a weapon."

"A weapon?" asked her daughter, surprised that their two thoughts were running in the same direction.

"Well, yes - this car is nothing less than a gigantic bullet, propelled along by you and sharing the road with any number of similar bullets. The consequences of a misstep are obvious." Pennie sat quietly, remembering some missteps when she had been a passenger. She cleared her throat. "Your father often follows too closely, and you must decide not to let such a thing run in the family."

"Okay, Mom."

At the end of the exam, to no one's surprise the smiling girl came back through the door.

"Ninety percent!" she beamed, shaking the piece of paper in her hand.

Her mother smiled. "How's that Examiner?"

"Mom!"

"Just joking," said Pennie, holding out her hand for the temporary license. "Let's have a look. I knew you would do it." She sighed. "But I'm going to miss you out on the rows." She hadn't realized how much until this moment.

CHAPTER FIFTY

Sheer American Freedom

Jenny pulled into the driveway and caught the unmistakable aroma of barbecue. She didn't want to waste a single second of this birthday, but still took a moment to reflect that for the first time ever, she had driven, alone, along a highway. She'd had the choice of what time to leave one place, and arrive at the next. There was even the choice of whether to obey the speed laws, which of course she did, but it had still been her own decision. The sheer American freedom of this thrilled her, and she hoped to feel it for the rest of her life.

When she reached the back yard, Landon's T-bones were sizzling agreeably, gray smoke billowing up and around his face.

"Here she is!" he called out, waving at her with his tongs.

"Hey, way to go, Sis!" shouted Matt. "Mom told us about your license." At age twenty, he was a college junior and everything fabulous in her eyes.

"Thanks!" she grinned back.

Pennie brought out the potato salad and watermelon as Kathleen poured lemonade. The weather stayed hot, but nobody cared. In the middle of summer, what else could eastern Oregon possibly be? Ellen climbed up into the apple tree, hanging above them all like some ravishing little star. The tree was such that its one smooth bough could comfortably hold a person just about her size. She sat there now and munched an apple, her brown legs swinging back and forth as she listened to the conversations below.

It made for a lovely picture that day, the family situated around the green lawn, Landon serving up the steaks and everyone else digging in. Ann sat with William, laughing and holding their newly born daughter. William's visiting parents had settled on lawn chairs beneath the big maple tree, and Jenny wondered for a moment why, in all this heat, Mrs. Sanders was wearing her coat.

The telephone rang. Kathleen, standing near the door, set down the lemonade and went to answer it.

"West residence," she said into the kitchen receiver.

"Landon, please," said a woman's voice, sounding a little bit like the Operator.

"I'm sorry, Ma'am, he is busy cooking right now."

"I would still like to speak with him. Please, dear, do go and get him."

Kathleen set the phone down, and went back outside.

"Dad, it's for you."

"Okay. Matt, can you man this thing till I get back?" He went inside, and Kathleen followed. "I'll take it in the bedroom," he said.

She lifted the kitchen phone again, ready to hang it up as soon as her father answered the other line. She heard him say, "This is Landon", and started to hang up. But the lady's laughing voice rang out, saying, "Hello, you! Is our plan still on?"

"Of course," he said, "but I told you not to call me here." He sounded nervous, and nervously went on. "The Washington Hotel, July 6. I'll be there at..."

The words hit hard as Kathleen listened. July 6 was her parents' anniversary, so how could he be meeting someone - a lady, apparently - in a Portland hotel that day? Then she remembered her father's shameful confession, on the unforgettable day she'd been sick. Unable to stop herself, she shouted something incoherent into the phone, and slammed it onto the table.

"...Uh-oh," said the lady.

Kathleen stood in the doorway, breathless and red-faced.

"Mom? Can you come in for a minute?"

"What is it?" asked Pennie as they went inside. The girl pointed to the receiver where it lay on the table. Pennie quietly picked it up, listened, and in a few moments the serenity of the day was shattered by a shout. Jenny and Matt heard it through the open window and looked at each other, eyebrows raised in concern. The Sanders in their lawn chairs appeared to be as calm as if they hadn't heard a thing.

In the kitchen, Kathleen was saying, "I'm sorry, Mom, I'm so sorry..."

"It isn't what you think, Pennie," Landon interrupted. "Kathleen misunderstood." Her father's face became red as he stood between them, placing blame upon his daughter.

"Stop talking!" Pennie snapped. "After Kathleen heard you and that woman talking, I listened long enough to know what the two of you have planned for our anniversary."

"But," Landon said, backing away. "You've got to believe me...".

"I have, Landon, for ten years. And I don't believe you anymore." Grabbing his keys from the table, she threw them at his chest. "You can just get out!"

With a pitiful and pleading look, Landon turned and left.

Outside, Matt's face had become all closed up and hard. By now the last steak was badly overcooked, but he just kept on turning it. Jenny stood watching as her father's car sped down the hill, wondering if it meant they wouldn't be cutting her birthday cake.

"But where is Daddy *going?*" Ellen asked, coming down from the tree. Her mother looked formidable but did not speak, and Ellen's face went pale. She couldn't think what had made such a change from one moment to the next. She always loved a party, especially parties like this one where everyone's favorite foods were being served. Now it had all been spoiled, and Ellen didn't know what to do. So she went back to the apple tree, and stayed there until her mother came calling for her much later, when the guests had all gone and the sun was beginning to set.

PART NINE

HERE'S MY HEART, OH TAKE AND SEAL IT

CHAPTER FIFTY-ONE

The Empty Chair

Their father had gone, they knew not where. It shouldn't have felt so very different, accustomed as they were to his absences. But there seemed an eeriness now to the empty dining room chair, and they found themselves going around on egg shells. Their mother's grim face inhibited discussion.

Three days later Landon returned to the house, packed his things, and handed Pennie his keys.

"I won't be back," he said, and Pennie believed him. She cringed, and thought, *I would rather die than go through what I am going to have to go through.*

But she did not die. Instead, she drove to Pendleton and consulted a lawyer for the first time in her life. After a long discussion with him about the children, the house, and the money, Pennie walked to the nearby courthouse and filed papers for divorce. The action involved an enormous amount of paperwork, including one question she was, as yet, uncertain how to answer - *Grounds For Divorce.* The choices were:

Desertion
Adultery
Habitual Drunkenness
Mental Cruelty
Lack of Consummation
Insanity
Imprisonment

Although Adultery would seem the strictly natural choice, Pennie simply could not bring herself to choose it. In the end she decided upon "Mental Cruelty" for the broader truth it represented.

The rest of that summer, Pennie went about in what felt like a state of shock. She and Landon were Christians, getting a divorce, and her face went crimson each time she thought of it. She dreaded being asked any probing questions, especially the question of *why*. Landon had been such a respected member of the community in both town and church, that people were naturally shocked by the rumors. Night after night as she waited for sleep to come, Pennie prayed earnestly about these questions and how (or if) she could truthfully answer them.

Ida, finally put into the picture of what had happened to her eldest daughter, came to the rescue. "Let us take ourselves to San Francisco, Pennie," she said. "We can see the sights; eat in restaurants! Stay in motels..."

"Motels?" Pennie had said. "Goodness, Mother, the expense!"

But Ida had privately taken care of it all. With the girls away for the rest of the summer, the two women packed up their bags and drove south. It was not a vacation, for Pennie's burdens followed her into the city she had once known, and loved, with Landon. Reminders of him were everywhere: Fisherman's Wharf, Lombard Street, the Golden Gate Bridge. While visiting the lovely San Francisco City Hall where they had once posed for pictures, she became suddenly dizzy and collapsed on the steps. For years, the only thing Pennie remembered of that summer's journey was tearing her stockings as she fell.

Meanwhile, Landon discovered he had troubles of his own. Whenever a federal employee becomes divorced, an audit is done to be sure their financial accounts are in order. As Ida and Pennie perused San Francisco that summer, Landon's audit began. Irregularities surfaced and led to an investigation, an arrest, and months later, a trial. The debacle appeared in all the newspapers, and Pennie found it a slow and excruciating public ordeal as she, and the family, awaited the outcome.

CHAPTER FIFTY-TWO

A Year Without Him

News of the divorce did spread, but the townspeople were mostly generous toward Pennie and the girls. It could have run the usual gossipy gamut, tearing at her already wounded heart. But this had not happened. Her children had not been badgered, and for that, Pennie was thankful.

At least once each month, Pennie tried to think of something fun to do with Jenny and Ellen to lift their spirits. She remembered how her own mother had made the most ordinary outings turn into captivating ones.

"Girls, we are going to go and see a play!" she said one Saturday. "How does that sound?"

The girls looked at her, and blinked.

"A play? What play?" Jenny asked. Their mother held up a flier.

"It is called *A Thousand Clowns*, and is meant to be very funny. It ought to be, with all those clowns in it."

Ellen didn't really like clowns, and considered them creepy. But she asked, "Isn't it expensive?"

"Well, it would have been expensive, only some money has come to us that we can use on a play. So I've picked us out this funny one." And the girls smiled.

"I think you should put on your nice dresses," she said. "I will too, and then the three of us can go out and paint the town red." The two girls had never thought of painting towns in any sort of color, but they brushed their blond hair, put on their dresses, shoes, and gloves, and drove down the road toward Walla Walla.

Pennie asked, "Shall we go somewhere nice for dinner?"

The girls looked at each other. They had talked about this, hoping for maybe a Coke and a grilled cheese. But Pennie had something better in mind, and drove to the entrance of the spectacular Marcus Whitman Hotel.

"What?" Jenny cried. "We're going to the Marcus Whitman?" The Marcus Whitman had to be the nicest place to eat in Walla Walla, maybe even the whole county. "But Mother - it must cost the earth," she ventured.

"It is no more than we can spend."

Pennie parked the car, and the girls followed her inside, feeling confident in their nice dresses. The waiter approached and guided them to a table, calling them "ladies" and handing them menus.

"Would you like to peruse the wine list, Madam?" he asked. But Pennie politely declined, and they took their time picking out what they should eat.

They enjoyed their dinners, and the thought of seeing a play just down the road gave them chills.

"I have the chills," said the littler one.

"So do I," said her sister.

Their mother instantly declared that she had them too, for it made her happy just to see them happy.

Upon their arrival at The Little Theatre, they joined the animated crowds of people flooding in. There, a lady in red helped them to their seats in the balcony, high above the stage. The people around them chattered excitedly about the play, and someone said they had heard it was racy.

Ellen overheard this, and whispered, "What is 'racy', Mama?"

But the lights dimmed, and the orchestra blessedly began to play. Their mother did not think she had time to explain "racy", and dropped it.

As the play developed, Pennie and Jenny saw why it might be considered racy. The storyline included an unusually mature boy who lives with his perpetually unemployed uncle, and the shenanigans they get into while evading Child Welfare. Among these shenanigans, which Ellen found quite illuminating, was a naked Barbie Doll whose enlarged bosoms flashed on and off.

The audience thought it hilarious and howled with laughter, but Ellen came to her own understanding of the word "racy". She stared at the bosoms in scandalized shock, as her mother and sister laughed so hard their eyes watered. This modest little girl did not find it the least bit funny, and privately wondered if she would ever feel quite the same about her own dear Barbies.

"Well, girls, and what did you think of *A Thousand Clowns?*" asked their mother as they left the theater.

"I thought it was funny," said Jenny. "But that man wasn't really a grownup." Then she surprised herself by saying, "The boy was the real grownup." Pennie agreed, but had not yet thought of it herself.

"What about you, Ellen?" she asked. "What did you think?"

Ellen thought for a moment, and then, eyes wide, she said, "Oh. Well, I guess it was OK. But that Barbie Doll should have kept her little thingies covered up."

Pennie and Jenny were quiet and their faces solemn, but their shoulders were ever-so-slightly shaking.

CHAPTER FIFTY-THREE

At The Stroke Of Midnight

The girls saw Landon only once that year, on Christmas Day. The big kids were home from college, which helped a little. But it felt weird and uncomfortable because he acted like a stranger, and not their father. Pennie was polite but frosty, and he simply sat and *looked* at her as if hoping she might ask him back. She didn't. Then the gifts, the carols, and the turkey were labored, and not at all wonderful. They couldn't help but be relieved when it became time for him to go.

"Mother, is Dad coming back for New Year's Eve?" asked Jenny, watching as he drove slowly away in his old wreck of a car.

Pennie stiffened slightly. "I don't think so." The girls felt, but did not say, that it might be just as well if he didn't.

How strange it seemed, that things felt better now - a little easier - without him. More freedom, less turbulence. They could sense it in their mother, too. Gone were her snaps and snarls about how they dressed at home. In the past, if they came out of their room in short pajamas, Pennie would tell them to "Put on a bathrobe, for heaven sake."

"But why?" they would ask.

"Never mind. Just go do it." Her strictures were firm; but now their father was gone, and it didn't seem to matter anymore.

As the new year approached, no one felt very party-like. There didn't seem to be much point, because the big kids had gone back to college. Ann and William, who had moved with little Janet to Weston, would be down the hill in their own little house, the baby no doubt sleeping.

Jenny remembered the many New Year's Eves at home when things were fun, and funny. There had been delicious food to eat, and lovely family phone calls to make and to receive. At the end, they had all gathered around the television and counted down, as the glittering ball in Times Square began its descent. At last, and best of all, they sang the song they'd been waiting for all year:

Should Auld Acquaintance be forgot,
And never brought to mind,
Should Auld acquaintance be forgot,
For auld lang syne!

Robert Burns, Public Domain

The year before this year, before their world had changed, her father waited until the stroke of midnight, and then handed Jenny a little white box. She took in her breath, and looked up at him.

"What is it?" she asked. And then of course he said, "Open it up and find out."

When she did, the box revealed delicate white tissue paper wrapped around something small, round and slender. To Jenny's delight, it was the dear little white crystal watch she'd been wanting for Christmas, but had not gotten.

"Thank you!" she said, hugging both her parents. Her father had looked wonderfully pleased.

But now he had gone away. She thought about how such a man might have really been *two* men, two kinds of fathers, one who was thoughtful and planned ahead for things like watches, and another who mightn't think of daughters or watches at all, but could be counted on to think only of himself. She didn't know how both kinds of fathers could fit into one man.

Jenny and Ellen finally gave up and got into their pajamas. They had just collapsed onto the living room couch when they heard noises coming from the porch outside. There was laughter. There was shouting, as if some kind of wild party was starting up out there.

"Who..." Pennie began, but suddenly the door opened and in walked Ann and William, banging aluminum pans together and singing something funny. Sudden joy infused them all with the arrival of this happy little group. Even baby Janet smiled and giggled at them.

"You are a godsend," said Pennie, hugging her eldest daughter. They'd brought little paper hats and whistles, simple treats, and, wonder of wonders: a six-pack of cold, bottled *Coke-a-Cola.* Unheard of!

The somber evening suddenly gave way to all manner of silliness. They partied, told jokes, ate, and sang as the new year approached. Then everyone but the baby stayed up to see Dick Clark's countdown at Times Square. To Pennie this change of year came as a relief, for 1967 had ended and she would never live it again. If only her memories of it could just as easily roll off, down and away, like a Dick Clark ball in New York City's Times Square.

CHAPTER FIFTY-FOUR

A Return Of Appetite

The two girls had been sitting in front of the television, in rather a slump. They'd had an argument which nobody won, and sort of drifted toward the TV where the *I Love Lucy* on the screen was whining at Ricky. Jenny wondered if he ever got tired of her whining and wanted to leave. Their mother never whined, but their father had left. It seemed to be a question with no answer.

At that moment they heard their mother coming through the door.

"Come on, girls," she said. "Up you get! First sign of spring! "

First sign of spring? Their slump vanished and they switched off the television, suddenly excited. But they must first finish their chores, get ready, and only then, she said, would they solve the riddle.

Jenny filled the sink with dishwater while Ellen dusted. Chores weren't nearly so burdensome when they had something nice to look forward to. Jenny thought of the thousands of times she and Kathleen resented having to do the dishes. They convinced themselves that Mother had given birth to five children simply to make them do the dishes for her. What other reason could there possibly be? They had discussed this conundrum over and over again, for no one could deny that children did the chores. One day, their older and wiser sister, now a mother, pointed out that children have the effect of *producing* most of the chores. This concept did make some sense. But they liked their theory better than hers, and didn't discuss it in front of her anymore.

The first sign of spring would cost something, and as far as Pennie knew, there was no money in the house. A sudden inspiration sent her scouting for loose coins. After all, Landon had forever jangled the change in his pockets, and something must surely have fallen out. Sofa cushions, pockets, drawers, and closets were all searched, and in the end she came away with almost four dollars!

The house gleamed under their ministrations as they backed down the driveway with Jenny at the wheel. They began with the streets of Weston, but with a gentle hint from Pennie, they continued toward Milton. There, they drove past the high school where Pennie had first met Landon, and the stage where he had so brilliantly performed. Pennie sat looking straight ahead, thinking of the days when a Geometry test had been her biggest problem.

After one final turn, a familiar and beloved sign loomed into their view, a sign they had not seen lit since early fall.

"Turn left!" laughed Pennie, and Jenny did. Ellen shouted, "A&W!"

"That's the one," said their mother, "and that is your first sign of spring!"

"But why should root beer be a sign of spring, Mama?" Ellen asked.

"The A&W closes for the winter. March 20 is the first day of spring this year, which is why it's all lit up. I've always thought of it as the first sign of spring."

They checked the menus and ordered their food.

"Where did we get the money from this time, Mom?" asked Jenny.

"Your father provided it," Pennie said, with an arch look.

"He did? I thought..."

"Oh, he provided it quite it by accident. I just had to dig in the sofas and chairs. He was actually very generous."

They laughed, and for a while the burdens of life slipped away as they munched these simple treats. Jenny glanced over at her mother and thought she had never looked prettier. Ellen liked eating her Baby Burger from a tray attached to their car window. Pennie took a bite and thought a Mama Burger with french fries had been vastly underrated. They tasted positively scrumptious, far better than dried bread crusts. And these French fries! How in the world had she avoided them all these years?

Pennie had ordered coffee, but now saw Ellen's root beer float as a thing of rare beauty.

“Ellen?”

“Yes, mom?”

“What if I took a tiny taste of that?” The girls were astonished at this unexpected return of appetite.

“Sure, mom!” said Ellen, with a smile. “Have all you want.” And she did.

CHAPTER FIFTY-FIVE

Not Just Any Date

The Junior-Senior Prom would take place in April, and Jenny was hoping Melvin would ask her. Melvin was tall, blond, and had a crazy-sweet smile all the girls adored. She thought he might ask, because they'd already been on double dates for things like hamburgers or movies, or even just dragging the gut on a Friday night. But so far, no mention had been made of the vitally important Junior-Senior Prom.

One day she turned around in the school hallway - and there he was. Surrounded by a hundred noisy high schoolers going to class, Melvin said, "Uh, Jenny..."

"Yes?" she replied serenely, her heart racing.

"Well, what would you think of going to the Prom with me?"

Someone in the crowded hallway bumped into her, propelling her closer to Melvin. Their blue eyes met, and she said, "Oh! Um, yes. Yes, I'd like that..."

"Good!" He began moving down the hallway. "And my mom said to tell you my suit is blue!"

"Oh, blue is fine, blue is fabulous! I don't know my color yet, though."

"You can tell me later. Okay?"

"Okay!" And then with a wave, he was gone.

At home, she came skipping into her mother's room, eyes shining.

"I'm going to the Prom, Mom!", and Pennie wondered who had her daughter looking so happy.

"I figured as much. Who is taking you?" Pennie asked. She'd become accustomed to Jenny's dates, and had no concerns. She knew everybody's mother.

"Melvin!" said her daughter with a little hop. "But Mom, I've outgrown all my formals…"

It was true, they had no dress for her to wear, and no money with which to buy one. So the two of them browsed the fabric shop, discovering that the cost of the fabric and all the bits and pieces would come to over ten dollars! They hadn't so much as even one. What should she do? Pennie gave this important dilemma some serious thought and prayer as they made their way home.

The telephone was ringing as they came in, and through the line came the businesslike voice of Audrey Lieuellan, the school cook. She asked if Pennie would mind helping serve at the Athletic Banquet the next evening.

"We had enough ladies to do it, but someone had to cancel. Are you available?"

Pennie respected Mrs. Lieuallen, and said yes right away. Audrey, always in favor of the underdog (especially if the underdog happened to be a woman), hung up with satisfaction. She sure did like that Pennie West. What had that rascal of a husband of hers been thinking? She had never said a blessed word about it, and never would - but she'd always wondered. Sometimes you just couldn't make sense of the men.

Pennie went to the banquet the next evening, and did her part. It took ages, because the servers stayed for clean up. As Pennie got ready to leave, Mrs. Lieuallen handed her an envelope.

"Oh. What is this?" Pennie asked.

"It's your pay," the woman said.

"I hadn't realized there would be pay."

She didn't open it until she'd gotten home. By now it was late and both girls had gone to bed, but she turned on the hall light and opened the envelope. She gently drew out what she assumed would be a dollar bill. But it wasn't a dollar bill. She couldn't believe it.

"Ten dollars." It felt like a miracle. A gorgeous, green miracle.

She tiptoed into the girls' bedroom, peering through the darkness toward Jenny. "Are you awake?" she whispered.

"Yes, is everything alright?"

"Oh, everything is certainly alright. Everything is wonderful. Look..." and she held out the bill.

Jenny sat up and gazed at the money, which to her seemed like a fortune. "Where did you *get* that!?" she exclaimed.

"Heaven, I think. Straight from Heaven - in the form of Mrs. Lieuallan. We actually needed $10.01, but I think we'll be able to scare up that extra penny, don't you?"

* * *

Pennie made the dress, long and pink and Prom-worthy. Ellen stood watching her older sister getting ready, helping her with buttons and small suggestions.

"Shall I do the bow?" she asked, and did it. Jenny looked down at the pretty face of her sister and said, "You're good at this, you know. I never realized it before."

The doorbell rang, setting off a final flurry of activity in the back bedroom. When Jenny finally glided gracefully to the door and ushered

Melvin inside, they instantly caught the unmistakeable aroma of Old Spice aftershave. Wonderful! There was something very romantic about Old Spice, and she had hoped he would be wearing some.

"Hi," he said, and smiled.

"Hi!" She smiled back, and Ellen giggled.

Jenny remembered last year, when her father had been there to answer the door, tease her date relentlessly, and take photographs. She thought about the way it had made her feel, as if she could not compete with her charming father. But tonight it was just Mother, who was normal, and friendly, and would never in a million years tease anyone.

Melvin held her corsage, a selection of pink roses surrounding a white orchid. It looked as delicate as a spring cloud. Jenny caught her breath.

"It's beautiful..."

"Shall I pin it on?" He moved shyly forward to do this, but was so afraid of hurting her that Pennie good-naturedly offered to help. With this accomplished, Jenny picked up his boutonniere, a handsome affair consisting of two white roses surrounded by tiny leaves.

"Tell me if I stick you," she said, holding up the pin with a wicked smile. Laughter rang out as Pennie took the obligatory photographs, and followed them to the door.

Ellen stood at the picture window as the aroma of Old Spice began to fade.

"Momma?" she asked.

"Yes, Ellen?"

"When will I have a Prom?"Pennie smiled down at the blue eyed blonde and saw her through fresh eyes. The girl was so pretty, so honest, and becoming so tall. She would be ready for a Prom sooner than her mother wanted her to be.

"In due time, my girl; it will all happen in due time. But let's not hurry it too much. I want to keep you here with me for a little while longer. How does that sound?"

Her daughter nodded, and hugged Pennie's slender waist. It sounded fine to her, just fine.

Melvin had made a terrific start. As the event was only half a block away, they walked down the road hand in hand.

"I like pink", he said, and they both laughed.

It was a Prom to remember. As they entered the decorated gymnasium, friends waved and called out, "Hey! Over here!" After Jenny's purse and jacket had been safely stowed, the opening chords of a Beach Boys' song propelled everyone out onto the dance floor. Melvin turned, held out his hand with a flourish and said, "May I have this dance?"

It was simply perfect, and a thought came briefly to her mind - this boy was sweet and honorable, and nothing at all like her father. His unique humility had already won her vote, maybe even her heart.

The surprisingly talented band played the night away, belting out the great songs of the sixties as the kids danced and ate, laughing out loud whenever their teachers took to the floor.

Long before they were ready for it, the principal strode to the microphone and announced the final song of the evening, *You're Just Too Good To Be True*. It was Jenny's favorite, the song she had waited for all evening. Melvin looked at her, and without a word they walked back to the center of the room.

At the last chorus, everyone suddenly turned toward the band, holding hands and singing the familiar words; line after line they sang, louder and stronger until, in a joyous finale, their voices drowned out the instruments.

It was the highlight of the evening. At the song's end, everyone cheered - until the lights came on. At this, a general groan went up. It was like letting the air out of a balloon.

Melvin walked her home in the moonlight, stepping onto the lighted porch and taking her hand.

"Good night," he said.

"Good night. I had fun."

"The best!"

The porch light began flashing off and on, her mother's clear signal that their night was over. Quick as a wink, Melvin surprised Jenny by kissing her cheek, then said goodbye, and left. She stood, watching as he headed back down the road in his handsome blue suit. Under the streetlight he turned again, and waved.

How could he, or anyone else, have ever guessed that one day, not long from now, Melvin would be drafted into the U.S. Army; would be trained and made ready to fight; sent to Viet Nam, assigned to the Infantry; and would, in 1971, stand upon a hidden land mine, losing his life. No such thoughts could possibly intrude, not on a night like this one with stars shimmering in the warm, romantic evening of a High School Prom.

CHAPTER FIFTY-SIX

He Mourned It As A Death

On April 12, 1968, the town of Weston received a shock it never truly got over. Landon West - federal crop insurance salesman, family man, and pillar of the church - was convicted of embezzling from the US Government. Pennie had learned of it the day before, and finally understood their unpredictable bank account. Her husband had been in financial difficulties, and slipped some of the government's money into his personal account. He had meant to pay it all back, but the unexpected audit came too soon, and signaled the beginning of the end.

As the result of a guilty plea, the judge sentenced Landon to a two year probation in lieu of prison. In the divorce settlement, the house in Weston and Landon's one-third interest in the farm became signed over to Pennie. Landon now had no family, no job, no income, and no money. Walking out of the courthouse on that final day, the regrets he had evaded for so long a time at last engulfed him.

There were some things outside his control, things he could blame for what he had become.

He remembered, as a lad of fourteen, being required to sleep in the bunkhouse with the farm hands, only some of whom were honorable.

He remembered the farm-manager's wife following him there to relieve him of his virtue, age seventeen.

He remembered falling away from Pennie in those bright, early days of his marriage.

He remembered finding the only freedom he'd ever known, in the Gospel. Landon grieved now its loss, as he remembered. If only he had trusted in God rather than the irresistible government job that eventually felled him. If only he had fought the temptations that found him the first day, looking for the acceptance of men who had not cared about him. At the first signs of his disgrace, those men dropped Landon as they would a "hot potato". He did not blame them. He would probably have done the same.

Landon's existence dwindled now to a dreary single-wide trailer in a field outside the town of Helix. The children, he knew, would never see him there. He pulled up and parked the old wreck of a car he had bought with his last fifty dollars. There was no company car now, because he was no longer a company man. Stardom had eluded him, and he was a nobody. A nothing.

He walked up to his door, unlocked it, and went inside. As he looked around the hot, cramped and desolate space, he was assailed by sudden floods of rich memories, memories of a girl with soft brown eyes, and the babies she had borne; childish voices performing together on a stage; children practicing their instruments as he bellowed out corrections; Christmastime carols around the piano, his children's eyes shining in anticipation. He remembered it all now, and mourned it as a death; for it felt like a death, all of this loss. A loss of faith, and love, possessions and happiness, all gone from his grasp, it seemed to him, forever.

Landon had been a successful and talented man, basking in the praise of many. But what wouldn't he give for the admiration of a little girl named Ellen? He felt he would give up anything, for that - if he had anything left to give.

EPILOGUE

Landon, 1929

IT WAS A SIMPLE DESSERT, with simple ingredients - mostly cornstarch and milk. As puddings went, it stood right at the top of Landon's list of favorites, and he would do almost anything for a bowl of it. But one person in his life intensely disliked the concoction, and refused to make it. His mother.

Landon loved his mother, but could not comprehend this aversion of hers toward something he liked. He tried everything to persuade her, but Anna Compton West had her own opinions on child-rearing, opinions which did not and would not include the consumption of cornstarch pudding.

Still, Landon wanted it, and knew of a place he could get enough of it to satisfy any young boy's after school appetite. Grandmother's house.

Grandmother West approved of Cornstarch Pudding, and did not understand all the fuss. Why shouldn't the boy have some if he hankered for it? So Landon would make his way up the path to her welcoming red brick house, and eat Cornstarch Pudding to his heart's content.

"Don't tell Mother I've eaten this," he said.

"Our little secret," she told him, with a wink.

When he got home his mother would kindly ask about what he had done there, what had been talked about, and what had been eaten. He told her everything that first time, but after the ensuing storm he found it easier to, well, adjust the truth. He did not like to think of it as lying, but it became one of life's rules he gradually absorbed; a rule which followed him throughout his childhood and every year after it.

It was complicated keeping the lies straight; but he thought he had learned to manage it, at least most of the time. It became easier as time passed and he grew to be a man, but it never stopped being complicated.

It had all started with something as simple as a dessert and two opinionated women. Mother, Grandmother. And in the years to come, all the other women were cornstarch pudding.

THE FAMILY PSALM

Wish I could go back to the days I was little,
When my daddy and uncles seemed seven feet tall.
With their whiskery hugs, and their loud jolly voices
And Grandad the biggest, and loudest of all.

Wish I could go back just to sit at the table,
With good food and laughter on every side,
Holding hands for the blessing, eating turkey and dressing,
Looking round at the faces I loved most of all.

Wish I could go back to my grandma's big kitchen,
Smell the coffee pot perking at the back of the stove,
Hear my mother and aunties just talking forever,
While the littlest babies bang pans on the floor.

Wish I could go back just to play with my cousins,
Build forts and ride Viking ships just one more time,
Saying, "You be Roy Rogers, and I'll be Dale Evans,"
Playing games in the twilight til after bed time.

I can never go back to the days gone forever,
I can never go back and be little again.
Some I love went the wrong path, and some went to Heaven,
So there's no use to dwell on just what might have been.

But I have my children, and they have their cousins,
Their aunts and their uncles are the children we were.
Now we are the ones who stand tall in their memories,
We are the ones who seem seven feet tall.

Oh Lord, keep me true, oh Lord, keep me worthy,
Oh, Lord, keep me honest until my life ends,
That the children who love me will follow You safely,
And all at Your table may one day join hands.

-Karen Pierpoint Copyright © [1985]

Made in the USA
Coppell, TX
08 August 2022

81156952R10154